(D) Margaret June   Hoc/c

1 1 SEP 2007

1 4 JUL 2008

27 NOV 2009

24 Mar
6 May

2 4 DEC 2011
26/5/12
7/6/12

HULLBRIDGE
4/15

0 8 MAY 2019

This book is to be returned on or before the date above.
It may be borrowed for a further period if not in demand.

Essex County Council
Libraries

D0261167

REQUIEM FOR A DEALER

It's Brodie Farrell's night off, and she's taken her friend Daniel Hood for some driving practice, when an encounter with an hysterical girl leaves them both shaken. The accident is undoubtedly the girl's fault, so why is she adamant that Daniel tried to kill her? Brodie turns to Detective Superintendent Jack Deacon, who is trying to find the source of a new drug which is flooding the streets of Dimmock. Then the girl, Alison Barker, turns up in hospital not as an RTA victim but suffering from a drug overdose, claiming her father was murdered and that she'll be next...

REQUIEM FOR A DEALER

REQUIEM FOR A DEALER

by

Jo Bannister

Magna Large Print Books
Long Preston, North Yorkshire,
BD23 4ND, England.

British Library Cataloguing in Publication Data.

Bannister, Jo
    Requiem for a dealer.

    A catalogue record of this book is
    available from the British Library

    ISBN   0-7505-2531-2
    ISBN   978-0-7505-2531-2

First published in Great Britain in 2006 by Allison & Busby Ltd.

Copyright © 2006 by Jo Bannister

Cover illustration © The Old Tin Dog

The moral right of the author has been asserted

Published in Large Print 2006 by arrangement with
Allison & Busby Ltd.

Magna Large Print is an imprint of Library Magna Books Ltd.

Printed and bound in Great Britain by
T.J. (International) Ltd., Cornwall, PL28 8RW

Chapter One

Now they were committed, Brodie found herself wondering if she'd made a terrible mistake. There are some things that even friends, even good friends, shouldn't do for one another. Things that are better left to the professionals. Professionals who had seen it all before, and wouldn't laugh when you got it wrong.

But it was too late for second thoughts. Daniel would be hurt if she changed her mind. It had been, she knew, a long time since he tried this: if she put him off now, gave him instead the number of a girl she knew, left him with the impression that she had no confidence in his ability to come up with the right moves after so long, she thought he might never find the courage to try again.

She took a deep breath and tried to make herself comfortable. A dew of sweat was on her brow, which was ridiculous. There was nothing to be embarrassed about: this was something she did all the time. But not with him, and not giving a running commentary on how to do it.

At least he wouldn't be criticising her

technique. Daniel had told her candidly that he hadn't been much good at it even when he was getting a bit of practice. When Brodie suggested giving him a refresher course, at first he was doubtful. Then he seized the opportunity with enthusiasm. As he said, who knew when he would get another? So she really had to go through with it. It would be over soon enough.

'OK,' she said, hoping she sounded calmer than she felt, 'let's do this. Gently but firmly. There's no rush, but don't think it's going to bite you either. Take a firm grip and push it in ... that's it, that's good ... and then, gently, let the clutch out...'

As the car moved forward with barely a lurch, intense concentration furrowed the brow between the top of Daniel's glasses and his mop of yellow hair.

'Relax,' Brodie said softly, 'you're doing fine. Keep an eye on the mirror and check your position on the road.'

'Drive,' muttered Daniel.

Brodie misunderstood. 'You want me to take over? So soon?'

'No. I mean, we aren't on the road yet – we're still in your drive.'

Brodie started to laugh. The things they'd been through together, the things they'd survived, and this was what had reduced them to grunted communication through clenched teeth. 'I thought we'd save that for the second lesson.'

She wasn't exactly laughing at him, but Daniel wouldn't have minded if she was. He brought her car to the most controlled of halts, put on the handbrake and got it out of gear before he turned to look at her. 'You really don't want to be doing this, do you?'

She linked her arm through his and hugged it. 'Of course I don't,' she chuckled honestly. 'Let's do it anyway.'

'On the road this time?'

'On the road,' she nodded. 'You've got your licence, the car's insured, and you're not suddenly going to throw a handbrake turn at me, are you? You've every right to be on the road, Daniel, you know how to drive a car. You passed your test when you were eighteen. All you need to do is get your eye in again.'

'It's been a while,' admitted Daniel. He reached for the gear-stick, eased it into first. 'As the actress said to the bishop.'

Brodie had her mouth open to correct him but then let it pass. Either they could discuss the respective lifestyles of the apocryphal couple or they could get on with the driving lesson. 'Exactly. Now, check the road and if there's nothing coming, turn left. And somewhere along here you might want to try second gear.'

He tried second gear, then third. He made a right turn. He overtook a woman on a bicycle. The tense corrugations of his brow began to soften and a boyish grin lit his face. 'I'd forgotten how much fun this is...'

As if a malicious God had heard him, disaster shot out of a side street. They'd turned up Fisher Hill, passing Shack Lane where Brodie had her office. The short autumn evening had turned dark a couple of hours before and a fine rain was falling. There were street lights on Fisher Hill, but not many of them, and those that were working produced more glow than illumination. Neither Daniel nor Brodie saw more than a glimpse of the figure that, running in the rain, emerged from an alley between the old houses and went to cross in front of them. But the resounding bang off the nearside wing left no room for doubt.

The car was only doing fifteen miles an hour and Daniel braked to a standstill almost instantly. He spared a second to look at Brodie, the eyes of both of them wide with shock. 'I've hit someone,' he said quietly. Then he was out of the car. In another moment Brodie had found the handle on her side and joined him.

Her first thought – and she recognised immediately that it was a selfish one – was that they'd never had a chance of avoiding the accident. Someone who dashes in front of a car on a wet night wearing a long dark mackintosh is responsible for their own misfor-

10

tune. Even now it was hard enough to make out what the thing beside the car was. It didn't look like a human being. It didn't even look like a bundle of clothes. Mostly it looked like a black plastic bag blown into the road.

Daniel was bending over it, wondering if he dared touch it or if it would only make things worse. 'We're going to need an ambulance,' he said over his shoulder. His voice had the flat, hollow sound of someone refusing to panic.

Brodie nodded jerkily and reached back into the car for her phone.

But before she could dial the black plastic bag gave a sudden spasm and sat up. Brodie saw a white face spattered with mud down one side and a white hand held up shakily to fend off the stooping man. A woman's voice rose in a tremulous crescendo. 'Get away from me!'

On the bright side, thought Brodie, she didn't sound like someone hammering at death's door. She put her phone down on the car seat and went to see if she could help. 'It's all right, don't be afraid. You've had a bit of an accident but we'll take care of you. Are you hurt?'

As soon as it was out she thought it was a bloody stupid question: the woman had bounced off a moving vehicle and hit the road, of course she was hurt. She wasn't sitting in the gutter because she liked the view from down there.

And then she wasn't sitting in the gutter at all. With remarkable strength for someone who'd just head-butted a car she staggered to her feet and backed away until she met the wall of the Fisher Hill cottages. They came in various colours: this was a pale pink one, rosier than usual in the soft-focus light from the street lamp.

By contrast the woman – or maybe she was only a girl, late teens or early twenties – had no colour at all. Her face was ashen, her long wet hair dark, her long wet coat black. But there was no blood that Brodie could see, and none of the crippling awkwardness that betrays a broken limb.

Brodie reached a hand towards her. 'Won't you sit down for a minute? Sit in the car while we work out if we need an ambulance or if we can safely take you to A&E ourselves. What do you think – is there much damage done?'

Afraid the girl might have injuries she was not yet aware of herself, Brodie touched her shoulder with no more than a fingertip, to guide her to the car. The girl's reaction was out of all proportion. Unable to retreat further she spun sideways, her eyes staring wildly, keeping close to the wall. 'Stay away from me!' she yelled again, her voice cracking.

By now the noise was attracting attention.

They didn't twitch net curtains on Fisher Hill – they opened their front doors and stood on the steps, watching with undisguised interest.

'You need to calm down,' Brodie said, allowing a trace of firmness to creep into her voice. 'You need to calm down and sit down, and I'll call the police and let them know what's happened.'

'Yeah, right!' snorted the girl. The shock was giving way now to anger: such anger that she shook and panted with it. 'With half a dozen witnesses I don't suppose you've much choice. Well, tell them what you want. Tell them it was an accident; tell them it was my fault. They'll believe that – they think my whole damn family's suicidal. But I know who sent you. Give him my regards. Tell him, better luck next time.'

Daniel was peering at her through his thick spectacles, his plain round face bewildered. 'I don't understand. Are you saying ... you think I hit you *deliberately?*'

The girl managed a wild, half-hysterical laugh. 'Whatever would make me think a thing like that?'

'I don't know you. Why would I want to hurt you?'

'I don't think you wanted to hurt me,' spat the girl. Hatred vibrated in her voice. 'I know what you wanted to do. And I know why you wanted to do it. And who knows, maybe next time it'll all work out for you. But think about this. That'll leave *you* as the last soul alive who knows what Johnny Windham is capable of.'

And with that she was away, running, across the road and into another of the Fisher Hill entries, vanishing in the darkness.

For what seemed a long time Daniel and Brodie looked at one another, and at the woman in the floral pinny and the man in the sleeveless pullover who'd come to the door with his dishmop still in his hand. Finally Brodie gave herself a shake. 'I suppose I'd better tell Jack about this.'

Daniel's frown was disapproving. He was embarrassed by Brodie's habit of bending people to her use. 'Jack's a detective super-intendent – this was a traffic accident. I'll go round to Battle Alley and report it to the duty sergeant.'

Brodie shrugged. 'It'll go in the book.'

'It *should* go in the book. That girl could be hurt. Someone ought to find her, make sure she's all right.'

'She looked all right,' sniffed Brodie, using a long-fingered hand to push the cascade of dark curls away from her face. 'You know what vets say – you don't have to worry about patients you can't catch.' He went on regarding her with that quiet reproach that was harder to ignore than an argument. 'Oh, all *right*, let's do the thing properly. Do you want to drive or...?'

But he was already in the passenger seat and refused to meet her gaze.

Sergeant McKinney saw them on the CCTV, put down the mug of tea he'd been looking forward to and went out to the front desk. There would be other tea-breaks. But a man who took an interest in events in and around Dimmock couldn't afford to take his eye off this pair for too long. 'A problem, Mrs Farrell?'

Brodie explained what had happened.

'And Mr Hood was driving?' Daniel nodded. 'Can I see your licence and insurance?' Daniel produced the one, Brodie the other. 'Well, that seems to be in order. She ran out of Hunter's Lane, you say?'

Daniel gave his lopsided shrug. 'She must have. She was running, and there was nowhere else she could have come from. But I didn't see her until she hit the wing.'

'Me neither. You know what the lighting's like up there,' said Brodie. 'And she was wearing a long dark coat of some kind.'

'And afterwards she got up without assistance?'

'Got up and ran off,' nodded Brodie. 'Into The Ginnell. Whether she had a car parked up there or was making for one of the cottages I don't know. I was too surprised to follow.'

15

'And you didn't get her name.'

'There wasn't much time,' said Daniel apologetically.

'Then it's hard to see what more you could have done,' conceded Sergeant McKinney. 'I'll check with the hospital to see if she turned up there. But it sounds to me it was more her fault than yours and there was no great damage done anyway. If she makes a complaint I'll get back to you; otherwise you should probably forget about it. Only next time you fancy a driving lesson, Mr Hood' – he lowered one eyebrow meaningfully – 'perhaps a nice sunny day would be more suitable than a wet night.'

'We'll bear that in mind,' said Brodie, a shade tartly. She still thought they could have met the letter of the law by recounting the incident to her partner. 'Can we go now? My babysitter will be wondering where we've got to.'

After they'd gone Constable March, who was manning the desk, said, 'Wasn't that...?'

'That's right, son,' said Sergeant McKinney, deadpan.

'She's a bit of a looker, isn't she?'

'Out of your class, that's for sure.'

'And she and Detective Superintendent Deacon...?'

'Exactly.'

'And the guy with her – Daniel Hood. He's her ... bit on the side?'

16

Sergeant McKinney bent a censorious eye on him. 'You're new around here, lad, so I'll give you a word of advice. Mrs Farrell and Mr Deacon are an item, Mrs Farrell and Mr Hood are not. They are friends. Nothing more, nothing less. You don't have to understand it, I don't have to understand it. We don't even have to believe it. But those of us who don't want to wake up with a crowd round us and the imprint of Mr Deacon's fist on our noses would do well to remember it.'

Chapter Two

Twice the following day Daniel phoned Battle Alley, and seemed surprised to learn he wasn't the subject of a manhunt. Both times he was assured there were still no unexplained bodies in the morgue at Dimmock General Hospital, and that pending any such development there was nothing more he could or should do.

But Daniel was a born worrier and couldn't dismiss the accident as part of life's rich pageant. He blamed himself. He thought that someone who'd kept his hand in behind the wheel, who'd driven a car more than half a dozen times in the nine years since passing his test, would have reacted quicker or more

17

appropriately and managed to avoid the girl running out of the rain at him. He knew he hadn't been speeding. He thought he'd been careful. But he ended up hitting someone, and now she'd disappeared so he couldn't even be sure she was all right.

And then there was what she said. What was that all about? Did he *look* like someone who ran people down deliberately? Why should she think such a thing? He knew – of course he did, panic was a subject he was intimately familiar with – that people say strange and stupid things in the heat of the moment, with the adrenalin flowing and the blood pounding in the temples. She could have called him all the names under the sun and he'd have understood, even agreed with her. But she'd accused him of trying to kill her. Even though she was wrong, whatever had happened in her life to make her think that? What explained the transfixing hatred in her eyes when she looked at him?

Daniel couldn't begin to understand it. But he knew someone who just might.

Brodie recognised his light step on the Shack Lane pavement and opened her office door as he went to knock. She left it locked as a matter of habit. The services she offered were confidential and often required a degree of discretion: she didn't encourage people to wander in off the street. Either they made an appointment, or they knocked and waited until it was convenient for her to see them.

This Tuesday she was alone, working on the phone and the Internet, doing the business equivalent of housekeeping which had built up over the weekend. As a one-woman firm Brodie couldn't always manage a nine-to-six five-day week, but she kept Saturdays for the sort of expedition she and her six-year-old daughter could enjoy together. Combing the antiques markets of the south coast, perhaps, or anything that involved animals or machinery. These trips, and Paddy's Sunday morning riding lesson, were highlights of the week for both of them.

But the housekeeping didn't do itself, it waited until she got round to it. By Tuesday afternoon she was glad of a distraction. She waved Daniel to the tiny sofa. 'Do you want coffee?'

'Thanks.'

'You know where the kettle is.' She waved him towards the tiny kitchen. 'What's up?'

'I'm worried,' he admitted.

'What about?'

He stared at her. 'Gee, I don't know, Brodie. It's not like anything unusual just happened!'

'The girl? Daniel, you'd have heard by now if there were going to be repercussions. Anyway, it wasn't your fault. You didn't hit her, she hit you.'

Daniel thought that was probably true. It was no help with the other thing. 'She thought I was trying to kill her!'

'She was wrong.'

'But why did she think it?'

'Because she'd just seen her life flash in front of her eyes. Because she was in a state of shock and she wanted to blame someone. Hell, Daniel, that close a call's enough to make anyone tetchy. I'd have shouted at you too.'

Her friend considered. 'You shout at people all the time, Brodie, me included. I'm not sure that proves much.'

'I don't shout!' retorted Brodie indignantly. Then, because she tried not to lie – at least not to Daniel, at least not when she wasn't going to get away with it: 'I may express my opinions forcefully from time to time. I may occasionally allow an understandable irritation to show in my voice. If the need arises, I see nothing wrong with putting my foot down with a firm hand...'

As always, being with her was helping him get things into proportion. As far as Daniel could see, nothing worried Brodie. She saved her energy for changing things that needed changing and enjoying things that were fine just as they were. Where he dwelt on the past, she lived in the present and looked to the future. Her attitude was the perfect antidote to his. He could feel the burden of anxiety lifting from his shoulders as she talked.

That didn't mean he was going to let her get away with lying. A moderate and a liberal in every other respect, he took a zealot's view of lying. He didn't do it himself, even when he really needed to, and he disapproved of it in others. 'Brodie, you shout all the time. You can do it without raising your voice. You shout at people for stopping at traffic lights. You shout at people for being old.'

She thought for a moment. 'Only when it makes them really slow,' she conceded then, eyes lowered. 'All right, Daniel, so I shout. I have no patience. That's who I am. I can't help it.' She risked a sly grin. 'It's why you love me.'

'No,' he said sternly, 'it is not why I love you.' But he couldn't resist her grin. 'I love you in spite of it.'

She ducked forward over her desk and kissed him. On the brow; breaking his heart.

He turned away, just quickly enough that someone with a quite modest degree of sensitivity would have wondered why, and busied himself with cups in the kitchen. 'You think I'm worrying for nothing, then?'

'I'm sure you are. But then, you always do. It's why I love you.'

A person of any sensitivity at all would have wondered at his silence. But Brodie just wished he'd hurry up with the coffee.

Only in the sense that this was when he worked was Detective Superintendent Deacon a twenty-first century policeman. Now in his late forties, many of the developments which had turned criminal investigation from an art into a science had come too late for him to learn with the job. He'd had to study them, to ponder their implications, to work out how to use them and how far he could trust them and when to trust instinct instead.

The problem with that, of course, was that even his instincts were resolutely twentieth century ones, involving intimidation and the occasional haymaker.

Now he was looking at a piece of paper – and it was only a piece of paper because he'd insisted on having a printout rather than peering at a computer screen – covered with a lot of letters that formed no words he could recognise. He turned his heavy head slowly and fixed his sergeant with a jaundiced eye. 'This is it?'

DS Voss nodded. 'That's it. The full chemical breakdown. Like we thought, it's a new compound – so new Forensics are still putting together a profile on it. But it's what killed the Hanson brothers and put three other kids in Intensive Care, so it's likely we'll be seeing more of it.'

Deacon didn't doubt it. In a world of few

certainties, one thing you could count on was that a new designer drug would always have teenagers queuing up to try it. There would be more weeks like this one, going from one pleasant middle-class home to the next, searching children's rooms and reading their diaries and asking their parents about their friends and social activities; and waiting patiently and asking again when the disabling tears had passed, although the bottom line was that whatever they knew hadn't been enough to keep their children from harm.

Deacon had done a lot of these interviews in his career. He'd asked grief-stricken parents where their sons and daughters might have got hold of heroin, cocaine, LSD, Ecstasy. Even in his experience, this week had been difficult. The Hansons had produced an heir and one to spare, and lost them both during the longest two days of their lives. The fifteen-year-old went gently into the good night in the early hours of Monday morning, the seventeen-year-old fighting a rearguard action for another ten hours before he too finally succumbed.

At that point no one could even tell the Hansons what had killed their sons, except that it was pretty obviously a drug overdose, apparently taken at a party in the Woodgreen Estate on Saturday night. Their parents found them collapsed in their rooms the following morning.

Deacon tapped the sheet of paper with a blunt fingertip. 'These letters and numbers. Chemicals. If the doctors had had these on Sunday – had known what they were dealing with – would it have made a difference?'

'Probably not,' said Voss. 'The biggest problem with this is not that it's different from anything else on the market, but that it's so powerful. The biggest difference between the boys who died and their friends who're still holding their own seems to be the number of tablets they took. A lot of kids tried them out on Saturday night – they were new, they wanted to give them a test-drive. I talked to some of the Hanson boys' friends. Those who took one tablet experienced visual disturbances, euphoria then hallucinations before losing consciousness. Some came round before the party was over and got themselves home, some were taken home by friends. Sick and hung over, but none of them needed detoxing.

'Judging from the blood-work, the kids in Intensive Care took two apiece. The Hanson boys apparently took three each. Even if the toxicology had been available then, it's likely that Sunday morning was already too late to save them.'

So even picking it apart and nailing its components to a printed page wasn't enough to stop it killing people. Deacon's jaw clenched till his teeth ached. Which made it his job. Wasn't it always? Defending the general populace from sudden death was always the job of some tired and frustrated policeman. Even when they were asking for it. Even when, God help their stupid souls, they were paying for it.

He scowled at the jumble of letters in front of him. 'Why are we getting bodies? Who-ever's selling this stuff, it's not in his interests to wipe out his customer-base. Is the stuff contaminated? Or is it that the compound itself is intrinsically lethal?' He heard himself and shuddered inwardly. He was spending way too much time with Charlie Voss. Two years ago he'd never have said *intrinsically*.

'Not dirty, just very strong,' said Voss. He was almost twenty years Deacon's junior, a different type of policeman and a different type of man. It was a constant source of surprise to those they shared Battle Alley Police Station with that they could work together at all, let alone well. 'I don't think either the supplier or the buyers have figured out yet how little it takes to produce the desired effect. And then, this isn't an expensive drug. It's not in the dealer's interests to tell customers they can get out of their skulls on a few quid's worth.'

'What are they calling it?'

Voss pursed his lips, pointed at the print-out with his freckled nose. 'Er – that. I can't

25

pronounce it.'

Deacon sniffed at him. 'Well, if you can't, sober, on a Tuesday afternoon, how do you suppose drunk kids in clubs on a Saturday night are going to manage? What are they calling it on the street?'

That was easier. 'Scram.'

'All right. Scram. Now get back onto Forensics and ask if Scram...'

Voss hated having to do this. He thought it would get him shouted at. 'Forensics don't call it Scram. They call it Horsefeathers.'

When Deacon went still like this it was as if the big man had turned to stone where he sat. Voss felt he was being watched by a mountain. Or rather a volcano, which when it had done watching would blow its top.

'Horsefeathers.' When the need arose the superintendent could filter all the emotion out of his gruff voice. This was more a statement than a question. But Voss knew it required an answer.

'That's what the letters are about. They represent the constituent parts. Most of them are common or garden chemicals you can obtain in this country with little or no paperwork. The exception, the catalyst that turns the whole thing into pixie-dust, is a heavy-duty veterinary tranquilliser currently being trialled in Germany. Hence Horse-feathers. It's Forensics' idea of a joke.'

Deacon nodded ponderously. 'Remind me

26

to laugh sometime when I haven't got three teenagers on life support and two in the morgue.'

This was hypocrisy. In a business that dealt with horror as a commonplace, sometimes all that kept people sane was a bad-taste joke. Deacon had made enough of them in his time that he shouldn't have taken exception to this one. But self-awareness was not one of Jack Deacon's strengths.

'Being trialled?' he said then. 'It isn't in general use even in Germany?'

'Apparently not. They're doing clinical trials: it won't be widely available until next year.'

'Then why the hell is it killing kids in Dimmock now?'

If you asked him about the town where he'd lived and worked for ten years, Deacon would say he despised the place. That it represented all that was worst about Middle England. That it was grey and repressive and self-satisfied and faded, lacking in either style or grace. A late Victorian dowager still giving orders though the servants had all left and the ceilings were falling in. Yet when the old lady faced a threat of some kind, Jack Deacon was first on the barricade. Dimmock might be an old baggage but it was his job to protect her.

'It shouldn't be,' said Voss, shaking his ginger head. 'It's supposed to be strictly controlled. The trouble is, it's designed for large animal work. What would be a reasonable dose for a bull would provide the active ingredient in hundreds of tabs of Scram. There won't be vast quantities of the stuff missing from the records, just a few litres written off as a dropped bottle or a book-keeping error.'

'Fine. But why is it our problem, not Dusseldorf's?'

'Maybe it's their problem too and they just haven't realised yet. We don't know the Hanson boys were the first victims in this country, just that they were the first to be identified. Where the cause of death didn't fit the usual parameters and the agent was recognised as something new. Dusseldorf may have a morgue full of similar cases just waiting to be identified.'

He was saying that a lake was filling up and the Hanson brothers were the first crack in the dam. Tomorrow there could be a flood of dead and comatose teenagers whose condition could now be attributed to Scram. In Dusseldorf, and also in Dover and Brighton and Bognor Regis. 'How's it coming in?'

Voss was beginning to feel he was doing all the work here. 'The same way anything else is smuggled in, but easier because you're talking about small quantities. If Customs & Excise can miss whole truck-loads of human beings, how are they going to pick up a few bottles of clear liquid?'

Deacon blew out his cheeks in a gesture of acceptance. 'They can't, can they? We have to find the factory. Nail whoever is introducing this storm-trooper German tranquillizer to our nicely-brought-up English pharmaceuticals and producing the drug from hell.

'Well, if Dimmock is the first place it's been identified, maybe it's the first place it's been sold. If so, the probability is that the factory putting the stuff together is within ten miles of this spot.'

Voss nodded slowly. 'In that case, the casualties from Woodgreen were the tip of an iceberg. If they're getting their catalyst in from Germany and they've got the facilities to produce the stuff locally, we're going to start seeing more of it. Much more of it.'

'Shut your mouth, Charlie Voss,' growled Deacon, 'God may be listening. You're right, of course. We have to get on top of this, quickly. If this is still essentially a local problem we have a chance to contain it before it spreads. Before there are Scram factories up and down the country. Once it's endemic we'll never get the genie back in the bottle. Imagine cheap heroin: it'll be everywhere. We'll never again have the opportunity to stop it in its tracks.'

'Like fire,' mused Voss, 'or a disease. Once

it gets through the pinch-point it grows exponentially. You have to stop it while it's small. Or you may never stop it at all.'

'Throw everything we've got at it while everything we've got might be enough,' agreed Deacon. 'Starting with friendly visits to everyone in the area that we know is dealing in drugs. Less with the expectation of shaming one of them into a confession, more in the hope that someone who's losing business to a cheap new wonder drug might be sufficiently pissed off to point us in the right direction.'

'It's worth a try. They wouldn't normally talk to us,' said Voss, 'but this could be different. This could put some of them out of business.'

Deacon gave his sergeant a wolfish grin. 'So now we have a decision to make. Which of us goes to see Joe Loomis?'

'Me,' said Voss quickly.

'Last time you went to see Joe he left you in a pool of blood.'

'Last time *you* went to see him you broke his fingers with a monkey wrench!'

Deacon gave a negligent shrug. 'I thought he was reaching for a gun. Besides, it's too late for him to complain now. Joe and I have a sort of understanding. If he has a problem with me he doesn't take it out on my officers.'

Voss wasn't sure how to word this. 'What

does he get in return?'

'When I go to interview him I leave the monkey wrench in the car.'

Chapter Three

Overnight there was another admission to Dimmock General that rang all the same alarm bells. It was a girl this time, a little older than the Hanson brothers and their friends, and if she'd been at the party in the Woodgreen Estate she mustn't have taken what she bought there immediately because after three days she would either have died or recovered.

But everyone in A&E was now atuned to the possibility of Scram overdose. Although the initial call-out was to a suspected RTA, her age and the lack of any witness to a road accident were enough to make a canny registrar have her blood screened for narcotics. It came back positive for Scram. A lot of Scram: four or five tablets.

She wasn't dead only because, instead of staggering off to bed and sleeping undisturbed for ten hours, she'd stumbled out onto Fisher Hill and either fallen down or been knocked down, with the result that she was in an ambulance within an hour of taking the things. A stomach-pump removed some of the substance undigested, then it was a matter of cleaning her blood and hoping that what had reached her brain hadn't reached the concentration necessary to fry it. That wouldn't be known until she woke up.

Charlie Voss heard about it before Deacon did because his fiancée worked in the hospital. She woke him up when she got home because she thought he'd want to know. While Voss was putting together a sort of hybrid meal that would do Helen as a late supper and himself as an early breakfast, she told him what she'd heard.

'Her name's Alison Barker. She doesn't live in Dimmock – she was house-sitting for some friends. She rides horses for a living.'

Voss's sandy eyebrows climbed. 'She's a jockey?'

'Not racehorses, show-jumpers. One of the nurses says she's quite well known. She was short-listed for some team or other.'

'I don't imagine she fell off a horse on Fisher Hill!'

'I don't think so either,' said Helen Choi calmly, 'I'm just giving you all the background so you don't accuse me of withholding information later. But if you're going to be silly I won't tell you the other really interesting thing I know about her.'

When it comes to gathering intelligence, a bit of bribery is often efficacious. 'You can have my bacon butty.'

The Chinese nurse thought for a moment, then nodded. 'Done deal. She was found lying in the road about two o'clock this morning, yes? But the accident was reported earlier.'

How much earlier?

'Monday evening.'

Voss frowned. 'You're telling me she was lying there for thirty hours?'

Helen shook her dark smooth head. 'If she'd been lying there for six hours she'd be dead now. Whatever happened to her had only just happened.'

'Then how...?'

'You tell me,' shrugged the woman. 'But check your incident book: it'll be there. Your Sergeant McKinney phoned the hospital on Monday evening, looking for the missing victim of an RTA. Then, we had no one fitting the description. But Alison Barker fits it exactly, down to what she was wearing. Now ask me who reported the accident.'

Voss was still trying to get his head around what he'd been told already. 'How the hell am I supposed to guess that?' But something in her expression pulled him up short. The mere fact that she asked the question meant he should know the answer. And when it came to the bizarre and inexplicable, one name was always worth an each-way bet. 'Daniel?' His voice soared.

'Daniel.'

It had been dark, it had been wet, both of them had been shaken and the girl had quickly turned angry. Even allowing for that, and the fact that the photograph Voss produced showed a white unconscious face hung about by tubes against a white sheet, Daniel had no doubt it was the same girl. He nodded. His voice was low. 'I thought we'd got away with it. She ran off: she seemed fine. I checked the hospital. They couldn't find an admission that fitted.'

'That's because they only got her early this morning.'

Daniel flinched. 'What was the problem – internal bleeding? Instead of getting better she was getting worse?'

'She's got a few bruises that probably date back to Monday, but that isn't what knocked her out. It was a drug overdose.'

For perhaps half a minute Daniel just went on staring at him, with no idea how to react. His instinctive response was relief, because whether or not he was to blame for the accident he certainly didn't give her drugs. Then he felt guilty for considering his own position when she was fighting for her life in hospital. Finally he decided that she'd still be in hospital if it *had* been his fault, so it was better that it wasn't. He swallowed. 'By drug overdose you mean illegal drugs?'

'Indeed I do,' nodded Voss. 'Scram.'

'Scram?'

'I hadn't heard of it a week ago either,' admitted Voss. 'It's new, and potent. Three or four tablets seem to be a lethal dose.'

Daniel was reassessing the accident in the light of this information. 'Is that why it happened? Was she high on Monday as well? Is that why she ran out into the road, and why she jumped up and ran off afterwards as if colliding with a car was nothing special?' Behind the thick lenses his mild grey eyes sharpened. 'Is that why she was saying those crazy things? She wasn't lucid?'

Voss shrugged. 'It seems quite likely, doesn't it? Maybe she'll be able to tell us when she comes round. If she comes round.'

Daniel winced. 'There's some doubt about it?'

'Oh yes. She took a lethal dose. What we don't know yet is whether they got the treatment started in time.'

Daniel shook his head in disbelief. He'd worried, at the time and since, that he might have cracked her ribs. It never occurred to him that two days later she could be dying. It seemed it wasn't his fault; but simply being Daniel was enough to make him feel guilty. 'Who is she?'

Voss told him what he knew. 'She doesn't actually live in Dimmock. She was staying at a friend's house.'

'What does the friend have to say about all this?'

'Not a lot. She's in Australia – Alison was house-sitting for her. So far as the friend or the neighbours know she was staying there alone. She wasn't dressed for partying – the same dark riding mac she was wearing when you knocked her down, jeans and a sweat-shirt underneath. She wasn't a habitual drug user so she must have had something special in mind last night. It's hard to be sure but it could have been a suicide attempt.'

Daniel let out a long, soft sigh. 'Her whole damn family's suicidal.'

Voss blinked. 'What makes you say that? Do you know her?'

'No. It's what she said to me. When she thought I was trying to kill her. She said I should blame her for the accident – the police would believe me because you thought her whole damn family was suicidal.'

'It sounds like there's a family history,' said Voss. To him it was sounding more like suicide all the time.

Not to Daniel. 'No, that's not what she was saying. She was saying – I *think* she was say-ing – you'd written something off as suicide when it wasn't. Something had happened to someone in her family, the police had thought it was suicide but she didn't. And now something else has happened, and she's in hospital and maybe she's never going to wake up. That can't be a coincidence.'

He had Voss's full attention. 'You think someone fed her those tablets? Knowing what the result would be?'

'How would I know?' shrugged Daniel. 'But if I was the investigating officer I'd want to rule out the possibility before I did anything else. If she took them herself, that's stupidity. If they were forced on her, that's attempted murder.'

'It's not impossible.' Every detective is aware that a proportion of drug deaths are not the result of self-administration: what no one can judge is how high a proportion. The other thing every detective knows is that, usually, what appears to have happened *is* what happened. 'But she thought you were trying to kill her and you weren't. Maybe she's just a disturbed young woman suffering from paranoid fantasies who'd finally had enough of the chaos inside her head.'

It made sense: almost enough for Daniel to stop beating himself up over it. If she was out of control when she ran in front of the car it wouldn't have mattered who was behind the wheel. In fact, a better driver would have been going faster and probably killed her outright. 'She just seemed so angry.'

'People who're suicidal often are.'

Daniel nodded sombrely. 'Thanks for coming round, Charlie. I don't know if all this makes it better or worse, but at least I don't have to wonder what happened to her any more.'

Voss nodded. 'The accident was nothing to do with you. You were just in the wrong place at the wrong time.'

'I'm having that engraved on my tombstone,' said Daniel glumly.

'They think my whole damn family's suicidal.'

'Sorry?' Brodie closed the door of Paddy's room to a crack and went on standing there, listening for any sound of bedclothes being tented, torches lit and books opened. Now the child could read she thought bed-times applied to other people.

'That's what she said. Alison Barker – the girl I ran down. She said the police would believe it was an accident because they thought her entire family was suicidal.'

'I wish you wouldn't say that,' Brodie said irritably. 'You didn't run anybody down. She ran into us. Then she got up again and ran off, and the following night she took enough rocket-fuel to put herself into orbit. Why is that anything to do with us?'

'I'm not saying it is,' said Daniel. 'It's just – why would she say that?'

Brodie's attention was still on the darkened room beyond the cracked-open door. 'What?'

'It makes no sense. Not if she thought it

was my fault, and not if she was trying to top herself.' Daniel wasn't very good at slang. He was always out of date. 'She thought I tried to run her down. And she thought the police wouldn't take it seriously because of something else that had happened. Something they'd decided was suicide. But she didn't. She thought it was...' He heard where he was going with this and stopped.

Brodie gave up listening at the door and came and sat on the sofa, facing him. 'Murder,' she said quietly.

'What?'

'If she thinks the police wrote it off as suicide and she thought it was more serious than that, there's really only one thing that qualifies. Murder.'

'That's what I came up with too,' he admitted.

'Thinking it doesn't mean she was right.'

'But thinking it means she's in trouble.'

Brodie was troubled too: she knew what he was doing. 'Half the world's in one sort of trouble or another. It doesn't all have to be your problem. Let it go.'

'She could be in danger.'

'She's in hospital, with healthcare professionals clustered round her like flies. When she wakes up the police will ask her what happened. If she has anything to tell them, that's her chance.'

Brodie made some coffee. She offered to

run him home but Daniel preferred to walk. As she saw him out he hesitated on the front step. 'You didn't.'

He'd lost her again. 'Didn't what?'

'Let it go. When I was in hospital surrounded by professionals. What happened to me was nothing to do with you, but you didn't leave me to deal with it alone.'

These days they hardly talked about how they'd met. But neither had forgotten. It was like a volcano in the background: on a nice day it was just part of the scenery, but its mere existence cast a long shadow. Brodie said softly, 'What happened to you *was* something to do with me.'

He shook his yellow head stubbornly. 'It wasn't your fault I got hurt. You were doing your job: you had no way of knowing what it would lead to.'

'I took money to find you for a man who was prepared to kill you and almost did,' Brodie said plainly. 'I believed the story I was told. I didn't know I was being used. But I should have.'

'That's hindsight talking. Maybe you made a mistake, but it was an honest one. I never blamed you for what happened. Not then and not since.' He looked at her with wrenching honesty. 'What I remember is that when I woke up, with no idea what had happened to me or why, you were there. And you stayed with me until I got some

40

sort of a grip on reality. I know it wasn't easy, that it would have been less painful to leave it to the professionals. But you were my lifeline, Brodie. You kept me sane. That's what I remember.'

Tears pricked her eyes. His generosity flayed her, no less now than two years ago, and more rather than less because it was absolutely sincere. That was how he felt. That what he'd gained from knowing her was worth more than what he'd lost: several days, a lot of skin, a lot of blood, and the chance of ever feeling entirely safe again.

She touched the back of his wrist with her fingertips. 'Then maybe you should do what I did. Go and say sorry. Even if you're not quite sure what for. Even if there's not much chance of her hearing you.' She flashed him a quick, brilliant smile. '*Especially* if there's not much chance of her hearing you.'

Daniel's face lightened too. 'Yes, I'm sorry about that. I imagine it fairly put you off your stride when I opened my eyes.'

'I thought you were at death's door. I only went to see you because I thought I could apologise without having to explain.'

'Sorry,' Daniel said again.

Chapter Four

Due to circumstances beyond his control, Daniel was well known at Dimmock General. It bought him a certain amount of licence. When he shyly explained the reason for his visit, expecting – perhaps even hoping – to be shown the door, one of the nurses took him to Intensive Care. Alison Barker was in an end bed. She didn't look as if she'd moved since Voss's photograph was taken.

'Five minutes,' murmured the nurse. 'And if anyone asks, you're a relative.'

Now he was here there was really nothing Daniel wanted to say to the girl. If she'd been awake he might have gently questioned her – about what she'd said, about what tragedies had befallen her. But she was comatose, and it didn't take a toxicologist to know she was nowhere near ready to wake up yet. Her face was grey, sweat beading the brow where the long brown hair was scraped back. Her eyelids looked bruised. A drip ran clear liquid into a vein inside her elbow and a plastic tube was trickle-feeding her oxygen. Somehow these vital, life-saving pieces of equipment turned her from a deeply vulnerable human being into an object, part of the hospital machinery. It seemed absurd even trying to speak to her.

But getting him in here had been a kindness and Daniel didn't want the nurses to wonder why they'd bothered. So he pulled a chair up to the foot of the bed and sat down, feeling vaguely ridiculous, hoping no one he knew would see him. He waited the five minutes he'd been given, then – with a sense of relief – got up to go.

A woman was watching from behind the glass screen. Daniel's heart tripped as if he'd been caught out in something improper. He thought the woman was Alison Barker's mother, that she'd been told he was a relative too and knew it was a lie. She must wonder who the hell he was and what he was doing here that needed disguising behind a falsehood.

In the circumstances he couldn't pass her without speaking. 'I'm sorry if I held you up. I met Alison a few days ago. When I heard she was in here I came to see how she was.'

'And how is she?'

The least frown gathered Daniel's light brows. Clearly he'd misunderstood: whoever the woman was, that wasn't something Alison's mother would say. 'I don't really know,' he answered honestly. 'She's still unconscious. Er – I'm Daniel Hood.'

'Mary Walbrook. Ally's father was my

43

business partner.'

Daniel looked around. 'Is he here?'

The woman shook her head. She was a small, neat individual in a well-tailored coat and high heels. He put her in her early forties. 'Stanley is dead,' she said plainly. 'Ally has no family left. That's why I'm here. I thought she might need some things – clothes, toiletries. I wasn't sure there was anyone else she could ask.'

'How did you know she was here?'

'The police called. My number's on her phone.' Mary Walbrook's keen, intelligent eyes were openly assessing him. 'So you and Ally had barely met but still you're here at ten o'clock on a Thursday morning when most people are otherwise engaged. What are you, the new boyfriend?'

'Hardly. When I say we met I mean literally for five minutes. She... I...' The woman's gaze was tripping him, making him stumble. 'She ran out in front of my car. I hit her. I didn't think she was hurt, but when she ended up in here...'

'I was told she'd taken drugs.'

There was something about Mary Walbrook that reminded Daniel of Brodie. Not physically: she was smaller, less striking and ten years older than his friend. But there was a directness in her manner that probably came from the same place Brodie got hers: the knowledge of what she was worth in every sense including financially. Mary Walbrook was another businesswoman, another head of her household, another mover and shaker.

'I was told that too,' he said. 'I suppose I wanted to be sure it wasn't my fault she was here.'

'And are you? Sure?'

It wasn't exactly aggressive, the way she addressed him. It wasn't exactly rude. It was as if she was probing him for weaknesses before deciding what kind of label to slap on him. Daniel thought she'd got her work cut out. 'Yes. That doesn't mean I don't care what happens to her.'

When Mary Walbrook smiled you could almost hear the crash of boots as the palace guard went from *Attention* to *At Ease*. The sculpted planes of her face relaxed and the sharpness went from her eyes. Her voice dropped half a tone and lost its edge. 'Good. Ally could do with a friend. Before, but especially now.'

Daniel wanted to ask about Alison Barker, was looking for an excuse to stay until Mary Walbrook's visit was complete. But she just looked at the girl in the bed and shook her head. 'She's not going to want any clothes today, is she? I'll come back tomorrow.'

Daniel fell into step beside her as she headed for the exit. Her stride was shorter than Brodie's too, and he didn't have to tilt his head to talk to her. 'Have you come far?'

'Peyton Parvo. About half an hour. You?'

'I live on the seafront.' He smiled. 'It takes me about half an hour too.'

She stared at him. 'You *walked?*'

'Last time I drove a car I knocked someone down,' he said ruefully.

'I'll drop you off.' It wasn't an offer so much as a statement.

'It's out of your way.'

'It's five minutes out of my way. It's of no consequence.'

Daniel went to thumb for the lift but the woman was already halfway down the stairs. He trotted after her. 'Can you tell me about Alison? What sort of person she is, what sort of life she leads. I suppose, what got her into this situation.'

Mary stopped on a middle step and fixed him with her gaze. Her bright hazel eyes were indignant. 'Why should I tell you anything about Alison? What entitles you to know things about her that she hasn't chosen to tell you?'

She was right, of course. Embarrassed, Daniel nodded. 'I'm sorry, I don't mean to pry. Well, actually I suppose I *do* mean to pry, but only in the hope I can help. When we met she said ... some things. I know, she'd just bounced off a car, she probably wasn't thinking too clearly, but she believed someone was trying to hurt her. Could she be right? Has something happened that would make her think that?'

Mary took a deep breath and walked on, more slowly than before. 'Mr Hood, you've come in at the tail-end of a family tragedy. Ally's been through hell these last few months, it's no wonder she's paranoid. She lost everything that mattered to her – her father, her job, her horses, her home. And then she pretty much lost touch with reality as well. Whatever she said to you, it would be a kindness to forget it.'

'What happened?'

For a moment she debated whether to tell him. Then she did. 'We had a run of bad luck. We almost lost the yard. Stanley and I were partners in a bloodstock dealership. Horses,' she said in plain English, seeing his confusion. 'Ally worked with us, on the yard and as our show rider. It was an advertisement for us and an opportunity for her. But when the bailiffs came knocking we had to sell everything that was worth money. Keeping the jumpers was a luxury we could no longer afford. The Barkers' house and my cottage went as well. The yard pulled through, but only just.'

'She must have been very upset.'

'Of course she was,' said Mary sharply, 'she'd been very successful with those horses. She was being considered for the British show-jumping team. And she'd done it all herself with just some promising young horses that came onto a dealer's yard. Now other people were going to benefit from her work and her skill, and even the money was owed elsewhere – she didn't see a penny of it. Of course she was upset. But she knew it was necessary. She'd have done anything for her father, the way he'd always done everything for her.'

'And then he died?'

'Yes. She gave up her career for Stanley and then Stanley died. Three months ago. She was inconsolable. I was afraid for her sanity. And I suppose' – she glanced back the way they'd come –'I was right.'

'It makes sense to you, then,' said Daniel. 'That she'd take an overdose.'

Mary Walbrook sighed. 'I'm afraid it does, Mr Hood. The state she's been in the last few weeks I've kept waiting for the phone to ring. It was no surprise at all when the police called me.'

Daniel was nodding slowly. 'What about her mother? Does she know what's happened?'

'Ally's mother died when she was three. A brain tumour. It was always Ally and Stanley, as far back as she could remember. Now she's alone.'

'She must have friends?'

'She *had* friends,' agreed Mary. 'Six months ago she was on the crest of a wave and she had a lot of friends. When the yard got into trouble, suddenly she hadn't quite as many. None of us had. When she lost the horses a few more disappeared. But her real friends, the ones who cared about her, hung on in there until she made it impossible for them. She was crazy after Stanley's death, thrashing around looking for someone to blame. People tried to help her – she wouldn't let them. She flung wild accusations at everyone. One by one she exhausted their sympathy. Her behaviour caused a lot of hurt. In the end people walked away. There's only so much abuse anyone's prepared to take.'

Daniel gave a sombre smile. 'So why are you here?'

The woman chuckled. 'Because if we're not exactly family we nearly are, and family can't cut and run when the going gets tough. I knew what she was going through, I made allowances for it. Somehow we managed to stay on speaking terms after Stanley's death. Until just now I thought I was the only person left who cared what became of her.'

It wasn't an accusation but he defended himself as if it was. 'She just seemed so – alone. So angry and alone. And I was afraid that she was in danger.'

'Like I said, she became very difficult. She thought the world was against her.'

'She was fantasising?' said Daniel. 'You're sure?'

'As sure as I can be. When her father died she wanted the police to launch a murder inquiry. They listened politely to what she had to say but there was no sense in it, no basis in fact. They were sorry for her too, but they couldn't give her the kind of help she wanted and she wasn't interested in the kind of help she needed. I begged her to go for counselling. It was the closest we came to a bust-up. She slapped my face. It was good advice but I knew before I opened my mouth that she wouldn't take it.'

They'd reached the front of the hospital. Mary Walbrook led the way to her car. Daniel was expecting something racier than this elderly Land Rover. He caught himself staring and looked away, hoping she hadn't noticed. Of course, she had. 'There are two reasons I don't drive a Ferrari. One is, it wouldn't tow a horse trailer. The other is, I can't afford it.'

'Do you ride horses too?'

'Not so much these days. The ground gets harder once you pass thirty. That's why I stopped competing and started dealing.'

Daniel knew nothing about horses, and it seemed he knew nothing about dealers either. He thought they were men in flat hats, checked suits and canary-coloured waistcoats. He thought smoking cigars was probably compulsory. 'In show-jumpers?'

'Competition horses generally. What we've

started calling sports horses – they're worth more that way. Show-jumpers, eventers, dressage horses, hunters. All the way from the Hickstead or Badminton hopeful down to children's schoolmasters. There are a lot of horses out there, but most of them are rubbish. You can waste a lot of time and money looking for a good one. Or you can pay me to find it for you.'

Daniel laughed. Mary Walbrook raised a surprised eyebrow. Chastened, he explained. 'I have a friend who does the same sort of thing. Not with horses but just about everything else. She calls her business *Looking For Something?* and uses exactly the same sales-pitch.'

'That's because it's true.' Mary pulled out of the car park and onto the ring road. 'The average person wanting to buy a riding horse will travel a thousand miles to look at half a dozen. There'll be something wrong with five of them. None of them will match the advertised description. The 16.2 warmblood will be a 15.3 Thoroughbred ex-hurdler with no mouth that won't go anywhere on its own. The nine-year-old all-rounder will be fifteen with spavins and navicular disease. The promising newcomer, potential in any sphere, needs bringing on, will have been overworked and overfaced before it was six and now needs a JCB to shove it into a ring.'

Daniel smiled. 'You exaggerate.'

'Not even slightly,' said the woman. 'In fact, there'll be things wrong with the sixth horse too, but after the other five he'll look great and you'll heave a sigh of relief. You'll ride him round a couple of times, and when he doesn't try to hang you in a tree and the vet says he's got the right number of lungs you'll hand over your hard-earned cash and think you've done pretty well. The likelihood is, though, he'll have problems that either limit what you can do with him or mean he'll be on the market again within a year. He might be a good enough horse, just not right for you. He might be a nice horse but not up to the standard you want to compete at. Or he might be monster once he's taken away from a yard where it habitually took three professionals to get the tack on and sedatives to get him shod.'

'That happens?' asked Daniel, shocked.

'All the time. There are a lot more ways of getting this wrong than getting it right. And it matters. More than buying the wrong car or even the wrong house. You don't just stand to lose money on the wrong horse – it can kill you. You buy through me and it'll cost you more but you'll end up with an animal that's suitable for the job you want it to do. Long term it'll save you money. And you'll have a lot more fun with it.'

Daniel thought it was probably good advice though there wasn't a cat in hell's chance he'd ever have a use for it. Paddy's riding school pony came up to his hip and was rarely caught with both eyes open, and even it made him nervous. But then, he was a mathematician. If you could plot all the world's pleasures on a graph, horses with their mad brains, lightning reactions and iron-clad extremities would come at one end and numbers weaving pretty patterns on a page at the other.

He said, 'What happened to Alison's father?'

The woman must have decided to answer his questions. 'I told you: we had a run of bad luck. We thought we were going to the wall. Only while I was working my butt off and calling in every favour I was owed, and asking people who didn't owe me a thing to let me owe them for a bit, Stanley was drowning his sorrows. First he drowned them in whisky, then he walked down our back field and drowned them in the water jump.'

Daniel recognised that her flippancy was a defence against the brutal reality. 'Suicide?'

She shrugged. 'He might just have stumbled around until he fell in and been too drunk to climb out again so the police called it an accidental death. Ally didn't believe that either. She didn't want to believe that it was Stanley's own actions which led to his death and the business going into free fall. She still believes he'd have fought for it

– for her – to his last breath.'

'But you didn't agree.'

She considered for a moment. 'Well, I knew Stanley Barker better than his daughter did. We were business partners for ten years; for some of that time we were partners in every sense. He was a good man, a kind man, but he wasn't a strong man. And then, he was a lot older than me. I think he couldn't face losing the business and having to start over.'

Her eyes shadowed with the memory. After three months it had begun to settle into the background, to lose its edge and inch towards history. Having to explain these events brought them back into the forefront of her mind. 'It takes a lot of work, a lot of energy, a lot of self-belief to build something from scratch. In your thirties, even in your forties, you know it'll be worth it – you have time to get where you want to be and then sit back and enjoy it. When you're pushing sixty the figures stack up differently. I think he was too tired and dis- pirited to do it all again, and too ashamed to take the easy way and go bankrupt. Maybe it was an accident, but it's my belief that he sat on the log over the water and drank himself insensible, knowing there was every chance he'd never wake up.'

There was a thread of anger underlying her voice that Daniel wasn't sure she was aware of. They'd been partners, they'd faced hard times, and he'd left her to deal with it alone. And she'd succeeded: she'd saved the business. But it would have been easier, less traumatic, to have done it together. She hadn't forgiven him for running out on her.

They had reached The Promenade. Daniel indicated the netting-shed on the beach. 'This is where I live.'

Mary Walbrook stopped the Land Rover and regarded the stubby black tower rising out of the shingle shore. 'Of course it is.'

'Will you come in for a coffee?'

She shook her head. 'I'd better get back. I've a shipment due in from France this afternoon. I need to be there when they arrive.'

'Thanks for the lift. And...'

'Mm?'

'If Alison's feeling better next time you see her, wish her well for me.'

'Will she know your name?'

'No,' he said.

'Will she remember you at all?'

Daniel smiled. 'Probably not. Do it anyway.'

Chapter Five

All he had to do was leave it alone. It was none of his business: everyone was agreed on that. He'd had a reasonable explanation of Alison Barker's state of mind from some-one close enough to her to know. He'd been told the police had investigated her allega-tions and found nothing to suggest she was genuinely in danger.

At that point a wise man would have backed away gracefully, maybe sent some flowers and a Get Well card, been sorry for her unhappiness but glad it wasn't his fault. Perhaps he would have taken some guilty comfort from knowing he wasn't the most screwed-up person on the south coast after all, but after that he would have forgotten her.

Daniel wanted to help her. He asked Brodie what she thought.

'I think you're insane,' she said frankly.

'No, really,' he said with a ghost of a smile. 'Don't be polite, tell me what you really think.'

Brodie gave a little snort that was half exasperation, half affection. 'Look, Daniel – I know what's going on here. I know where this is leading. You're going to do what you always do. You're going to get involved in somebody's troubles – offer her a shoulder to cry on and an ear to rabbit into – and you're going to get dumped on. Again. There's a reason why some people have no friends and no luck – they're bad news. They are the authors of their own misfortune. They can't – won't, even – *be* helped. I don't doubt that people who know Alison Barker better than you do and owe her more tried to sort her out and failed and had to give up long before you came along.

'But you always think you can do better, don't you? That other people didn't try hard enough, or tried too hard, or didn't go about it the right way. Your way. You always have to get involved. Hasn't it struck you by now that you're not a very good judge of character?'

Usually when Brodie subjected him to one of her tirades it meant she was worried about him. He tried not to take it personally. Plus, he couldn't actually argue with anything she'd said. 'I'm not planning to adopt her. I just want to make sure she's OK.'

'But she isn't OK. We know that. We knew it before you talked to Mary Walbrook. She's – let's be kind here and call it unstable. Now, maybe she's unstable because of things that have happened to her, and maybe things have happened to her because she's un-stable, but either way it isn't the services of a maths teacher that she needs right now! If she wouldn't let her friends help her, what makes you think she'll let you?'

Daniel considered for a moment. 'A man gets thrown into prison for a crime he didn't commit. He writes to everyone he knows, asking for help. His doctor writes back enclosing a prescription for Valium. His priest sends him a prayer. His MP says he'll vote for the next Criminal Justice Bill.

'Someone else he wrote to turns up at the prison and yells at the guards until they throw him in the same cell as his friend. Who is, as you can imagine, pretty disgusted. "A lot of help you are," he shouts. "Now there's two of us in here!" His friend gives him a wink. "But I've been in here before," he says. "I know the way out."'

Brodie went on looking at him, still waiting for a punchline she could understand.

Daniel sighed. He knew he shouldn't tell anecdotes: he was no better at them than at slang. He explained in words of few syllables. 'I know Alison Barker isn't making much sense right now. I know she's exhausted every friendship she ever had. I know she thinks the whole world's against her and every random misfortune is part of a global conspiracy. I know she took enough Scram to kill a donkey, and that probably wasn't a mistake.

'But Brodie, that place where she is – I've

been there. Someone helped me out, and I want to help Alison. Not because I owe it to her but because I can. Please help me.'

Most people don't know how to say please. Either they whine or they make a demand of it. When Daniel asked a favour he did so with a kind of quiet dignity that made you feel like a rat for refusing. So mostly he got what he asked for. Not only from her, Brodie had noticed, but from other people as well. Even Deacon, though he might spit and storm first, tended to end up doing as Daniel asked. It was no wonder, she reflected, that the big man resented him so.

She gave a gusty, ungracious sigh. 'What do you want me to do?'

He hadn't expected her to acquiesce so quickly, didn't have an answer ready. 'I suppose the most important thing is to rule out the possibility that she's right – that her father was murdered and she's in danger too. Mary said the police dismissed her claims. But did they look into them thoroughly or just decide she was hysterical?'

'You mean, is she completely off her head or just mildly paranoid,' Brodie para-phrased.

If she was going to help him, Daniel could forgive her the odd unkindness. 'I suppose. Until I know that, how can I help her?'

'How indeed?' She sniffed. 'Leave it with

me, I'll see what I can find out.'

There's no point sleeping with a detective superintendent if you can't get access to the Police National Computer when you need it. She asked Deacon what he knew about Alison Barker.

But all he knew or cared was that she'd taken Scram and was in no condition to tell him where she'd got it.

'You know she thinks her father was murdered.'

He reared his thick body up on one elbow to look at her. 'He was a horse dealer. He fell in a pond.'

'His daughter thinks he was pushed.'

'Still? I thought she'd probably come to terms with it by now. That's – what? – a couple of months ago?'

'Three. You're sure it was an accident? Or, at least, that nobody else was involved?'

'There was no evidence to suggest anyone was with him when he died. His partner found him in the morning and called us. The PM showed he'd been drinking heavily. It may have been an accident, it may have been suicide. I do know he wasn't murdered by the man Alison Barker blamed. He was driving a lorry in Europe at the time. His tachometer was a pretty good witness for the defence.'

'OK, so the girl's paranoid. But Daniel's

concerned. If you could just reassure him that there's nothing to worry about...'

'Oh – *Daniel's* concerned, is he?' Everything about Deacon – the craggy face, the heavy body, the gruff and venomous voice – was built for sarcasm. 'You should have said sooner. Of course I'll drop what I'm doing to make enquiries about some druggy girl who's so scared someone's trying to kill her she thinks she'll save them the trouble! It's not like I've got anything better to do. Anything at all urgent.'

'You think it was a suicide attempt?'

'Actually, I doubt if it was,' he conceded. 'Suicides don't usually go for a walk while they're waiting for a drug to take effect. They try to avoid being found while there's still time to save them.'

'What if she wanted to be found?'

'The cry-for-help thing? It's possible,' said Deacon. 'Maybe insisting her father was murdered was the same sort of thing. She wanted someone to pay her some attention.'

Almost against her wishes Brodie found herself empathising with the troubled girl. 'The poor kid's had a packet to deal with in a short period of time. Before she lost her father she lost just about everything else.' Then annoyance tacked up the corner of her mouth. 'It doesn't say much for society, does it, that a girl her age can be so alone this is the only way she can get someone to listen to her.'

'It's working, though,' growled Deacon. 'She's not even awake yet but she's got Daniel's attention. That's as much being listened to as would last most people a lifetime.'

Brodie grinned. Although it gave her problems from time to time, the antipathy between the two men in her life was an endless source of amusement. Except it wasn't exactly antipathy, more a total and mutual lack of understanding. Jack Deacon could understand the deep, dark workings of violent minds; Daniel Hood could understand people whose own mothers had given up on them; they just couldn't understand one another. The harder they tried – and they *had* tried, for her sake – the wider the gulf yawned between them.

'I know. Well, look at it this way – better she wastes his time than yours. So for everybody's sake, especially mine, can I tell him that she really hasn't any reason to be afraid? That you're convinced the murder only occurred in her imagination?'

'Yes,' said Deacon. 'Look, people get drunk and have fatal accidents every day of the week. Not all in Dimmock, thank God, but you know what I mean. There were no suspicious circumstances. His business had been failing for months. He'd sold everything he owned – horses, house, everything

– and it wasn't enough. He didn't know where else to turn. So he turned to drink, and maybe to thoughts of suicide.

'If Daniel's looking for a worthy cause, maybe Alison Barker qualifies. She might even benefit from his undivided attention. But he needs to be careful, because this girl could be a disaster looking for someone to happen to. If she isn't actually suicidal she's certainly reckless. She's accused a plainly innocent man of murder, she's run out in front of a moving vehicle and now she's taken a lethal dose of Scram. To me, that sounds like someone out of control. Now, maybe Daniel can get her feet back on the floor. But he needs to be careful that she doesn't draw him into her fantasy world instead.'

Detective Sergeant Voss believed passionately in the place of women in the modern police service. He didn't think they should be kept for domestic abuse and child protection cases: he thought they should be represented in every department. Particularly CID. Since the arrival of Detective Constable Jill Meadows he was no longer the only person on the top floor of Battle Alley who could work the computers.

On Friday morning she was the only detective working in the squad room. Voss walked the full length of it to ask if she was making any progress with the task he'd given her.

Her fellow constables had freed her a desk beside the coffee machine. At first it gave them an excuse to keep wandering past her. Later, when the novelty had worn off, they thought she could bring them top-ups. That didn't last long either. Even Huxley, who was slowest on the uptake, got the message after he'd had to go home to change his shirt three days running. Meanwhile his colleagues had run a sweepstake on whether he'd still be optimistically calling for a strong one with three sugars while he waited for his skingrafts to take.

'Any luck fleshing out the background on the Barker case?'

Jill Meadows liked Charlie Voss. Everybody liked Charlie Voss: he was a gentleman in an age, and indeed a profession, not noted for them. Even Detective Superintendent Deacon seemed to have a soft spot for him. When he wanted to shout at Voss, quite often he closed the door first.

'Luck,' she said with a smile, 'had nothing to do with it.' She printed off a couple of tightly-packed pages.

When he'd read them Voss knocked on Deacon's door. Correctly interpreting the snarled '*Now* what?' as an invitation, he went inside.

'Jill's put together a history on the

Barkers, father and daughter.'

Almost against his better judgement, Deacon had been spurred into taking a fresh look at the death of Stanley Barker. He had no reason to suspect foul play, but that didn't mean there wasn't a crime for him to investigate. Alison Barker had bought a dangerous drug and somebody else had sold it to her, almost certainly on the streets of Dimmock. That made it his business. In all likelihood knowing more about her wouldn't help him to find out where she'd got her Scram, but he wouldn't be sure until he'd tried.

'Anything we didn't know and should have done?'

Knowing he was busy, Voss tried to keep it short. But it wouldn't make sense if he edited too ruthlessly. 'You have to go back about five months. Stanley was the senior partner in a business buying and selling horses, with a yard in Peyton Parvo. They had a run of bad luck – a couple of horses died in transit, the yard was hit by a virus – anyway, word got around that they were unreliable and they lost a lot of clients. The business started going under.

'Up to that point Alison Barker had led every little girl's dream-life. But with the business failing her own horses had to be sold. Everything went. The Barkers' house, Mary Walbrook's cottage – everything. They used the equity to pay off their debts, but there wasn't much left. Miss Walbrook moved into a flat above the stables but Stanley and Alison had nowhere to go when the sale of their house completed. They paid off their debts but it cost them everything they had.'

'And Stanley hadn't much relish for starting again,' mused Deacon.

'Apparently not.'

'Except Alison didn't think it was suicide. She thought it was murder. And said so, loudly and frequently, to anyone who'd listen. Us first, then everyone else. Her friends, casual acquaintances, then shopkeepers and people she met in the street. She couldn't bear the truth.

'There's nothing unique about that,' he said, settling deeper into his chair. 'Faced with a tragedy, people behave in one of a fairly limited number of ways. Number five is, Externalise. Blame everything on a third party. If there isn't a third party available, make one up.'

Voss was impressed. 'As it happens, there was a third party available. It took a leap of the imagination to blame him for Stanley's death, but Alison managed it.'

'The lorry driver. What was his name again?'

'Johnny Windham. He runs the transport firm that carried Barker & Walbrook's horses. Alison blamed him for their problems. If he'd been more careful they wouldn't have lost horses in transit, they wouldn't have got the virus, their business would be thriving, she'd still have her competition string and her father would still be alive. The whole lot was Windham's fault. She overheard them arguing. She believed Windham came back later and pushed Stanley in the pond.'

'But she was wrong,' said Deacon.

'She was certainly wrong about that. We know he was abroad when Stanley Barker went swimming in his water-jump. I don't know, maybe Windham let them down, or maybe they were just unlucky. But the general rule is that if you have livestock, from time to time you have deadstock. Their real mistake was over-extending themselves – they hadn't a buffer to see them through a sticky patch.'

Deacon sucked his front teeth. 'And Barker died rather than deal with the situation, and now his daughter's turned to drugs for pretty much the same reason. God, what a mess.'

For a policeman, Voss had an improbable optimistic streak. 'Sometimes people have to hit rock bottom before they can start to climb back. Maybe ending up in hospital with an overdose was what needed to happen to Alison Barker. Maybe now she'll get the help she needs.'

'Maybe she will, Charlie Voss, maybe she will.' Deacon's face darkened. 'But maybe she'll get Daniel.'

Chapter Six

Deacon told Brodie what Voss had told him, and Brodie told Daniel. He listened carefully, without interrupting. She wasn't sure if he was persuaded or not until she'd finished.

Then he sat back – he'd been leaning forward with his elbows on the table between them, the remains of lunch pushed to one side – and nodded slowly. 'I'm very grateful,' he said simply. 'You'll thank Jack for me? It doesn't sound as if she's in any danger after all. Except mentally, of course, and there's not much I can do about that. At least I'm not going to open *The Sentinel* next week and read that she's been murdered.'

Brodie regarded him with her head tilted slightly to one side, the dense dark curls clustered on her shoulder. The driftwood greys of Daniel's living-room provided a foil for her dramatic, almost gypsy beauty. Everyone she knew considered her a strikingly handsome woman, and though she demurred in public, privately she was inclined to agree. 'You really thought that was a possibility?'

'Yes,' admitted Daniel. 'I know it sounds melodramatic, but what she said scared me witless. I couldn't get it out of my mind.' He looked at her with hunted eyes. 'I kept thinking how awful it would be if something happened to her, after we'd had the chance to help and hadn't taken it. If she'd known someone was trying to kill her, and she'd told me, and along with everyone else I dismissed it as an over-active imagination. If there was a moment when I could have saved her and I let it go by.'

These days Brodie wasn't much bothered by thoughts of what might have been. She fended off such problems as she saw coming and dealt with those she didn't, and if she got herself, her child and her business through the week without any major disasters she reckoned she'd done well enough. She wasn't prepared to feel a failure because she couldn't see into the future.

Curiously, when her marriage had been on track – or at least she'd thought it was – she took small upsets much more to heart and blamed herself for everything that went awry. Though the divorce was the last thing she'd wanted, in some ways it had been good for her. She'd learned it's the big things that matter, not the minutiae. She would never again worry whether her ironing was up to

69

scratch. And when something went badly wrong, she exhausted all the alternatives before even wondering if it was her fault.

But Daniel agonised over every decision and every mistake, like a pocket Atlas carrying the sky, and while she considered it stupid and told him so, his open-ended sense of responsibility was one of his more endearing qualities. It might be a foolishness, a conceit even, but it wasn't done for effect. He really did care about things like right and wrong and the suffering of strangers. She knew it was no exaggeration when he said he'd been worried sick; that it was quite likely he hadn't slept since the incident on Fisher Hill.

'Repeat after me,' she said calmly, 'you're a blithering idiot.'

'I'm a blithering idiot,' Daniel said obediently. 'And you're a princess to put up with me. And Jack...'

Brodie stopped him there. 'I think, if we're wise, we won't accuse Jack of philanthropy. We both know what was in his mind when he did it. Let's just say you got what you needed because he thinks the world of me and I think the world of you.'

It was one of those now-or-never moments. Either he said something or he put the thing irretrievably out of his mind – walled it up, locked it up, buried the key in concrete and dropped the concrete off the

Forth Bridge. Daniel didn't lie. He despised lying. But he was coming to realise that concealing the truth for as long as he'd now been doing it was hardly any better.

He'd known for months that what had begun as a close platonic friendship had somehow – with no encouragement from him, when he wasn't even looking – evolved into something else. But only on his side. He knew Brodie didn't feel the same way about him: she took his hand, kissed his cheek, made pronouncements like the one she just had far too easily. Not that it wasn't true when she said she loved him – he knew it was. He'd felt the same way about her, not that long ago. He wished from the bottom of his heart he still felt that way. Friendship he could do – he was good at friendship. This other thing made him foolish.

And it wasn't even a secret any more. Somehow Deacon had guessed. He hadn't said anything to Brodie yet, because Daniel had begged him not to, but Daniel knew that one day he would. It was vital that he get it said first, if only to kick it into touch. To let her know that he didn't harbour any ambitions in that direction. That he wasn't going to sacrifice their friendship, which was the most important thing in his life, in the vain hope of having something more.

They were alone. This being Saturday, Brodie had brought Paddy for what Daniel

71

had come to think of as family lunch, when he did Proper Cooking instead of getting something from the freezer. But now the food was gone the child was on the gallery, looking out to sea and pretending the wooden house was a ship. Daniel took as deep a breath as he could manage with his chest constricted and said, 'There's something I need to tell you.'

Brodie had started clearing away the pots. 'Something urgent?'

'No, not urgent,' he said. 'In fact, it's been on my mind for a while.'

'Important, then?'

That was harder. 'Not history-book important. Not even front page of *The Sentinel* important.'

There was a *but* implicit in that, but she was in too much of a hurry to hear it. 'Well, if it isn't important and it isn't urgent, could it wait? Paddy and me are doing the antique fair in Eastbourne this afternoon. Do you mind if I leave you the washing-up? Pop round tonight if you want a natter.'

She had the front door open and in a moment she would call her daughter and be away. And he'd never pluck up the courage to start again, and she would never know.

'Brodie,' he said, his voice taking on the stridency of desperation, 'the other day. When I said I love you? I meant it. In every way.'

She turned in the doorway with a smile as brilliant as starfire. She took a quick step back into the room and dropped a kiss on top of his yellow head. 'Of course you did, sweetie.' Then she was gone.

Daniel not only hadn't got the response he wanted, he hadn't even got the response he expected. It was, he conceded as he reviewed the exchange in his mind, entirely predictable that when he finally took the plunge and said that to someone he would be so cack-handed as to give the impression she was right there on the list of "Things I Love" with shaggy dogs and home cooking and a nice bottle of Chianti. When it came to the life of the heart he was a disaster area.

He once told Brodie his whole family were emotional cripples, but that wasn't quite it. He was not lacking in emotions. He was not without sensitivities. His feelings were, he imagined, similar to everyone else's. It was in giving expression to them that he failed so comprehensively. You could blame lack of practice, but he was articulate enough when it came to finding words for other people's hopes and fears. Yet when he tried to describe his own he ended up getting a motherly kiss from the woman of his desires!

In spite of which, and curiously, he felt better for having said it. The fact that Brodie had misunderstood altered very little.

Indeed, if she'd taken him up correctly she would have been embarrassed and unsure what to say next time they met. It was probably better that she hadn't followed his meaning. There was still a degree of satisfaction in having got it out, however incoherently. When he was an old man, and still alone, at least he could console himself with the knowledge that, just once, he tried to break the mould. That he may never have won the race but he did, at least once, get as far as the starting-blocks. It took some of the burden of failure off him, left him oddly cheered.

He was in the kitchen, washing the pots – which Brodie *always* left for him – when the phone rang. It was the hospital.

They didn't have a next-of-kin for Alison Barker, and she'd received only two visitors. One was a woman none of the staff knew or knew how to reach. The other was a young man whose contact details were on the computer and whose blood type they knew by heart.

Alison was awake, groggy and disorientated, distressed and confused. What she needed was someone she knew to come and sit with her and talk to her and help her to sort through the maelstrom that was her mind. 'But we couldn't find one,' said Staff Nurse French. 'We wondered if you'd do it.'

Daniel was taken aback. 'I'm not a relative. I'm not even a friend. We only met when Brodie was giving me a driving lesson and I ran her down. I apologised, she shouted – that was it.'

'You cared enough to come and see how she was. It would help her if you'd come again.'

Daniel could never refuse an appeal to his better nature. 'All right. Of course. Now?'

'As soon as you can make it. Thanks, Daniel.'

She didn't even recognise him. He saw her eyes light on him as he walked down the ward towards her, and explore him anxiously for signs of familiarity, and slide away disappointed when she found none. What she wasn't was alarmed.

Daniel didn't know whether to be offended or relieved. It was beginning to look as if he was the only one to take Alison Barker's fears seriously, Alison included.

But then, today she wasn't half the girl he'd seen that night, running too quickly for her own good, fast and agile and angry. But nor was she the unconscious girl he'd seen here on Thursday, still in the bed but for the odd restless twitch, white, blind and hung around with tubing. Her eyes were open now and intelligent if confused. The nurses had raised her head a little so she could see something other than the ceiling.

Daniel smiled in what he hoped was a reassuring manner and refrained from pulling out the chair until she asked him to sit. 'My name's Daniel Hood. We met a few days ago, on Fisher Hill. You were crossing the road, I was driving up it.'

Alison Barker frowned so carefully it must have hurt. 'I know you?'

Daniel remembered this: waking from a nightmare only to find that reality had nothing much to recommend it either. That the world had changed fundamentally while you were asleep, and it was alien and scary and you didn't know how it worked, and right now you couldn't see any way of catching up.

'Not really,' he admitted. 'I knocked you down.'

For a second she shrank from him and her eyes were afraid. He hastened to explain. 'It was an accident. I didn't mean to hurt you.'

Her eyes were brown, like peat-pools in the pallor of her face. Daniel watched the fear in them subside and a kind of puzzlement take its place. Her voice was a breathy murmur, rusty with lack of use. 'I remember...'

'We wanted to call an ambulance,' said Daniel. 'My friend and I. But you dashed off, and I hoped that meant you were all right. And then I heard you were in here.'

It was difficult to judge if she was remembering or just taking in what he was saying. 'An accident. That's why I'm here?'

So no one had told her. He wasn't sure if it was his job or not. But he wasn't going to lie to her, and he couldn't think of a good reason not to answer so he did. 'Well, no. The police think you overdosed on – I can't remember the name, some drug. Scat or Scratch or something.'

For the first time he got a flash of the girl he'd met in the rain. Her eyes spat contempt at him. 'Don't be stupid.'

'I may have got the name wrong...'

'I drink coffee. I drink wine with a meal. I don't smoke and I don't take drugs.'

Daniel didn't know what to say. 'Well, I'm pretty sure that's what they're treating you for.'

'Drugs?' The confusion in the girl's face slowly gave way to anger, and behind that a resurgence of the fear. 'Dear God. So he found a way.'

Daniel bit his lip and said nothing.

Finally she noticed that he was standing at the end of the bed as if expecting to be thrown out at any moment. She jerked an unsteady hand at the chair. 'Sit down, will you, before someone hangs a drip from you.'

Daniel did as he was told. Alison Barker went on watching him for perhaps half a minute. Then she said, 'I don't understand what you're doing here.' Her voice was frail and fractious, impatient with her weakness and with him.

He gave a shrug. 'I'm not entirely sure myself. When you started waking up the staff wanted to find you a familiar face. I was the best they could do.'

'The guy who knocked me down.' She laughed at that – bitterly, immoderately enough to trigger a coughing fit that racked her abused body. Daniel helped her to sit while she caught her breath. When she could speak again she said roughly, 'Which says pretty much all there is to say about my life.'

'That's silly,' Daniel chided gently. 'I know you have friends. One of them was here – Mary Walbrook? But the staff nurse knew where to find me and didn't know where to find her. She'll be back. She said she'd bring you some things.'

'Mary was here?' Alison nodded fractionally. 'She *is* a friend. She's been a good friend to me, and I've been bloody ungrateful. Will you call her for me? I know the number.'

'Of course I will. I'll go find a phone now, if you like.'

The girl looked puzzled again. 'Find one?'

He got this from Brodie too. 'I know. It's just, I try not to clutter my life up with things I don't need.'

She thought she understood. 'I'll pay you for the phone-call, as soon as I find my clothes.'

She wasn't being sarcastic: she thought it might matter to him. Daniel wasn't going to take offence where none was intended. 'There's no rush. Don't go anywhere, I'll be right back.'

'Funny guy,' she growled. But there was the hint of a smile in it.

Chapter Seven

Deacon heard that Alison Barker was awake soon after Daniel did. His first thought was to send Voss to interview her, perhaps accompanied by Jill Meadows because – so he'd heard – women were good at these things. At reassuring the frightened and encouraging the reluctant. At probing deeper by pushing gently than by shoving hard. At not losing their tempers when obstructions were put in their way. Deacon had heard these things about women often enough to believe they were probably true, although – the woman he knew best being Brodie Farrell – he couldn't vouch for them from personal experience.

But then he thought that perhaps the

gentle touch wasn't what was called for here. Alison Barker wasn't in any real sense a victim, except of her own foolishness. She had taken a drug so new that virtually nothing was known about its effect, let alone its side-effects. Presumably she had done so in a spirit of adventure. Well, she could look on this interview in the same light. He took his coat and headed for the car park.

Staff Nurse French saw him coming and fell into step with him. 'You won't have to stay too long. She's still very disorientated. You may find she simply doesn't remember what you need her to. She almost died. Nobody's brain comes out of a coma in the same condition it went in.'

Deacon gave her a crocodilian smirk. 'A lot of people have trouble remembering things when I first talk to them. You'd be surprised how much better they do with a little help.'

Sharon French had been a nurse for twelve years: she saw scarier things than Jack Deacon every day. She said without rancour, 'You want to use thumbscrews, you wait till she's off my ward.'

He tried to look hurt. 'Staff Nurse French, you know we don't do things like that.'

He'd forgotten she worked with Charlie Voss's fiancée. 'Where was it you lost that monkey wrench again, Superintendent?'

He dropped his chin onto his chest and gave his tie a secret smile. 'Let's put it this way. The vaseline must have worked or he'd have needed your help to get it out.'

The nurse left him at the entrance to the ward. Over her shoulder as she went she said, 'Daniel's about somewhere.'

It was a bit like having mice in the attic. At first it drives you mad and you try every-thing to put a stop to it. But when the poison and the traps and the swearing fail, left with nothing else you start coming to terms with it. The noise doesn't annoy you any less but it doesn't distress you in the same way. Daniel Hood was the mouse in Deacon's attic. He no longer felt his whole body clench at the sound of Daniel's name, but the way his life overlapped with Deacon's in so many varied and unexpected areas was a constant irritation.

'Never mind,' he said with restraint.

Anyone who knew this girl a week ago would have been shocked at the sight of her, her face white and strained, her slender body, that in health looked only fit and toned, so diminished by illness that it barely lifted the sheet off the bed. But when Deacon last saw her she was teetering on the edge of the abyss, and he was surprised how much better she looked today.

He told her who he was, then he told her what he wanted to know. 'Where did you get the pills, Miss Barker?'

She couldn't have sat up without the

support of the pillows and her voice was wafer-thin. But it seemed her mind was clear enough to understand the question, and even to evade it. 'I didn't.'

Deacon breathed heavily at her. 'We don't really have to do this, do we? Pretend that you've no idea what I'm talking about until I produce the blood-work and we discuss it like intelligent people? I know what you took. I want to know where you got it.'

Some people you can bully, some you can't. If he'd thought about it rather longer Deacon would have realised he was unlikely to intimidate a girl who threw half-ton horses at five-foot fences for fun. Even lying half-prone in the bed, Alison Barker managed to glare back at him. 'Superintendent Deacon, watch my lips. I didn't take any drugs. I know – I've been told – they got into me somehow, but I didn't take them. I didn't buy them, I don't know where they came from and I don't know how they got into my system.'

Deacon sighed. He pulled out the chair recently vacated by Daniel and sat down. 'Miss Barker, are we back to this "There's a murderer on the loose" business?'

She was no stranger to scepticism. She'd seen the look that was on Deacon's face now too often to go on being surprised. On the faces of friends and of professionals – people whose job it was to listen, to understand and to help. Some of them policemen. She bared her teeth in a smile that would have been fierce if it hadn't been so frail. 'That's right. He killed my father and now he's tried to kill me.'

'That's what you said when you ran into Daniel's car,' Deacon pointed out, not unreasonably.

Alison nodded. 'I was wrong about that.'

'Perhaps you're wrong about this.'

'You mean, perhaps I spent money I don't have on drugs I don't want and took them without noticing?'

One thing was clear: she hadn't much in the way of brain damage. 'Then how do you explain it?' asked Deacon.

'My food was spiked. It's the only way.'

'Who by?' Deacon hadn't a lot of time for grammar.

'Johnny Windham.'

'The livestock transporter?'

Alison hadn't expected him to remember. She'd imagined that once the file was stamped *No further action recommended*, everyone who'd handled it would forget. She nodded.

'You've seen him recently?'

Alison shook her head without lifting it off the pillow. 'He knows better than to let me see him. He must have broken into the house when I wasn't there.'

Deacon wondered if she had any idea how

foolish she sounded. 'Miss Barker, when you accused Mr Windham of murdering your father we had a good look at him. We found out exactly where he was the night of the accident. He was in Germany, collecting a lorry-load of horses. He'd been there for thirty-six hours and he stayed there another day. There is no way he could have been involved in your father's death. Which makes it kind of silly to keep accusing him.'

'You don't know him. I do. I know what he's capable of.'

Deacon wasn't prepared to go down that road again. He was only here because he'd hoped she could help with his Scram inquiry. If she wasn't going to, his detective's instinct was to move on and leave her to the hospital psychiatrist. What stopped him was the outside chance that there was a grain of truth in what she was saying. That she was in danger. Also, Scram had got into her system somehow. Whether he liked it or not, what had happened to her was part of his investigation.

'All right,' he said. 'Tell me why you think Windham tried to kill you.'

For a moment she didn't answer. He felt her eyes assessing him. 'Because you'll do something about it? Or because, once I've got it off my chest, we can talk about the drugs?'

Deacon suspected Alison Barker had a

history of making it hard for people to help or even like her. 'Because you seem to believe it, and I want to be sure you're a crank before I bin it.'

Alison gave a little snort with something like a chuckle in it. 'At least that's honest.'

'They say it's the best policy. Especially, I suppose, when you're a policeman.'

'All right,' she said, 'I'll tell you. But why should you believe me this time when you didn't three months ago?'

In fact Deacon hadn't interviewed her himself. Stanley Barker's death had never seriously looked like a crime. 'Maybe I won't,' he agreed. 'But I'm willing to listen, and you're not going anywhere...'

Dead on cue, the mouse in the attic started to scratch. Daniel came back from the phone. 'Jack,' he said warily, keeping his distance.

'Daniel,' growled Deacon.

'Is this official? I can come back later...'

Deacon would have accepted his offer but Alison waved him to the end of her bed. 'Superintendent Deacon wants to know why I think Johnny Windham wants me dead. I expect you do too.'

It took a moment to organise her thoughts. 'Don't suppose I don't know how this sounds. People I've known most of my life won't talk to me any more. They think my dad's death somehow turned my head.

That's what Mary thinks.' She caught Daniel's eye with her own. 'She told you as much, didn't she?'

He didn't answer. He didn't make a habit of betraying confidences.

Alison took his silence as consent. 'Don't worry,' she said tiredly, 'you're not telling me anything I don't already know. Mary's been a good friend to me, but I know she thinks I dreamt this up because I needed someone to blame for Dad's death. But then, she thinks he killed himself. I know better.'

'What do you think happened?' asked Deacon, his voice wiped of expression.

'I think he was murdered,' said Alison bluntly. 'If you tell me there was no way Johnny could have done it himself, I believe you; but he was behind it. Dad stopped using him after the problems he caused us, and word got around. Windham Transport ended up in nearly as bad shape as us. He was reduced to local moves and ferrying people to shows and things – which was a come-down for someone who was used to spending half his time in Europe.' She couldn't resist a small, vindictive smile.

'I heard them arguing about it a few days before Dad died. Johnny wanted to carry our horses again so people would think they'd resolved their differences and follow suit. He offered Dad a discount, to help with some of his losses and to bury the hatchet, but Dad wasn't interested, not at any price. He said he wouldn't let Johnny carry his horses for free, and if people thought that was because he didn't trust him that was fine by him.'

Her voice grew hard. 'I heard him say that, Superintendent, and five days later my father was dead. I don't much believe in coincidence. I think when Johnny couldn't get Dad on-side again he settled for shutting him up instead.'

Daniel could see she was tiring herself. She took a moment to rest. 'I know everyone else thinks it was suicide. But I know he wouldn't have killed himself. He wouldn't have left Mary and me knee-deep in debt.'

Deacon wasn't buying it. 'Even if you were right, and there's no earthly reason to suppose you are, why would Windham want to kill you?'

Her answer was disarmingly candid. 'Because I have a big mouth. Just because I couldn't get him charged with murder didn't mean I was going to forget. I made sure everyone I met heard what had happened and whose fault it was. I lost my home and my horses, and Mary nearly lost the business, because Johnny Windham is a lazy, good-for-nothing cheapskate. And I lost my dad because he thought his poxy reputation mattered more than a good man's life.'

Deacon blinked. 'You want to explain that?'

'In this business, reputation is everything. If people buy a horse from us and it works out well, they talk and we get more business. But if they have trouble they don't just talk, they shout it from the rooftops. This is a word-of-mouth business: dissatisfied customers are bad for a dealer's reputation. Enough dissatisfied customers can wipe him out.'

'That's what happened to Barker & Walbrook?'

'We lost two horses in transit. We delivered another three that were sick and one of them died. All in the space of two months. After that the yard was like a ghost-town. Nobody was buying from us, nobody was selling to us. The average horse is in our care about a fortnight, some of them just a few days. If we can't keep them safe till their new owners take delivery we're doing something wrong. By the end of those two months, *I* wouldn't have used us either.'

'Did you work out where the problem was?' asked Daniel.

'Don't you listen?' snapped the girl. 'We were using Windham Transport when we'd have been safer ferrying the horses around in clapped-out old beast-boxes. The guy's supposed to be a professional. It's supposed to be a professional operation – we were certainly paying professional prices. And he was delivering us sick and dying horses.'

'What killed them?' asked Deacon, becoming interested despite himself.

'Different things. One was a twisted gut. One was a bad reaction to a sedative. Others were blamed on a virus.'

'And these things shouldn't kill horses?'

'These things kill horses every day, Superintendent. We'd lost horses to every one of them before. What shouldn't have happened was so many incidents in so short a time, and every one of them involving Windham Transport. It had to be something he was doing, or not doing. He wasn't cleaning the lorry out properly between loads. He was setting off with horses that were already unwell and should have been put back in their boxes till the vet passed them fit. He wasn't feeding or watering them when he said he was, or else he was being rough and getting them upset. I don't know what he was doing, Superintendent Deacon!' she cried. 'But I know he was doing something, and because of it our clients lost some good horses and we lost a lot of good clients.'

Deacon nodded. 'And – this being a word-of-mouth business – you said so. Loudly and publicly.'

'Of course I did,' said Alison fiercely. 'People thought it was something *we* were doing. That we were passing off sick animals as sound. That we couldn't spot when a horse needed a vet, or we were trying to avoid call-out fees. The business was heading down the pan. People we'd had dealings with for years wanted nothing more to do with us. I had to sell my own string to meet the bills.'

She swallowed. 'When Dad died, people we knew – people who'd respected us – started saying that proved who was to blame, that he'd killed himself rather than face the consequences. I wanted them to know what Johnny Windham had done. It mattered more than anything.'

It might be absurd – Deacon knew it *was* absurd, Windham hadn't killed anybody and it wasn't the sort of thing professional assassins get involved in – but he thought Alison Barker believed what she was saying. 'And now you think he's had a go at you. Broken into your house – or rather, a friend's house, somewhere you don't usually live – and put the latest designer drug into your cornflakes.'

Her eyes were disappointed. As if, just for a moment, she'd allowed herself to hope she was finally getting a hearing. 'I knew you wouldn't believe me.' She looked at Daniel but Daniel was keeping his thoughts to himself. She shook her head, angrily. 'If I'm imagining all this, how the hell did I end up overdosed on drugs?'

Deacon nodded. 'Which was the first question I asked you.'

Alison's lip curled. She wasn't a pretty girl, except that most people – boys and girls – look pretty good at twenty-two. But there was character in her narrow face, a kind of mental toughness. 'Tell you what, Mr Deacon. Go to my house – my friend's house in The Ginnell. Take samples from all the food packages. And when you find traces of your drug, come back here and we'll talk some more.'

Though Detective Superintendent Deacon was not in the habit of allowing himself to be dismissed, he saw no point in remaining longer. He wasn't going to get the answers he wanted from her. Either she didn't know where she'd come by the Scram or she wasn't telling. He nodded. 'All right.'

Surprised, Daniel watched the big man walk down the ward and out of sight. Then he looked back at Alison. 'Will he find something?'

She shrugged. 'Will he look?'

Daniel considered. 'Yes. He won't want to risk missing something that might be significant.'

'Not because he believed every word I said, then,' the girl said sourly.

'He's a policeman,' said Daniel apologetically. 'I don't think he sees it as his job to believe or not to believe what he's told. He'll try to find proof.'

She went on looking at him in that

disconnectingly direct way she had. 'You're not a policeman.'

He smiled. 'No. I teach maths.'

'Do you believe me?'

It was a very simple question. There were only two, possibly three, answers. Still he hesitated. 'The honest truth?'

'It's the only kind that's worth a damn.'

'Then yes. Yes, I rather think I do.'

He'd knocked her down, he'd seen her afraid for her life, he'd seen her waking in a strange place with no idea what she was doing there or what had happened to her. For the first time he saw tears in her eyes. 'Thank God,' she whispered.

He went to offer her a handkerchief. Instead she took his hand in both of hers and held it as if she'd never let go. 'Thank God,' she said again; and then again. 'Thank God.'

Daniel was right. There was something about Alison Barker that made Deacon want to get to the bottom of her story. Partly because, if by any chance what she was telling him was the truth, the girl had shown courage and Deacon admired courage. And partly because if he found illegal substances in her biscuit barrel it would be a lead into the Scram network which he hadn't had before. He'd need to take another, closer look at Windham Transport.

So as soon as he left the hospital Deacon had Billy Mills – until his retirement Sergeant Mills, now civilian Scenes of Crime Officer Mr William Mills – head over to the house in The Ginnell with his satchel full of sample bottles.

It would be tomorrow, and probably late tomorrow, before the samples came back with a full-spectrum analysis for all likely narcotics, hallucinogens, amphetamines and barbiturates. But Deacon knew that Billy Mills, whose experience of places where people had done unpleasant things to one another was unrivalled, would have a fair idea what to expect from the state he found the place in. He had a nose for a crime scene as good as a sniffer dog's. As soon as he got back to Battle Alley Deacon called him to his office.

'Well?'

It was getting to be a long time since Billy Mills had looked like the cutting edge of criminal investigation. He was the wrong side of middle age, he was rotund, and when he got down and dirty with a bit of almost invisible evidence, sometimes he had trouble getting up again. But he was very good at his job.

He shrugged heavy shoulders. 'It all looked pretty normal to me. There were no obvious signs of tampering.'

'I don't suppose there were,' said Deacon

shortly. 'If someone *had* drugged her food he wouldn't want her to notice while she was preparing it.'

'Still, she wouldn't know what to look for, and I do. If someone was messing around in her cupboards he had a good tidy-up afterwards.'

Disappointed, Deacon nodded. 'OK, Billy, thanks. I suppose Forensics might turn something up?'

SOCO wasn't a big a fan of the Forensic Science department. He considered that they took a lot of the credit that rightly belonged to him. 'You never know your luck,' he said doubtfully.

Chapter Eight

Sunday morning was the sun at the centre of the Farrell family system, the fixed point around which everything else revolved. Working hours, meal-times, shopping and housework – all these were moveable feasts which could be made to fit in with one another according to shifting priorities. But Sunday morning was when Paddy Farrell went riding, and hell hath no fury like a six-year-old girl deprived of her weekly fix of ponies.

Sometimes Brodie took her, sometimes

John and his new wife Julia did. This weekend the John Farrells were visiting Julia's parents, so Brodie pulled Appletree Farm duty. It was no hardship to her. Admittedly, she spent some of the hour-long lesson with her hands over her eyes, and about once a month she had to spread a blanket over the seats before heading home because the child had fallen off in a puddle. But set against that was the heart-choking pleasure of watching the person who mattered most to her in the world doing the thing that mattered most to *her* in the world.

Paddy on top of a pony, bouncing round inexpertly and hanging onto the mane with both hands, was the human equivalent of the Cheshire cat – a smile wearing a child. Brodie felt privileged to be part of that. If her business ever took such a dive that it couldn't fund the weekly riding lesson she would re-invent it as a knocking-shop. Luckily enough she wouldn't even need a new shingle: that discreet slate beside the front door with the legend *Looking For Something?* would serve her just as well in her new career.

So Sunday morning came and, as with every Sunday, Paddy was ready for her eleven o'clock lesson by nine-thirty and sitting on the stairs in the hall with her hard hat on by ten. It was a fifteen-minute drive to Cheyne Warren – twenty if they bought ice creams on the way. But by twenty-past ten Brodie could feel her child's longing like a magnet pulling her towards the front door. She gave in with a sigh, left what she was doing and headed out to the car, Paddy cavorting joyfully around her like a springer spaniel.

Which is how they came to be at Appletree Farm while Dieter Townes was still getting his ponies ready.

Brodie had met him before, when she first went to enquire about lessons, and had exchanged a wave with him across the yard on a number of occasions since. But she hadn't sat and chatted to him while he brushed mud off half a dozen ponies of assorted sizes, colours and degrees of shagginess, and she found herself enjoying his company.

At ease in his natural habitat, freed of the need to impress a new customer, he seemed younger than she remembered: a couple of years her junior, she guessed, maybe thirty or thirty-one. He was as tall as her, strongly built and athletic, the muscles of his arms prominent where he pushed the sleeves of his sweatshirt up out of his way. It served to remind her that his was a very physical job: not just riding horses but working with them eight or ten hours a day. Brodie had gone to pick up a bale of hay once, for Paddy to use as a mounting block. She'd been surprised at the weight of the thing. Even the child-sized saddle she used was heavier than seemed necessary, and an uncooperative Shetland pony is stronger than the strongest man. It all helped keep him in shape.

A shocked little quiver ran through Brodie when she caught herself thinking that. But what the hell: a person's thoughts are her own, she has nothing to apologise for unless she acts on them when she shouldn't. And all she was doing, and all she intended to do, was sit on a bench chatting to the man while he worked, and occasionally passing him a tool from his extensive and arcane collection.

'Can I have the hoof-pick next?' He had a pleasant, even-tempered voice, without any inflection that would hint at his background. 'Er – that's the curry-comb.'

Brodie tried again, came up with a sweat-scraper. In an agony of embarrassment, Paddy reached into the box on the bench beside her and passed her the required item.

'I suppose you were born knowing this stuff,' said Brodie.

'Not really,' said Townes. 'My father was a soldier, my mother's a teacher. Neither of them had any interest in horses. I don't know where I got the idea from but I always knew I wanted to ride. Like Paddy.' He smiled at the little girl, who blushed with pleasure. 'By the time I was twelve I knew I wanted to do this for a living.'

'How long have you had this place?'

'About four years. Before that I worked in other people's yards.'

'Teaching?'

'Teaching, grooming, schooling, competing – anything I got the chance to do. The scary thing about horses is not how big they are or how fast they can travel: it's how much there is to learn about them. How easy it is to do the wrong thing. How much it can matter.'

It wasn't that she wanted further information on Alison Barker, more that she was enjoying talking to him. Even though she was committed elsewhere, Brodie didn't begrudge herself a little pleasant conversation with an attractive man. Deacon was many things, some of them quite admirable, but he was nobody's idea of a conversationalist. 'Someone was telling me much the same thing the other day. They'd been having all sorts of problems transporting their horses.'

Townes nodded. 'Body-brush, please. No, that's the dandy-brush. That's the water-brush. That's the curry-comb again.' Finally he got what he was waiting for. 'Everybody has a horror story about travelling. Trailers coming unhitched. Horses going through the floor. Horses having panic attacks and kicking the box to pieces. You just have to remember how many horses travel how many miles in any given year, which puts it in perspective.'

'They almost lost their business over it,' said Brodie, still chatting for its own sake. 'People started thinking they were jinxed.'

'You're talking about Barker & Walbrook.' Townes released the feathered fetlock he was holding and straightened up. 'Who were you speaking to?' He wasn't closing the subject. He was just smart enough to know that if she had an agenda he needed to know what was on it before he answered any more of her questions.

'I met Alison Barker the other day,' Brodie said, which was true if somewhat disingenuous. 'She seems to have had a terrible time. And she blames the transport firm.'

'I know she does,' said Townes quietly. 'Like you say, she's had a terrible time. She may not be the best judge of whose fault it was.'

'That's what I thought,' said Brodie, nodding agreeably. 'You know Alison, then?'

'Sure. This is a small world: we all enter the same competitions. I saw Alison at all the shows, until her horses had to go.'

'That must have been a wrench.'

It was in his eyes as he looked at her that he thought she had no idea, that she was just making sympathetic noises. 'Of course it was a wrench. They might be worth money – well, some of them are – but they're not just possessions. They're people. They're people that you've worked closely with, that you've taught and learned from, that you've trusted your life to. If the point comes that you can't afford to feed them you have to sell them, and you know that you've no further say in what happens to them for the rest of their lives. You hope you've found them a good home, but you can't know how long they'll be there or where they'll go next. You hope their next owners will understand that it isn't badness but an atavistic fear that makes them behave stupidly sometimes.'

Brodie wasn't really an animal person. She'd never had a dog. Deacon had a cat called Dempsey that was the reincarnation of Jack the Ripper, that expected food but had no truck with stroking, making it less a pet than a garbage disposal unit. These ponies were probably the animals she'd got closest to, and she remained deeply wary of them. But there was one thing she had noticed about animals: often they brought out the best in people. Men of Dieter Townes' age, young men with their way to make in the world, aren't famous for acknowledging responsibilities beyond what the law and the needs of their immediate family place on them. But clearly he had an emotional investment in his animals that went beyond expecting a fair day's work for a fair day's oats. He respected them and wanted to do right by them.

'My ex wrote me a reference that said pretty much the same thing,' she murmured, straight-faced.

The joke redeemed her in Townes' eyes. He grinned. 'Then all you need is a vet's certificate and we'll take you to the sales.'

If Alison Barker felt the same way about her horses that Dieter Townes did about his, selling them must have been the last resort, after every other option had failed. She had to feel bitter. Bitter enough to want to hurt the man she blamed. But perhaps also bitter enough to blame someone who was not in fact responsible. Brodie was still on the fence.

'What about Windham Transport?' she asked. 'Had Alison a point, do you think?'

Townes shrugged. 'I've never used them myself so I can't really comment.'

'It's a small world,' she reminded him. 'What's the feeling in the business? Are they to be trusted?'

He'd gone back to his brushing. But he stopped again for a moment to regard her over the piebald apple-shaped bottom of Paddy's favourite pony. 'Apart from Alison, I've never heard anyone say they aren't. Yes, they've had problems. Anyone in that line of work has. Hell, anyone who works with horses has. I don't think Windham's have had any more problems than any comparable firm. Barker & Walbrook were just unlucky to keep drawing the short stick.'

'So if you had to hire a carrier,' Brodie pressed him, 'you'd be happy enough using Windham?'

'Yes. He's experienced, he's local, and as far as I know his overall track record is good enough. I know he's careful who he employs, and that counts for a lot when it comes to handling horses.'

Brodie was curious. 'How do you know that?'

'I asked him for a job once. He didn't think I knew enough.' Again the easy grin. 'Can't fault him for that.'

'Bet you'd get the job now,' said Brodie supportively.

'I'd like to think so. But actually, I pretty much like the one I've got.'

In another few minutes the ponies were clean and saddled, and half a dozen children, from Paddy's age to around eleven, were springing or struggling on top. Brodie stood at the rail and watched them trotting round the sand school, and tried not to look away when Paddy and the piebald Ursula essayed their first jump.

Brodie and Deacon went out for supper the following evening. By then he had results from Forensics that backed up Billy Mills' gut instinct. There were no traces of Scram in any of the food samples taken from the house where Alison was staying. He was ready to dismiss Alison as a hysteric, and in no way persuaded to do otherwise by Daniel being inclined to believe her version of events.

Brodie was used to sitting on the fence between them. Sometimes it was a nice bit of post-and-rail, and sometimes it was barbed wire.

'There's no physical evidence to support anything she says,' said Deacon. 'All these things that she says have happened – I just don't believe somebody's trying to wipe out her family, and he's so good at it we can't find any trace of him even when we look.'

'What about Windham?' asked Brodie. 'Was he abroad again this week?'

'As a matter of fact he was,' said Deacon. 'Which doesn't actually prove much, one way or the other. If someone did sprinkle pixie-dust on Alison Barker's food, it didn't have to be the same day she became ill. It could have been days earlier. Depending on what food was involved, it could have been weeks.'

She eyed him impishly. 'So it is just about possible.'

He glared at her. 'It's possible. So is winning the lottery – every couple of weeks somebody beats odds of fourteen million to one. I can't spend time and public money investigating fourteen million potential crimes in the hope of catching one criminal.'

Brodie considered. 'Could Alison be right about what's happening and wrong about who's doing it?'

'*Whoever's* doing it left nothing for us to find in her kitchen. And these days, with modern forensic techniques, that's an achievement in itself. We used to say that absence of evidence is not evidence of absence, but these days it almost is.'

'Then how did the Scram get into her bloodstream?'

'The same way it gets into everybody's,' he shrugged. 'She bought some tabs and took them. She just isn't admitting it.'

'Why not? What does she have to gain by lying? Or what does she *think* she has to gain?'

Deacon pondered. 'One of two things; possibly both of them. She's blowing a smoke screen, possibly to protect herself, possibly to protect her supplier. She doesn't have to prove she was poisoned, only create a reasonable suspicion in people's minds that she might have been. If she took those tablets willingly she committed a criminal offence, which I can hold over her until she sees the wisdom of letting her dealer take the rap. But if she insists they were slipped into her food or drink, she's a victim until I can prove otherwise. Come to think about it, it's not a bad defence.'

'And the other?'

'That she's still trying to make trouble for Windham. Again, she doesn't have to prove anything. She slings enough mud around, sooner or later some of it will stick. I don't know if she has good reason to hate the guy or not, but we know she does – out of all proportion, if you ask me. Maybe he isn't the world's best transporter of horses, but their remedy was taking their custom elsewhere. Or suing him, if they really thought he'd ruined their business. I couldn't figure out why she was quite as bitter as she obviously was.'

'Maybe they have some history,' speculated Brodie. 'Personal history.'

Deacon thought about it. 'Actually, that's possible. She always calls him Johnny. Which is curiously cosy if they're mortal enemies.'

'It shouldn't be too hard to find out,' said Brodie. 'It's a small world, the horse-owning fraternity. If Windham and Alison Barker were ever a number, you could find out with a couple of phone calls.'

Deacon sniffed disparagingly. 'If this is a personal vendetta I don't propose to get involved. My only interest in Alison Barker is how she got hold of the garbage that nearly killed her. She's made it pretty clear she's not going to tell me and I can't afford to waste much more time pressing her. If I can track down how it's being produced – how the catalyst is coming into the country, who's turning out the tablets and where the factory is – I may get the whole distribution network including whoever supplied Alison Barker. At which point I shall want another talk with her. Until then, let her think she's pulled the wool over my eyes. People have thought it before. Some of them are knitting mailbags now.'

Brodie laughed. 'Do they still do that?'

'I doubt it,' growled Deacon. 'I think they spend their time being psychoanalysed and doing degrees in Information Technology.'

The next day Daniel brought sandwiches to Brodie's office. But he still got left with washing the coffee mugs.

She told him what Deacon's investigation had discovered. Daniel was plainly surprised. 'You really think she made all this up?'

'I doubt if she thinks of it that way. It's quite possible she believes it herself,' said Brodie. 'Look, her whole life's been turned upside down in the past six months. It's no wonder she hardly knows what she's doing.'

Daniel shook his head slowly. 'It's just, that's not how she comes across. At least, not to me.'

'And you're such an expert on young women,' Brodie said slyly.

He grinned, unoffended. 'OK, maybe I'm better on the theory than the practice, but I've taught a lot of girls not much younger than this one and I got pretty good at reading them. I don't see her as either a liar or a neurotic. I can imagine she's difficult to get on with. She's very strong-minded, determined to the point of obstinacy. And she may be wrong. I can imagine her taking a view on something and refusing to amend it in the light of subsequent developments. If she decided this man killed her father, wild horses wouldn't persuade her she was wrong. But why would she think it in the first place unless she had a reason?'

Brodie tried out her own theory on him. 'Perhaps she had a reason to mistrust him before any of this happened.'

Daniel's mild grey eyes were astute. 'You mean, perhaps they meant something to one another once and he let her down. And after that she laid everything that went wrong with her life at his door.'

'What do you think? Possible?'

'Maybe. Losing her father left her both bereft and intensely angry: I can imagine her trying to displace all that emotion onto someone. But the drugs are different. If she bought them or was given them and took them willingly, she knows Windham wasn't responsible and she's lying when she claims he was. Not wrong, not deluded – lying.'

Brodie gave an elegant shrug. 'Not everyone takes your zealous view of truth. Most people are prepared to be economical with it when it suits them.'

'Putting a slant on the facts is one thing. Accusing an innocent man of trying to kill you is very much another!'

'If he hurt her and she's paying him back, it may seem like justice by other means.'

Daniel watched her. 'Would you do that?'

'If I did, I wouldn't tell you!'

'Seriously.'

She considered. 'No. If someone hurt me enough I'd want revenge, and at some point I'd probably take it. But lie to the police about him? It's too likely to backfire.'

'That's the only reason?' He sounded disappointed.

Brodie laughed. 'I've told you, Daniel, don't look to me for high moral standards. I'm a pragmatist. And for a pragmatist, that is not a sensible way to proceed. I'd look for something with a much higher benefit-to-cost ratio. Of course, Alison might feel differently. You may not be an expert – and just for the record, men never are, *especially* those who claim to be – but even you must know that all women do not think and act the same way.'

He shook his head. 'You and Alison *might* think and act the same way. You have a lot in common.'

Brodie's dark eyes widened indignantly. 'You said she was difficult, obstinate and self-deluding!'

Being unfair to people was another kind of lying: Daniel took pains to avoid doing it. 'Two out of three ain't bad.'

Chapter Nine

A week after they died the bodies of the Hanson brothers had given up all the information they could. The funeral was held on Tuesday.

DS Voss made sure he was there: to show his respects, and also to see who else was there. He spoke to all the teenagers present, and found a lot of them had been at the party in the Woodgreen Estate. Now, reeling from watching two of their number shovelled under ground, was a good time to get their cooperation – to get them to talk about things of which yesterday or tomorrow they would have feigned ignorance. He asked them about the drugs scene in their particular age-group and circle. Who was taking, who was buying, who was selling. And he showed them a photograph of Alison Barker.

By close of play he had some answers for Detective Superintendent Deacon, though they weren't particularly helpful. None of the youngsters he'd spoken to had seen or even heard of Scram before the elder Hanson boy produced them from his pocket and handed them round. Treating them, he'd said. Try this, he'd said, it's new. It's the best ever. After this, he'd said, you'll never take anything else.

'So they couldn't give you a description of who was peddling the stuff?'

Voss shook his head. 'I expect it was one of the usual suspects – the guys who always peddle drugs to kids at parties. If we found him he wouldn't tell us who supplied them. It's more than his life is worth, he'd rather do the time. Anyway, it's not the dealers we need. All right, nice bonus, wouldn't say no, but what we need to stop these deaths are the people who're manufacturing Scram. We need the factory.'

'Horsefeathers,' said Deacon pensively.

Voss had long ago decided that taking offence at his governor's casual rudeness would be a full-time occupation. 'Well, if you know a better way...'

Deacon breathed heavily at him. 'That's what Forensics call it. Pay attention, Charlie Voss – you told me that! Horsefeathers: the German tranquillizer. That's the long thin neck where we could take the head clean off. It's the vital component, it's hard to get hold of, it only comes from one source and it has to be smuggled into the country. If we find out how they're doing it we close them down like that.' His fingers were a bit thick for snapping: he had to try twice, which rather spoilt the effect.

'Nobody's going to share information like that with a bunch of teenagers.' Voss blew out a disconsolate sigh that lifted his front hair. 'One more thing. None of them remembered seeing Alison Barker.'

Deacon was unimpressed. 'There were a couple of hundred kids in that clubhouse – what are the chances you'd ask one who saw Alison?'

'That's kind of the point,' said Voss, 'they were kids. Average age about sixteen. A girl of twenty-two *would* stand out.'

'Maybe,' conceded Deacon. 'So maybe she wasn't at the party. But she got Scram somewhere. Maybe she knows someone on the inside – someone who's involved in producing this stuff.'

'And he gave her some tabs without telling her what constitutes a safe dose? And she waited until she was alone before experimenting?'

'It doesn't sound too likely, does it? Oh God,' Deacon growled, 'I'm going to have to interview her again, aren't I?'

'Or I could,' suggested Voss.

Deacon eyed him suspiciously. 'Are you going to bully her? Are you going to stand over her and shout a lot, and convince her the only way she's going to get rid of you is by telling you what you want to hear?'

Voss was a good policeman who was also a decent human being. He looked both startled and shocked. 'Of course I'm not!'

'Didn't think so.' Deacon sniffed. 'Better do it myself, then.'

'Nothing?' Either Alison Barker was genuinely taken aback or she'd anticipated this moment and prepared an expression for it. 'There was nothing in the food except food?'

'Nothing,' said Deacon. 'Forensics knew what they were looking for and they looked carefully: they wouldn't miss it.'

'I was so *sure...*' Alison was still in hospital but out of bed and dressed now, waiting for the word to go home. A certain pallor was all that remained from her brush with death.

'Do you remember what you ate that evening?'

She tried to. 'I didn't cook. A cheese sandwich, I think, and a packet soup. Later I had a cup of tea and a biscuit.'

'Any alcohol?

'A can of cider out of the fridge.'

All of which accorded with the analysis of what was pumped from her stomach. Except that somewhere along the line she'd taken four tablets of Scram as well.

'A new can?' asked Deacon.

She didn't understand, answered with a puzzled frown.

'I'm asking if you opened the can before you drank from it,' Deacon explained patiently, 'or if it was already open.'

Alison tried to remember. It was several days ago now, it was a minor detail, and a lot had happened to her since. But she knew that it mattered. 'It was open. I'd had some at lunchtime and sealed the can with clingfilm. It was a bit flat but it was OK.' Her gaze steadied on him. 'Except that it wasn't, was it? That's where it was – dissolved in the cider.'

'It's possible,' said Deacon diplomatically. 'To drug your drink, though, someone would have had to get into your house and there are no signs of a break-in. It's much more likely you came by it outside. Did you go out that evening? Before you were taken ill, I mean.'

Alison wasn't interested in an alternative theory. 'If it was in the can, Forensics should have found traces.'

Deacon checked back his notes to confirm what he was saying. 'My Scenes of Crime Officer didn't find a cider can.'

'For pity's sake!' she exploded in exasperation. 'I didn't put an empty can back in the fridge! Didn't he check the rubbish?'

'He checked both the kitchen bin and the wheelie-bin in the yard. There was no cider can.'

Her expression flickered as she thought about challenging that, realised it would be foolish and moved on. A little hollow note of shock sounded in her voice. 'He's been back. He went back to the house after he thought I was dead and removed the evidence.'

Deacon resisted the urge to break his pencil. 'You think he broke in not once but twice, still without doing any damage?'

'I think if he managed it once he could do it again, yes,' she retorted sharply.

'By *he* you mean Johnny Windham,' said Deacon.

'Damn right I do.'

If they were back to this they might as well confront it and deal with it. 'Did he know where you were living? Have you seen him since you moved there? The person whose house it is' – he checked his notes again – 'Bella Goss, is she a friend of Windham's? Might she have given him a key?'

Alison was shaking her head. 'Bella doesn't know anyone in the horse world. I've known her since school. She's the only friend I have I didn't meet through the business.' There was no mistaking the bitterness in her voice. 'Perhaps that's why now she's the only friend I have.'

'OK.' Deacon put down his notebook and

114

looked at her levelly. 'So you're still insisting that the only way you could have taken these drugs is if a man who all the records show was abroad at the time traced you to a house that you don't own, that's owned by someone he doesn't know, and forced an entry in order to doctor your food – and broke in *again* in order to tidy up after himself so well that neither my Scenes of Crime Officer nor the Forensic Science Laboratory could find any sign that he was ever there. Is that what you're saying, Miss Barker?'

She wasn't blind to the weakness of her story. 'Sounds likely, doesn't it? But yes, that's pretty much what I'm saying. I can't think of any other way I could have taken drugs without knowing it.'

'And you're adamant that you didn't take them knowingly.'

'Yes,' she said, 'I am. Look, Superintendent – if it wasn't Windham then two different people killed my father and tried to kill me. That's even more bizarre.'

Deacon went on regarding her for a moment longer before responding. 'Miss Barker, I don't know what happened to you. I'm trying to work it out, because if someone is trying to kill you I don't want him to succeed. But it occurs to me there's one possible alternative. Do you want to hear what it is?'

With a spread hand she invited him to continue.

'A lot's gone wrong with your life in the last six months. Your family business failed. You had to sell a bunch of horses you were obviously attached to, and that left you without a proper job. You had to sell your house, and then your father died. A person would need a heart of stone not to succumb to depression after that lot.'

She looked away quickly, suggesting he'd scored. Deacon nodded. 'You got through it somehow, but I think it took more of a toll on you than you realise. I think you're suffering from depression now. I think you were depressed on Tuesday night – deeply depressed, sick of the whole sorry business – and you went out looking for something to cheer you up.

'You're not a big drinker, are you? One can of cider in the fridge and you didn't finish that at a sitting. So if you needed a boost, maybe you thought you'd try tablets. Maybe you'd never tried them before, but the way you were feeling there'd never be a better time.'

He was watching her closely, waiting for the flicker of an eyelid, the intake of breath, that would indicate he was hitting close to home. It didn't come, not yet. He pressed on.

'You found someone who was dealing, and you didn't know what to ask for so you took what he had. It happened to be Scram, and it happened to be stronger than either you or he realised. Once you'd got the stuff you couldn't wait to take it and stop feeling the way you did that night. I don't think you ever got home. I think you took those tablets in the street, and within minutes the world was spinning. And that's the only reason you're alive, Miss Barker. You collapsed in the street instead of behind a closed door.'

He wasn't sure what he was expecting. Not arms round his neck, a flood of tears and a tremulous apology: he didn't think Alison Barker was the dissolving-in-tears type. But if that was anything like the truth he'd offered her a way out. She could retreat from her accusations against Windham under the cover of emotional confusion, and rather than be charged with wasting police time expect nothing but sympathy. It would be interesting to see if she took it or not.

For a moment she seemed to consider it. But it involved too much of a retreat: she shook her head. 'I'm sorry, Superintendent. If I had a satisfactory explanation I'd give it to you. I haven't. But you haven't either.'

Deacon was watching her through narrowed eyes. 'I will have,' he said grimly. 'If I keep looking into this I will get to the bottom of what happened, and who did what to who, and then I'll charge everyone who's committed an offence. Is that what you want, Miss Barker? Do you want me to

117

investigate what happened to you?'

With barely a hesitation she said, 'Yes.'

The John Farrells were back home so Paddy was staying with her father the next night. She'd been looking forward to it for a week. So had he. So had Brodie. But Deacon had most of all.

Deacon's house was a small stone building under the shelter of the Firestone Cliffs that had been built in Georgian times as Dimmock's jail. It still had some of the original ironwork. Dimmock wasn't a very big town then so it wasn't a very big jail: by the time a kitchen and bathroom had been installed, and the guardhouse turned into a living-room, there were only enough cells remaining to adapt as one large bedroom and one small one.

In the large one, in the large oak bed, under the enormous feather duvet, at one o'clock in the morning, Brodie – who should have had her mind on other things – said pensively, 'I keep coming back to the horses.'

Deacon stopped what he was doing as if shot with a gun. 'What?'

'Horses,' she repeated, gratified by his interest. 'I mean, Dimmock isn't Newmarket. It isn't even Exmoor. When did you last have a conversation about horses with anyone? And yet they keep cropping up.'

With a restraint remarkable in the circumstances, Deacon put his best moves on hold while he dealt with this unwelcome distraction. 'Because that's the business Barker & Walbrook were in. If they'd been taxidermists the recurring theme would have been tiger-skin rugs; as they were horse dealers it's horses. Alison Barker rode them because she was Stanley Barker's daughter. Johnny Windham transports them because that's how Alison knows him. Everyone Alison knows does something with horses. She told me that herself.'

'What about the tranquillizer?'

'Horsefeathers? That's just what Forensics are calling it. It doesn't prove anything except they've got a funny sense of humour and way too much time on their hands.'

'But it is a veterinary tranquillizer used for large animals. Which means, the odd circus camel aside, cattle and horses.'

Brodie was right, there was a thread running through these events which might be considered to connect them – but where it wasn't lumberingly predictable it was diaphanously tenuous. The only real puzzle, the one thing that they knew for sure had happened and still couldn't explain, was that somehow Alison Barker had taken Scram. Except for that she was just a neurotic girl with a history of misfortune. But even if the attacks she complained of were illusory, the drug that almost killed her linked her to real and important crimes. The possibility that Alison Barker was his key into that secret world was all that stopped Deacon consigning everything he knew on her to the round file.

'All right,' he allowed. His elbows were getting sore so he shifted onto his back beside her. 'Suppose there is a connection through the horse trade. Somewhere in Germany a vet is rerouting an experimental drug he's supposed to be using on horses and cattle – and the odd circus camel – and passing it on as spare parts for Scram, to be assembled in England, probably not too far from here. If his social circle is as limited as Alison's, maybe it's people in the horse world who are smuggling it over here for him.'

Brodie liked that. 'There's a fair bit of coming and going, isn't there? Horses competing at shows all over Europe. Big lorries carrying loads of gear. You could probably smuggle fifty gallon drums of the stuff if you wanted to.'

Deacon shook his head. 'Customs weren't born yesterday. If they've reason to, which includes not having done it for a while, they'll take every bit of cargo off any kind of carrier and strip it down to the chassis. Live cargo won't stop them. They have people perfectly competent to off-load some horses.'

'You suppose they've had a look in Johnny

Windham's lorry?'

'I'd be surprised if they haven't. If he's crossing the Channel regularly he's bound to have had a shakedown from time to time. But if you'd something to smuggle, particularly if you could do it in small quantities, you'd farm it out to people whose faces weren't known, driving family hatchbacks with a couple of kids and a stack of suitcases in the back.'

'I suppose.'

He waited for her to say something more. When she had a bone she tended to worry it to the marrow. But Brodie remained silent. Thinking, possibly.

After a minute Deacon cleared his throat. 'So, if we've dealt with that, do you think we might possibly get on with ... um?'

She was, she was thinking. His polite enquiry brought her back with a start. 'What? Oh, yes – of course. Sorry. I was just... Sorry.'

He waited for her to get with the programme. When she showed no signs of doing so he vented a heavy sigh. 'Do you think a little enthusiasm might be a possibility?'

'Switching to enthusiasm mode right now,' she promised him. And to be sure, he had no grounds to call her a liar.

But over breakfast she said, 'I think I might pay Johnny Windham a visit.'

Deacon froze with his coffee halfway to his

face. 'Why?'

'Why not?'

'He hasn't done anything. The only person who thinks he's done anything wrong is Alison Barker, and he can prove he didn't do what she thinks he did. He *has* proved it. We have no further interest in Johnny Windham.'

'Then I can't possibly cause you a problem by visiting him, can I?' Brodie replied smoothly.

'But why would you want to?'

'Because his name's come up and I don't know where to file it. You're probably right and he's the innocent victim of a one-woman smear campaign. But just in case Daniel's right and there's some truth to what Alison's saying, I'd like to meet him for myself.'

'On what possible pretext?' demanded Deacon.

She gave him her most seraphic smile. 'Jack, I'm not a policeman. I don't have to tell him the *truth*. I'll ask him about transporting a horse for me.'

'What horse?'

'That's kind of the point about lying,' she explained patiently. 'There doesn't have to be a horse.'

Chapter Ten

The secret of lying, as with cookery, is preparation. Having all the ingredients to hand before you start. Knowing what order you'll want them in, and being ready to add that little unexpected something into the mix that will make all the difference to the finished product.

Brodie began with what Windham could most readily check. 'My name is Brodie Farrell. I'm a finding agent – I find things for clients who haven't the time or know-how to look themselves. I've been asked to find a pony for a man in Dimmock and I'm going to need someone to bring it in from Europe for me. This is not my field but I'm told' – she hit him with her most dazzling smile – 'it is yours.'

'Indeed it is.' Johnny Windham reached for a pad of consignment forms. 'Where is this pony?'

'I don't have the final details yet,' she said, 'but I believe it's in Germany.'

He looked taken aback. 'You *believe* it's in Germany.'

'That's right,' she nodded blithely. 'We've had a few false leads, but I think we're finally on the trail of The Saracen's Daughter.'

Windham was a man in his mid-thirties with the spare, rangy physique of a horseman. He had collar-length fair hair, expertly cut in a style that other men might argue was a couple of years too young for him, and eyes of that particular faded blue that comes with spending a lot of time out of doors. His voice hinted at an expensive education, and his clothes – suitable and hard-wearing but obviously good quality – suggested his business had been successful before the recent problems.

The other thing Brodie could tell from observing him was that he didn't know quite what to make of her. He was used to working with owners, riders and dealers; to transporting horses for people who had just bought them, those who were relocating and thought them worth the expense of taking along, and those entered for shows or expected at studs across half of Europe. Brodie was something else. For one thing, she wasn't part of the horse world and so was that rare thing in his experience, a stranger, an unknown quantity. Yet she was clearly a professional in her own field – if he'd had no other way of checking, her manner alone would have confirmed it.

But he was puzzled. Why would a man looking for a horse consult someone who freely admitted to knowing nothing about them? There was no shortage of professional horse dealers along the south coast, men and women of vast experience who could between them guarantee to find just about any mount for any rider. Why would someone seek help elsewhere? And who the hell – Brodie could see the question in his eyes – was The Saracen's Daughter?

'Pardon my ignorance,' he said, 'but who's The Saracen's Daughter?'

This was verifiable too, if he cared enough. 'The Saracen was an Exmoor pony stallion that stood in Milton Abbas from the mid-1960s until his death in 1984. He carried a very pure bloodline and was considered an outstanding example of the breed. But as you know, interest in purebred Exmoors diminished to the point where they became an endangered species. In particular, it was believed that the last of the Saracen line had gone.'

Brodie looked at him sidelong from under her eyelashes. He was following, she noted with satisfaction, with a rapt interest that had little to do with the survival of the Exmoor breed. She carried on.

'But my client was told that a filly-foal from his last crop was exported to Europe, and that it's still alive and still breeding. The Saracen's Daughter, twenty-three years old but carrying his bloodline and still passing it on. My client wants that pony.

'And the answer to your next question,' she added smoothly, 'is that he came to me rather than a dealer because he's had some unhappy experiences with dealers. After all, finding it didn't come down to what I do or don't know about ponies – it came down to what I know about finding things. Which is – and I may have mentioned this – extensive.'

'So you've found the pony?'

'I believe so,' said Brodie. 'Look, I really can't go into too much detail at this point. If it turns out I haven't got it yet, I will get it. If it turns out it isn't where I think, it won't be far away. What I need from you today is an agreement in principle to collect it from Germany and deliver it to Dimmock, and an estimate of costs.'

Johnny Windham shrugged. 'Sure. Give me an address in Germany and we'll collect your pony. We'll organise the paperwork and tell you what your client and his vendor need to provide. We'll bring the pony to our own yard initially, put it in an isolation box and have our vet check it over. When he passes it fit we'll deliver it. We not only comply fully with the 1997 Welfare of Animals (Transport) Order, we exceed its provisions, so the journey'll take about four days door to door. Does that sound satisfactory?'

Brodie had no idea. 'Yes thank you.'

'The cost will depend on a couple of things. Germany's a big country. Also, it'll be cheaper if we have a full load for most of the trip than if we have to go way out of our way to fetch it. But I'll prepare you some figures.'

'Yes, would you? Then I can get approval from my client and give you the go-ahead as soon as we know we're in business.'

Windham shook his head, bemused. 'An Exmoor pony, huh? I've had Badminton winners in that lorry. I've had an Olympic dressage horse.'

'And now,' said Brodie, 'if you're very lucky, you're going to have The Saracen's Daughter.'

Before she left he showed her round his yard. It wasn't pretty – there were no roses twining round the stable doors and the views in all directions were over the flat landscape bordering Romney Marsh – but it was workmanlike. The buildings were in good repair, the yard clean, and the aristocratic heads of blood horses peered out of a handful of loose-boxes.

Windham invited her to inspect one of his lorries. The other, he explained, was on a run to Europe right now. With Alison Barker's accusations at the back of her mind Brodie ran a critical eye over everything, but so far as she could tell Dieter Townes was right – the man was scrupulously careful about looking after his clients' animals. The lorry and the empty stables were scrubbed clean between incumbents. Any viruses that managed to evade his counter-measures could not fairly be blamed on Windham Transport.

He saw her to her car. 'I'll need your client's name,' he said. 'I can't do the paper-work without it.'

She saw no problem obliging him. After all, there was no pony. In a few days she'd phone him back and say the trail had gone cold, and promise to contact him again when she got a new lead, and do nothing of the kind. 'Hood,' she said. 'Daniel Hood.'

'But I don't want a pony,' said Daniel, perplexed. Brodie had called at his house on her way home.

'That's just as well,' she said, 'because there isn't one. But if someone from Wind-ham Transport contacts you, there *is* a pony – an Exmoor pony – it's in Germany and it's called The Saracen's Daughter.'

Daniel's eyes flared wide. 'Windham? As in Johnny Windham?'

'Yes.'

'The man who tried to kill Alison Barker?'

'The man Alison Barker *claims* tried to kill her,' Brodie corrected him. 'The man she claims can be simultaneously in different countries and pass through locked doors in his desire to wipe out her family. That Johnny Windham. Yes.'

'And he wants to sell me a pony?'

'No, he wants to collect a pony that I've bought for you.'

Daniel tried to find another way to say this and failed. 'But I don't want…'

'Daniel, I know! It isn't a real pony. It's a subterfuge. I just need you to back up my story if he checks it out. All right?'

If anything, that gave him more problems than the imaginary pony. 'You want me to lie?'

Brodie rolled her eyes to the ceiling. 'Of course I don't want you to lie! If a man who may be threatening the life of a young girl asks you if I'm on the level I want you to tell him no, I'm making it up, I'm trying to establish if he's a murderer or not. You tell him that, Daniel, and we'll soon know whether he's got a mean streak.'

He'd been the object of her invective before; he knew to batten down the hatches and sit it out. When she'd finished he said, 'Are you serious? You're trying to con this man? *Why?*'

'Because if Alison's telling the truth she deserves to be taken seriously and protected. And if she's pursuing a vendetta against him, Windham deserves to be cleared.'

'Fair enough,' agreed Daniel. 'But why *you?* Why not the police?' The corrugations on his brow deepened. 'Did Jack ask you to do this?'

Brodie's laugh was scornful. 'Don't be silly. It *should* be the police. But Jack's up to his eyes with this new drug – he hasn't the time or manpower to reinvestigate allegations that have already been dismissed.'

'That still doesn't make it your business!'

'I'm tired of hearing about Alison Barker from the pair of you! Jack thinks she's hiding something, you think she's in danger. Neither of you has any evidence. You're inclined to believe her, he isn't. I want it settled one way or the other so I can sit down to a meal sometime and *not* know what the main topic of conversation will be.'

Daniel thought he'd given up being surprised by her. It turned out he was wrong. 'Brodie – what if Alison's telling the truth?'

'She isn't. I've met the guy – he's perfectly normal.'

'But what if she is?'

'Then Jack can arrest him, Alison can breathe a sigh of relief and we can start getting a bit of fun out of life again. Remember fun?' she asked snidely. 'It's what we used to do before you had a girlfriend.'

Daniel had his mouth open to deny it, shut it again. Right now that wasn't the issue. '*If* Alison's right, this is a deeply dangerous man. If he guesses what you're doing he may want to put a stop to it.'

Brodie shook her head dismissively. 'If Johnny Windham had done half of what Alison says he did there'd be some evidence of it. There isn't. I don't think Windham tried to kill her. I don't think anyone did.'

'Then why are you trying to trap him?' demanded Daniel. 'If Alison's right it's dangerous; if she's wrong it doesn't need doing. Brodie, you have nothing to prove – not to me, not to Jack. We know you can out-think anyone alive. We know you can get to the bottom of any mystery you take on. But you're putting yourself at risk for no reason. Leave it alone. When Jack gets his head above water he'll find the truth without endangering himself or anyone else. Leave it to him.'

Brodie's head tilted to one side, her dark eyes mocking. 'I thought Alison Barker was your latest lame dog. I thought you'd want me to find out what happened to her.'

'I don't want you to do anything that could get you hurt!'

'You'd better not let Alison hear you talking that way about another woman.'

Somehow, and neither of them could have said how, the thing had not only got personal but come between them. Perhaps there was an element of jealousy on Brodie's part, something so unreasonable she couldn't admit it even to herself. Certainly Daniel didn't understand her attitude. They

131

stared at one another in a mutual incomprehension that was tinged on her side with spite and on his with vexation.

Brodie could have set his mind at rest in a moment. She could have said, as she'd meant to, 'I just wanted to meet this man and judge for myself if what he's been accused of is credible. Now I have and it isn't, and I don't propose to meet with him again.' Something stopped her. Not mere irritation: though she was often irritated with Daniel it didn't usually undermine her fondness for him. Something had shifted in the tectonics of their relationship, and she'd felt the quake and hadn't yet located the epicentre.

Daniel too could have done more to avert the looming confrontation. In particular, he could have *not* said, 'Now you're being childish.' If he'd tried to explain how the piquant combination of fear and bravado he'd seen in Alison Barker's eyes had spoken to him, she might have understood; and even if she hadn't, she might have accepted that it was so anyway, and beyond him to do other than try to help the lost girl. They had made so many allowances for one another's mistakes and frailties. Yet both of them were aware that they had ventured now into an area where things could be said which would strain even the tolerance of love past its limits.

'Childish?' she barked back at him. 'You want to talk about childish? How about your infatuation with this girl and her fantasy life? She's playing you for a fool, Daniel, and you're making it easy. I know she's had a hard time. But she's made a conscious decision to live off it for the rest of her life. To tout her sob story around for whatever sympathy it'll get her. She's like an old colonel dining out on forgotten wars. She's a leech, and she's zeroed in on you as the softest suck around. Can't fault her for that, anyway.'

Hurt pooled in his eyes. Brodie quite enjoyed a good argument but Daniel hated them, most of all hated arguing with her. He could have stopped it. He could just have walked away, and though her first instinct would have been to triumph, in a matter of minutes that would have turned to regret. When she'd thought about it long enough she would apologise.

Of course, it's harder to walk out when it's your living room you're arguing in.

'You're right,' he said softly. 'I'm a mug for a hard-luck story. And yes, I look for the best in people. Sometimes I'm wrong. I may be wrong this time. But if I am, all that happens is that my friends get to laugh at me again. If I'm right, I get the chance to help a scared girl that no one else is prepared to. So laugh all you like, Brodie,

I'm used to it. I'd rather make a fool of myself by being too trusting than by seeing malice everywhere.'

'Your problem is,' snapped Brodie, 'you think the world's some kind of a mirror. If you're nice to people they'll be nice back.'

'And what do you see when you look in the mirror,' he shot back, 'that justifies how you treat people?'

With a second longer to think he'd never have said it. If they hadn't been arguing, if she hadn't been goading him, he'd have done what he always did: picked his words carefully and said nothing until he was sure it conveyed exactly what he wanted it to. He lost a lot of debates that way: people thinking they'd won and heading for the pub when he was actually still rehearsing his response. Instead for once he'd done what she did all the time: come back with a smart retort because he was clever enough to think of it and too stupid to keep it to himself.

He saw the shock ricochet through her face like a slap. Her lips parted and her eyes rounded with a mixture of pain and astonishment as if he'd raised his hand to her. Shame flushed darkly under his skin, and he couldn't think of a thing to say that wouldn't make it worse.

Brodie went on staring at him for perhaps ten seconds, disbelief warring in her face with the knowledge of what he thought of her. Then, without another word, she turned on her heel and left, her shoes beating a quick tattoo on the iron stairs.

Chapter Eleven

'Where will you go?'

'Home. Well – Bella's house in The Ginnell.' A thread of steel ran through the girl's voice. For a statement of just seven words it defined neatly the nadir to which her life had sunk. She had no home, no one to return to, just a little house in a dreary town that wasn't currently needed by its owner, where she hadn't been safe before and had no reason to believe she'd be safe now. The steel thread was because she was intelligent enough to know this, and to know that she had no alternative, and to know that her only option was to face her situation with courage.

At least, that was what Daniel thought. Brodie might have thought something different.

'You can't.'

'I have to. I can't afford a hotel.'

'Couldn't Mary put you up for a few days?'

'I didn't ask.'

He frowned. 'Why ever not?'

Alison didn't want to tell him. Two things she'd learned to dread in people's faces: sympathy, and the weariness that followed when the sympathy was exhausted. 'Because I asked her before I asked Bella and she said no. She wanted to, she was really sorry, but she didn't see how she could fit me in. She's knocked together a little one-room flat out of what was a hay loft over the stables. It doesn't cost her anything and she says it'll do until she's got the business back on track, but it would be pretty gruesome sharing it with someone.'

Daniel considered. 'I know a bed-and-breakfast. It's not very smart, but you get clean sheets and as much as you can eat, and a great view of the beach.'

She appreciated him trying. 'Daniel, I can't even afford a B&B.'

'You can afford mine.'

She regarded him levelly, not speaking until she knew she could control what she said. 'Why are you doing this?'

'Because I can,' he said.

'You don't owe me anything.'

'I knocked you down.'

'I ran into you! It was my mistake. Except...' She smiled, a tear trembling on the lip of it. 'It wasn't a mistake at all. It was the best thing I've done in three months.'

Daniel did his odd little lopsided shrug

that was a remnant of a broken collarbone. 'Ally, I'm not offering you very much. I can't sort things out for you. I can't make the police believe you. I can't make them believe *me* most of the time. All I can give you is somewhere to stay while you deal with it. I think you'll be safer staying with me than on your own.'

'I think so too,' she said softly.

'You get your own room,' he said proudly, showing her. 'Twelve months ago you'd have got my room and I'd have got the sofa, but I had to rebuild after a fire and I got a couple more rooms out of what used to be the boathouse. A guest room and a study.'

She was looking round the odd building as if she'd never seen its like. 'Daniel – what is it?'

'It's a netting-shed. The same as the other two' – he pointed through the window – 'except this was converted for living in and the others are just used for storage. They date back to when Dimmock had a fishing industry, with boats launching off the beach and cheery fisherfolk hanging their nets out to dry of an evening.'

'Cheery fisherfolk?' Ally echoed faintly.

'Oh yes. It was stipulated on their licence. That, and singing jolly sea-shanties as they hauled the boats out at the end of the day.'

'All this was a bit before your time, wasn't

it?' she guessed.

'Well, yes,' admitted Daniel. 'But I have it on good authority. I saw a Disney film once.'

She sat on his spare bed and kicked her shoes off. 'I'm glad the cheery fisherfolk have gone. Those sea-shanties must wear thin after a time.'

'Ah. Then you don't want me waking you up in the morning with three brisk choruses of "Fiddler's Green?"'

She pursed her lips. 'Let's say I'll let you know if I do.'

Brodie hadn't given a thought to Johnny Windham in three days when the phone rang and it was him. 'Just to let you know, I'm putting together a lorry-load of horses in Germany. If you're ready to go with the Exmoor pony I have a space for you.'

'That's very good of you, Mr Windham.' She made polite noises while her brain worked overtime. 'But don't you need to do some paperwork first?'

'Brussels requires an Animal Transport Certificate for any horse travelling further than fifty kilometres. But we get them by the bushel. If you're ready, it'll save you a bit of money.'

'That's very good of you,' said Brodie, and if she'd had a pony to transport she'd have meant it. 'I'm sorry to mess you around. My firm lead's gone a bit soggy. Perhaps you should count us out of the equation until I give you a call.'

He sounded a little disappointed. 'Yes, sure. I was just calling on spec. Get back to me when you've some news. Anywhere in Germany, France, the Low Countries – we're always putting a load together, we'll fit you in no trouble.'

'You specialise in Europe, then,' said Brodie, still only making conversation for long enough to be polite.

'Based where we are it makes sense. There are guys in Wales and the Midlands who pick up most of the Irish trade, and Yorkshire on up is a whole other territory. I haven't been north of Birmingham in years.'

'Very sensible I'm sure,' said Brodie, with the heartfelt little shudder of the born-and-bred Londoner; and with that and the promise to speak again they parted.

Deacon took her to his favourite French restaurant for supper. Friday evening was the nearest thing they had to a standing arrangement: neither of them broke it without good cause.

Although sometimes it would have been better if Deacon had admitted honestly that his head was too full of work to go on a date with anyone. Instead he talked to her as if she were Charlie Voss, there to act as a sounding board for his ideas. He talked about the brick wall he'd hit when he tried to find out who was manufacturing Scram and who was distributing it. About the people who should have known something but were saying nothing, even when he turned the pressure up. Even when he offered to show them his new monkey wrench.

'I don't think they know any more about it than I do,' he grunted, frustrated and disconsolate. 'Which means this isn't the usual suspects. Maybe it's organised from the German end and Dimmock's just the final link in the chain.'

Brodie gave up trying to talk about something that interested her. 'They must have some reason to be here. It would be safer to buy the common chemicals in Germany than to smuggle a restricted drug through British Customs.'

Deacon was nodding pensively. 'The catalyst is the most important but actually the smallest part of the cocktail. If this thing takes off as they hope, they're going to need big quantities of the other stuff. Big enough to attract attention. They're doing it here because this is where they have contacts.' He looked up. 'This is where they live.'

'Dimmock?'

'Here or hereabouts.'

'Then why does no one know about them? Not just you – the competition.'

'It's a new operation,' he guessed. 'Not just a new drug – the whole set-up. These aren't drug-dealers playing with chemicals, they're chemists playing at drugs. Or if not chemists, people who have access to chemicals – the German tranquillizer and what they need to turn it into tablets. That's where they started – with the chemicals, and the idea. We don't know about them because they have no track record. They're two or three respectable professional people with access to chemicals, the knowledge of what to do with them and a lockup some-where with a Bunsen burner and a sink. That's all they need. How the hell am I ever going to find them?'

Brodie was surprised. He was often angry, not infrequently worried, but she didn't remember hearing that note of despair in his voice before. 'You'll find them. It may take a little while, but you'll find them.'

'But while I'm looking, kids are dying. We know of six people who've overdosed on this stuff. Five of them were teenagers, two of them are now dead. That's a thirty-three per cent mortality rate. What are we going to be dealing with when the production-line is running at capacity?'

'OK,' she said, moved to help him, 'then let's think about what you know about them. The catalyst comes from Germany but pro-duction takes place around here somewhere.

You're looking for professional people with a knowledge of chemistry and secure premises. It's based on a veterinary drug. Maybe you should be looking for a vet.'

A generation raised on James Herriot stories finds it hard to see the saviour of the animal kingdom in a less flattering light, but it was a valid point. 'Maybe I should. Or someone else involved with large animals. Like a horse dealer. Or a horse transporter.'

For a long minute Brodie didn't answer. Then she said, 'You mean, maybe there's something in Alison Barker's allegations after all?'

'Those damn horses,' Deacon growled into his wine. 'You're right, aren't you? We keep coming back to the horses.'

'Mm.' There was nothing modest about Brodie Farrell: the only reason that she didn't fire off a resounding "told you so" was that she too was thinking. 'Jack – that argument that Stanley Barker and Johnny Windham had in the yard at Peyton Parvo five days before Barker was found in his water-jump. Is it on record anywhere what exactly they were arguing about?'

'Sure. Windham bringing Barker sick and dead horses.'

'Yes. But had these horses anything else in common? The same vendor, or the same buyer. Or maybe they all came from Germany?'

Deacon put his glass down and left his meal to go cold. 'I don't know. But we should be able to find out. Either from Alison Barker or Mary Walbrook.'

'Let's ask Mary,' said Brodie, just a shade too quickly, leaving Deacon wondering why.

'I'm not sure I have her number. But I can probably still catch Alison at the hospital.'

'No, she was discharged this morning.'

'Then I'll call at the house in The Ginnell. Come with me, if you like.'

'She isn't there.'

It was like drawing teeth. Deacon hung onto his patience. 'Then where is she?'

There comes a point in any game where trying to defend the indefensible involves more loss of dignity than conceding defeat. Brodie reached that point now. Her dark eyes crackled at him. 'Where do you think? Where do all the crackpots end up? She's at Daniel's.'

He didn't understand her annoyance. 'All right, then we'll drop in on Daniel.'

'Maybe you should phone first,' she said nastily, 'Lord knows what we'll walk in on otherwise.'

He'd been ready to leave. Now he let his weight sink back into his chair. 'Brodie,' he said quietly, 'what's going on here? You know Daniel's been worried about her. I'm not surprised she's moved in with him, so why are you?'

'I'm not surprised,' she said shortly. 'I just think he's letting himself be used. Again.'

Deacon shrugged. 'Does it matter?'

'It might. If Alison Barker is lying, she's conducting a hate campaign against a man she blames for everything that's gone wrong with her life. What if Daniel doesn't measure up to her expectations either?'

'You think she might turn on him?' Deacon wasn't sure what he was hearing. It hadn't occurred to him that Daniel was in any danger of being bitten by his lame dog. Thinking about it now he had to concede there was a chance, if only an outside one; but listening like a detective rather than someone who was involved it sounded more like an intelligent woman rationalising a quite primitive situation – two cats squabbling over a fish head. She sounded jealous.

'She might. If Mary Walbrook's right about her, Alison is a loose cannon. And Daniel ... is Daniel. For a smart man he can be remarkably slow on the uptake sometimes. And this is an area he hasn't had much experience of.'

'What is?' he asked softly. He felt it important that she say it.

She flicked him an irritated glance. 'You know what I mean. The whole emotional thing. I'm not sure he's ever had a serious girlfriend. It's foreign territory to him, and I don't trust him to pick up the warning signs

144

if it starts going wrong.'

'You think they're involved emotionally?'

'I don't know.' He didn't think Brodie heard the note of anguish in her own voice. 'I think they might be.'

'You think they might or you're afraid they might?'

'I don't want him to get hurt!'

'Getting hurt goes with the territory.' He was speaking from experience here. 'The only way to avoid it is giving the whole damn business a miss. Is that what you want him to do?'

Brodie stared at him, detecting a moment too late the minefield she'd wandered into. 'Of course not. I don't mind if Daniel has a girlfriend. I think it would be a very good thing. But I'd sooner he didn't take up with a bunny-boiler!'

For a moment Deacon came perilously close to confronting her. Just in time he pulled back. It would achieve nothing except animosity between them, and anyway he'd already said most of what he wanted to. She knew what he was saying. She'd come back to it when she was ready.

'Maybe we should try to establish once and for all who's actually telling the truth here,' he said. 'You thought there might be something between Alison and Windham that would explain her anger. We never got round to finding out. Maybe we should.'

She was mollified at being consulted on what was, after all, his job. 'Apart from the two of them, who would know?'

'Mary Walbrook,' said Deacon. 'But she might be too close to Alison to give us a straight answer.'

'I could ask Dieter Townes,' said Brodie. 'He knows both of them and has done for years. As everyone keeps telling us, this is a small world. If there was a relationship between them before the problems started, I bet he'd know.'

'Who's Dieter Townes?'

Sometimes Brodie forgot that Deacon wasn't actually part of her family. 'He owns the riding school. Paddy's going to marry him.'

Deacon grinned. Then the grin faded. 'Dieter Townes?'

'Yes. Why?'

'*Dieter* Townes?'

'What?'

He breathed heavily at her. 'Don't you watch *any* war movies? It's not exactly an English name, is it?'

It hadn't even occurred to her. It did now. She said, very carefully, 'It's German, isn't it?'

Chapter Twelve

Brodie wasn't the only one who was unclear how things stood between Daniel and Alison Barker. Alison wasn't sure either. At first it hardly seemed to matter. He'd been kind to her, and if he had reasons beyond the desire to do good he kept them to himself. She noticed right away that the bed in the guest room was a single. Admittedly, there wasn't room for anything bigger, but she still didn't think she was suddenly going to be presented with the bill for his assistance.

But it's human nature to look for the fly in the ointment. A man she didn't know, who owed her nothing, probably not even an apology, had chanced upon her in straitened circumstances and took it on himself to help. At first, with the hospital psychiatrist wanting to know if she'd tried to kill herself and the police wanting to know where she got the drugs, she was just so grateful for the quiet, undemanding presence of Daniel Hood that she didn't care if there were strings attached. She needed someone to believe her, or if he didn't believe her at least not to call her a liar to her face, so desperately she'd probably have paid whatever he asked in return. But he asked nothing. Now she was living in his house and eating his food, and even getting the occasional privileged glimpse through his telescope, and still there was no hint of an accounting to come.

At some point, the selfless wish to help others without reward becomes downright sinister. For Alison, that point came on the Sunday. She almost wished he'd try to jump her bones. At least she'd know then why he was doing this.

All her instincts urged her to have it out with him. To ask him to his face what his agenda was, what he hoped to get from her. If the man was no more than he appeared to be – a decent, kind, possibly simple individual who thought people should try to help one another – it would be embarrassing. But even that would be better than being afraid to ask.

Twelve months ago she'd have said she wasn't afraid of anyone. Subsequent events had made her revise that judgement, but the fact remained that she had, and knew she had, physical courage – what riders call nerve – to burn. It was the only way to get the job done. Only one thing persuades a horse, weighing in at maybe 500 kilos and capable of travelling at forty miles an hour, to do as it's asked by a slip of a girl balanced on top, and that's the belief that she's stronger and smarter and braver than it is and will always win any battle between them. Riders learn to be good at tackling obstacles head on.

What stopped her from confronting Daniel was the knowledge that if she didn't like what she heard her only option was to leave. And she really didn't want to do that. She felt safe with him. She would rather take the risk he would betray that confidence than analyse it too deeply.

Instead she watched him covertly, waiting for a sign that he was about to make his move.

He was marking test-papers when he became aware of her observation. Without glancing up he said, 'You're making me nervous.'

'Sorry,' she said quickly, and looked away. Then she steeled herself and looked back. 'I'm feeling a bit twitchy myself.'

Daniel stopped what he was doing and put his pen down. 'Anything I can do?'

'Actually, yes.'

She didn't come straight out and say, 'What are you expecting in exchange for what you're doing for me?' Nevertheless, he picked up the gist of it pretty quickly. She'd been afraid of making him angry, but Daniel was annoyed only with himself.

'I'm sorry, Ally, I'm not very good at this.

If I've made you feel uncomfortable I'm really sorry. I was trying to help. That's all I want: to feel I'm helping. The last thing I meant to do was add to your problems. Maybe I should find you somewhere else to stay. I have friends, I can probably call in a favour. How do you feel about the piano? Marta Szarabeijka would put you up, but it has to be admitted she teaches some very untalented young musicians.'

The girl felt a sudden flood of shame at the way her mind had been running. She shook her head, the long brown hair curtaining her gaze. 'No. Daniel, please... I didn't mean... You've been a star. You saved me. I didn't try to kill myself. I didn't take drugs to make the world go away. But that doesn't mean I've never wondered if suicide would be an easy way out of the mess my life has become.'

His eyes were shocked. He reached out a hand to her, then took it back for fear of crowding her. He didn't know what to say for the best.

Alison saw his distress and tried to reassure him with a smile. 'It's all right, I'm not going to get blood on your carpet. I'm not ready to give up yet. It's just, a year ago the thought would never have occurred to me. A year ago I thought I could deal with anything the world threw at me, and people who couldn't were wimps and losers. Now I can imagine being desperate enough for suicide to start looking like an option. Until I met you I was getting more desperate every day. Now I'm not. Now I feel I've got something to hold onto.

'I'll understand if you think you've done enough and it's someone else's turn, but if you want to know what I want, I want to stay here. I won't look at you when you're marking any more,' she offered hopefully.

Daniel laughed. 'If you want to stay, Ally, you're welcome. If I seem to be helping, use me; if I become part of the problem, we'll make other arrangements. But talk to me. Tell me what you need. I'm not good at guessing. I'm not very good at people. I get on better with numbers.'

'I don't know,' she said softly, 'I think you're pretty good with people too.'

'You'll stay?'

'If you'll have me.'

He nodded, relieved. 'Do you want to bring some stuff down from The Ginnell? You've been living out of a carrier-bag since you left hospital. If you want to pack a suitcase I'll help you carry it down.'

'I can do better than that,' said Ally. 'I've got a car parked up at the house.'

She'd managed to surprise him. 'I didn't know that.'

'It's not much of a car. It goes, that's about it. But it would make more sense to have it down here where I can keep an eye on it. I can park on the front?'

'You can park right here on the Promenade. Do you want to get it now? I can finish this later...'

Ally shook her head again. 'I don't need any help. I'll walk up Fisher Hill, pack some stuff and be back in an hour.'

'OK.'

You can't arrest a man for having a funny name. In an increasingly global village it's dangerous to make assumptions about people based on the vagaries of their birth. Coincidences happen all the time, and in all probability it was nothing more than coincidence that linked Dieter Townes with his riding school to a multi-national trade in drugs because of the involvement of a large animal tranquillizer manufactured in Germany.

But Deacon didn't get to be a Detective Superintendent by assuming people were innocent until proved otherwise. He got there by being a nasty suspicious bastard who took nothing on trust and assumed everyone was up to something, even if some people had yet to be caught.

The first rule of police interrogation – no, the second rule: the first is to call it *making enquiries* – is not to ask anyone a question until you've some idea what the answer should be. Before Deacon spoke to Dieter Townes he wanted to speak to someone about Dieter Townes.

Everyone kept telling him what a small world this was. Now, with questions to ask about Townes, Alison Barker and Johnny Windham, seemed a good time to put that to the test. Taking DC Meadows, he drove out to the yard outside Peyton Parvo to see if Mary Walbrook could help him understand how all these people fitted together; and if she could, whether she would.

Confirmation of one point he got very quickly, before he'd even got out of the car. It was certainly a small world. A lorry in the red-and-white livery of Windham Transport was parked in the yard.

He had one advantage and he played it. Neither Mary Walbrook nor Johnny Windham had any reason to recognise the police officers. They stayed in the car, waiting to see what would happen in the space before they had to declare themselves.

But all that happened was that a man came out of an outbuilding, walked to the lorry and climbed up. A woman watched from the doorway and waved as he drove off. Then she turned her attention to the car. 'Can I help you? I'm Mary Walbrook.'

'Detective Superintendent Deacon,' he replied, producing his warrant card, 'and Detective Constable Meadows. Yes, I hope you can. In fact, you already have. I was going to ask if you'd seen anything of Mr Windham recently, and I see you have.'

Mary Walbrook nodded. 'Mr Windham and I had some business to discuss. In fact I'll be seeing rather more of him in the future. He's going to start carrying my horses again.'

Deacon considered. 'You don't share Alison's view, then, that Windham was to blame for your problems.'

Mary gave a compact shrug. 'I'm fond of Alison, Superintendent, I care what happens to her, but I don't share her view of a number of things. Windham's role in our difficulties is one of them. Yes, it's possible he brought in a virus – you move stock around, that's something you risk. I don't think it happened because he was careless. I think we were unlucky, but more than that we hadn't taken steps to protect ourselves against a run of bad luck. We should have had a much bigger buffer against disasters. I shan't make that mistake again.'

Deacon looked around the yard, took in the number of doors that had horses' heads peering over them, the evidence of recent repairs and repainting – all signs of a business on the way back. 'You've got things ticking over again, then?'

She was pleased he'd noticed. 'It was uphill work for a while, but once I persuaded a couple of people to come back the word spread and we started seeing a few more old faces. We haven't anywhere near the turnover we once had, but we're in profit again. I think the business is safe.'

'Safe enough to use Mr Windham again.'

Mary frowned. 'I told you, Windham was only the problem in Ally's mind. We talked through everything that had happened, he offered me a good deal in recognition of the difficulties we've had and I took it. Alison won't be happy. But this is my yard now. She has a financial interest but not a controlling one. What she inherited on the death of her father was a share in an empty yard with massive debts. I don't want to sound mercenary, but I turned that around and I intend to reap the benefits.'

Whatever she wanted, she did sound mercenary. But Deacon couldn't fault her logic. If the work had been hers and the risks had been hers, she was entitled to the rewards. 'Before all this started – when Stanley Barker was alive, before your run of bad luck – how well did Alison know Johnny Windham?'

Mary wasn't sure what he meant. 'She's known him most of her life. This is...'

'A small world,' finished Deacon. 'Yes, I know. And he was transporting horses for you. Was that all?'

'You mean, were they ever a number?' There was a certain flatness to her voice that made Deacon think Brodie had guessed right. 'Well – not really. As a teenager, Ally had a crush on him. Johnny used to flirt with her. She thought it meant something, he didn't. He was amused and maybe a little flattered. They went out a few times as part of a crowd, after shows and things. I think only a teenage girl would have thought it was anything serious.'

'Could she have had a grudge against him because it never went anywhere?'

Mary pursed her lips. 'It's possible. She seemed to shake it off and move onto other things, but maybe she felt he'd treated her badly. She wouldn't have said anything if she did: not to me, not to her father. Ally doesn't wear her heart on her sleeve. There are two sorts of girls, Superintendent: one sort spends every spare minute thinking about boys, the other spends every spare minute thinking about horses. Ally's the second sort. I was myself. It doesn't mean we're not interested in men, just that they have to wait until the horses are done.'

'Could that explain why she was so determined to blame him for your problems?' asked Meadows. 'Why you saw a disastrous run of bad luck and she saw a conspiracy?'

Mary Walbrook nodded. 'It might.'

'Just for the record,' wondered Deacon, 'how did Stanley Barker see it? Did he blame Windham? He stopped using him,

156

didn't he?'

'He did.' She was working out how to put this. 'To be honest, Superintendent, Stanley blamed everyone but himself. It was Windham's fault, he wasn't looking after the horses in transit. It was the vendors' fault, they were sending sick animals. It was the vet's fault for passing them fit to travel when they weren't. At regular intervals it was my fault – I was buying horses that any fool could see were sickly. I suggested he do the next buying trip himself, see if he did any better. That didn't suit him either. I was trying to get him off the yard so ... oh, I can't even remember why it was I was supposed to want shot of him.'

She gave a sad little smile. 'He was going downhill even faster than the business. He was drinking way too much. I don't mean bad hangovers: I mean alcoholic poisoning. I tried to shield Ally from the worst of it, but maybe that was a mistake. What finally happened to him didn't surprise me in the least, but it knocked her sideways. Five days earlier she'd caught Stanley and Windham arguing in the yard. By all accounts it got personal and it got nasty. When Stanley died, Alison was convinced that was why. Not suicide, not an accident – murder. But no one else thought so.'

Which accorded pretty much with the picture Deacon had put together. He drew a

157

mental line under it and nodded. 'Actually, Miss Walbrook, there was something else I wanted to ask you. Do you know a man called Dieter Townes?'

'Townes.' The name seemed to mean something to her; after a moment she got it. 'He runs that little riding school at Cheyne Warren.'

'Appletree Farm. That's right.'

'Whatever can the police want with a man who gives riding lessons to under-tens? Oh – unless...'

'No, nothing like that,' Deacon said quickly. 'Only, it's an unusual name. Is he German, do you know?'

'I think his mother is,' said Mary. 'The way I heard it, his father was stationed in West Germany while he was in the army and he married a local girl.'

'So he may have family there,' said Deacon. 'Cousins and so on.'

'I've no idea,' said Mary Walbrook coolly.

'How long have you known him?'

'I wouldn't say I *do* know him. I've met him a time or two. We have some acquaintances in common. That's all.'

'You've never done business with him?'

Mary laughed out loud. 'I'm sorry, Superintendent, I don't mean to be rude. But the horses we handle have nothing in common with the animated hearth-rugs he uses. They're the same species. But you'd need to be an expert to know that.'

She hadn't told him much, but it gave him somewhere to start with Townes. Maybe the man had nothing whatever to do with the tranquillizer those wags at Forensics called Horsefeathers. But if he still had family in Germany, and if he did any visiting, and if it turned out his cousins had horses too, it was time Deacon gave Dieter Townes the opportunity to convince him of his innocence.

He and Meadows were back in the car, ready to leave, when a spit of stones and the squeal of dodgy suspension announced the arrival of a clapped-out hatchback of a type rarely encountered since the introduction of the MOT. It skidded to a halt and Alison Barker stumbled out, flushed with anger.

If she saw that Mary had visitors she didn't care. Distress twisted her mouth in awkward and ugly ways and her voice was thick. 'I saw him in the lane. What was he doing here? Tell me you sent him away. Mary, tell me you sent him away!' Her hands gripped the older woman's arms, shaking her.

Mary Walbrook broke her friend's grasp and her voice was firm. 'I wanted to tell you before you found out. But as you see, we've only just sorted it out. I was going to call you tonight.'

'Sorted what out?' But Deacon could see that she knew. She just couldn't believe it. Her whole body was rigid with shock.

'Ally, I have a lot of horses to be collected and delivered. Johnny did a good job for us for years, and now he's made me a very good offer. I can't afford to turn it down.'

'He tried to kill me!' The howl of anguish ripped straight from her heart.

Mary shook her head. 'I know you believe that, Ally, but it isn't true. And I wish I could afford to take your part, right or wrong, but I can't. I need this deal. I've told him I'll take it.'

Alison Barker backed up a couple of steps. Her body bent like a bow with the bitter force of her fury. 'I own part of this business. I won't let you do it. My father threw that man off the yard, and Johnny killed him because of it. Now he's tried to kill me too. And all that matters to you is saving a bit of money! I won't have it. Dad started this business, he was the senior partner. I'm his heir. You need my approval to make any kind of arrangement with Johnny Windham. And guess what? You're not going to get it.'

'I'm sorry, Ally,' Mary Walbrook said quietly, 'you're mistaken. I don't need your approval. The decision has already been made.'

The sense of betrayal is an emotion, an abstract, easy to describe but impossible to depict. Except that it was made manifest in Alison Barker's eyes. For the record, it looks like broken crystal. For a moment she couldn't find a voice to express it. When she did, all she could manage before she ran back to her ancient car and drove away was: 'It's the worst decision of your entire life. And it could be the last.'

Chapter Thirteen

Driving back from Peyton Parvo Deacon and Meadows considered, separately and together, what they'd heard. Specifically, whether it constituted a threat; and if so, whether it had been the sort of empty threat that angry people terminate conversations with, or the sort that subsequent inquiries hold to have been sufficiently significant and credible that a responsible officer would have acted on it.

Deacon didn't do his job with one eye on posterity – if he made mistakes they were honest ones and he was ready to answer for them. But the reality is, if something goes badly wrong somebody's head is going to roll. If something goes disastrously wrong – and it would count if one woman threatened another in front of two police officers, they decided it was just girl talk, and someone ended up dead – one of the privileges of rank is to be first to the chopping-block.

'I'm not sure it was a threat at all,' ventured Meadows. 'I think it was a warning. Alison Barker thinks Johnny Windham is a dangerous man who tried to shut her up by drugging her food. Now she finds out her friend is doing business with him again. She's alarmed – frightened for Mary's safety.'

Deacon wasn't entirely convinced. 'I thought she was more angry than alarmed. She thought Mary was letting her down.'

Jill Meadows had heard that too. 'Do you think Mary Walbrook is in any danger? From either of them?'

Deacon considered. '*She* didn't think so, did she? She didn't ask us for help of any kind. I don't think we have reasonable grounds to arrest Alison, and I don't think Mary would want us to even if we offered.'

'So what do we do about it, sir?'

'We *remember* it, constable,' Deacon said pontifically. 'That's what we do.'

From Peyton Parvo they headed across the Three Downs to Cheyne Warren. Meadows was thinking. 'There's something I don't understand, sir.'

'Only one thing?' Deacon was impressed. 'Perhaps you should be the superintendent.'

Detective Constable Meadows fully intended to be but thought it wiser not to say so. 'Sorry – not the case. Why is it Chain Down' – she spelled it out – 'but Cheyne Warren?'

'For the same reason it's Mennor Down but Manor Farm, and actually both of them were named after the standing stone – the menhir – on the top. For the same reason that gorge' – he pointed out of the driver's window, to where the roadside verge disappeared in forty metres of drop onto chalk boulders – 'is Ship Coomb. You don't really think they ever got ships up that little stream? Somebody lost some sheep down it once. But the rubes down here were illiterate until they punched through the road from London.'

'The Roman road?'

'The M23,' said Deacon sourly.

When he saw Dieter Townes' ponies Deacon understood Mary Walbrook's amusement. There wasn't one of them worth the trouble of importing. If he'd bought them at all it was from a rag-and-bone man. He might have been paid to take them away.

Then he remembered that one of these ponies – and even if it was the prettiest that wasn't saying much – was the dearest thing to Paddy Farrell's heart after her mother and Howard the stuffed dragon. She'd have been riding it this morning; half a dozen other little girls would be on it during the course of the day. Every one of these placid little beasts was the means of separating middle-class families from their hard-earned wealth. At that thought both the ponies and their

163

owner went up in his estimation.

Townes was teaching when they arrived. Deacon called him over, and the flash of his warrant card made Townes first frown and then call over a teenager who was working in the corner of the yard. 'Keep an eye on this lot for me. Get them doing Round The World. Anyone who falls off gets put back on. Anyone who falls off twice gets 10p and put back on.'

The girl ran a critical eye over his class. 'They'll make more money out of you than you do out of them.'

'Just do it.' He walked back to where Deacon and Meadows were waiting. 'Sorry about that, but I can't just abandon them. What's this about?'

It was always a balancing act, deciding how much to say. Of course, if Townes was involved in smuggling drugs in from Europe he knew what it was about, and if he wasn't, telling him wouldn't matter. 'We're talking to people involved in the horse trade in this area about the possibility that illegal substances are being smuggled across the Channel in horse transporters.'

Townes wasn't a fool: he didn't throw his hands up in horror at the very idea. He gave it some thought. 'It wouldn't be difficult. For obvious reasons, a horse lorry is a big, sturdy vehicle. A lot of them are built with double floors as a safety measure. It wouldn't be rocket science to create a cavity between those floors big enough to smuggle in almost anything you wanted. And to find out you'd need to do a proper search – unload the horses, remove the partitions, muck out the box, hose the floor, lift the rubber matting and then start looking for a way into the floor itself. What I'm saying is, you couldn't tell anything by just looking and tapping with a screwdriver.' When he realised he had more of their undivided attention than was strictly desirable he shut up.

'My goodness, Mr Townes,' said Deacon, 'you *have* given this some thought.'

Townes forced an embarrassed little chuckle. 'Not really. It's kind of obvious. Anyone who's travelled across borders with a horse-box knows that Customs would rather search a coach-load of deaf pensioners than start on a trailer with two ponies in it. If that mattered to you, it would be worth bearing in mind.'

Deacon let his gaze travel back to the sand school, where half a dozen small children were engaged in an exercise that, deliber-ately or otherwise, had resulted in several of them sitting back-to-front. The ponies either hadn't noticed or didn't care. 'Find yourself crossing a lot of borders, do you, Mr Townes?'

'With that lot, no,' said Townes. 'But I

worked as a groom in a number of competition yards and we spent half of every year travelling round Europe. If you want to know if I ever smuggled anything myself, the answer is no. The fact remains, it wouldn't be difficult.'

'No,' nodded Deacon. 'Where did you get to, then?'

'All round,' said Townes. 'France, Belgium, Holland, Spain, Germany...'

'Ah. Visiting the family.'

Townes had thought the questioning was essentially over, they were making conversation now. He blinked as he realised his mistake. 'That's right, my mother's from Germany. I have cousins in Hamburg. And yes, when we took the eventers to Luneburg Heath I paid them a visit. About eight years ago, and I haven't seen them since. Superintendent Deacon, I don't see how this is going to help you.'

'Are your cousins into horses too, Mr Townes?'

'No,' he said levelly. 'One is an accountant, one works in a brewery, two are academics at the university.'

'Veterinary science?' hazarded Deacon, who saw what was always a thin lead withering by the moment.

'Media studies and archaeology,' said Dieter Townes.

Deacon made himself smile. 'Well, thank

you for your insights. I'm sure we'll find them very helpful. If we should need another word with you...?'

'I'll be here. I always am.'

She'd said an hour. When two had passed and Alison still wasn't back Daniel put his books away and walked up Fisher Hill to The Ginnell.

He was expecting to find her there, with a suitcase open on the bed, debating what to bring and what to leave, unaware how much time had passed and how uneasy he had become. Instead he found the house empty and no sign of an old banger outside.

All Daniel's instincts were telling him something was wrong. Even so, before he did anything he made himself stop and think. There were a lot more likely explanations than that she'd been abducted in broad daylight. She might be on her way down to the shore right now, just not the way he'd come because she'd parked the car facing up the hill. If he walked home he might find she'd got there first, was sitting on his steps like an orphan because she hadn't got a key.

By then, though, she'd have been adrift for two and a half hours. Twelve days after what she claimed was an attempt on her life, would she have left him to worry for that long, when all she had to do if she'd been delayed was pick up the phone? If she knew his number. Daniel couldn't remember if he'd given it to her or not.

He turned round and headed home. If she was there, or there was a message on his phone, well and good; if not he was going to have to call the police. The chance that Alison was in trouble outweighed the risk of making a fool of himself.

In the event, Brodie walked out of Shack Lane as he hurried past. With Paddy at her father's for tea she'd taken the opportunity to do a couple of hours' work. So intent was he on getting home that Daniel didn't even see her: she had to call his name, with some asperity, before he stopped.

'Not talking to me, Daniel?'

They hadn't parted on the best of terms, but in fact he was desperately glad to see her. He explained the situation in a few sentences.

To her credit, whatever her feelings about Alison Barker and however irritated she was with Daniel, Brodie put that aside while they dealt with the crisis. 'I'll get the car. We'll check your house, and if she's not there I'll call Jack.'

She wasn't there. Daniel's heart plummeted. But while Brodie was dialling a decrepit car pulled up behind Brodie's. Daniel touched her arm.

Immediately Brodie's annoyance, her sense that something valuable to her had been stolen by this girl, returned. She was all set to give Alison a piece of her mind as soon as she came inside. But she didn't come inside. She didn't get out of the car. They could see her bent over the wheel, not moving. With a sudden surge of fear they hurried down the iron steps and up the shingle together.

Alison was uninjured. But she was crying as if she'd never stop.

Daniel wanted to touch her and didn't dare, afraid she might shatter like crystal. Brodie had no such reservations. She ducked down beside the weeping girl and put her arms around her, and guided her out of the car and down to the netting-shed. Feeling rather foolish – thieves aren't *that* desperate, even in Dimmock – Daniel locked the car and followed.

Brodie didn't even try to get any sense out of her until Alison was installed in an armchair with a mug of hot sweet tea pressed into her trembling hands. Then she said, 'Tell us what happened.'

In all honesty, what had happened barely explained the state she'd worked herself into. She had done as she'd told Daniel she intended: walked up to the house on The Ginnell. On the kitchen table she'd found a message from Mary Walbrook saying she'd popped by and found the house empty, and would Alison call to say where she was staying and that she was all right.

'I was going to phone. Then I thought, the car's out there, I'll drive out to the yard then she'll know I'm OK.' She packed what she was taking down to Daniel's, then headed for Peyton Parvo.

Half a mile from the yard, on a road that went almost nowhere else, she met one of Windham Transport's lorries with Johnny Windham at the wheel.

'I thought... I thought... I don't know what I thought! I *thought* she was my friend. I thought if Johnny offered her the same deal he offered my father she'd throw him out. I didn't think she'd be willing to forget everything that had happened for the sake of some cheap transport! But I was wrong.'

'And you were upset,' said Brodie softly.

'*Upset?*' The girl's voice soared. 'Mrs Farrell, I know you don't believe me. I know Superintendent Deacon doesn't believe me, and I'm not sure Daniel does. But Johnny Windham is a killer, and he's talked Mary into hiring him again. What's in it for her is cheap transport. What's in it for him is her standing up and saying that no, what happened to Barker & Walbrook – what happened to my father – wasn't his fault. The people we know will understand what it means when they see him delivering to our yard again. They'll understand it means Mary's backing him, not me.'

Daniel tried to find a little consolation for her. 'I suppose it was a business decision. She'll have had to make some difficult ones to keep the yard going. She probably felt this was another occasion when she just had to bite the bullet and do it.'

Alison pushed away the mug – most people don't actually *like* hot sweet tea – and put both hands to her face. But she wasn't crying any more. She was trying to say this without sounding hysterical in the hope of finally convincing someone who mattered. Daniel was sweet to believe her, but she had come to realise that Daniel had problems with his own credibility. She desperately needed a big gun to back her up.

'I'm not talking about yard politics here. I'm not angry because Mary's taking his side not mine. Well, I am, but that's not what this is about. It's about the fact that Johnny Windham thinks he's entitled to remove any obstacles in his way by any means that suit him. I'm afraid for her. I'm afraid that once the novelty of cheap transport has worn off she'll remember what kind of a man he is and want nothing more to do with him, and he won't let her walk away.'

Her chin cupped in one hand, Brodie regarded the girl without speaking for some moments. Finally she said, 'Can we put our cards on the table here, Alison? Say what we think?' Ally nodded. 'Then, there are a lot of things about your story that don't make any sense. But things that make no sense happen every day, and a lot of them I could just about believe with a following wind. Do you know what I can't believe? That Johnny Windham – that *anyone* – would want to kill either you or your father over a business dispute.

'All right, your father blamed him for the damage to some horses, and Windham blamed your father for costing him some customers. It's the sort of thing that happens every day – you lose one customer over a disagreement, you gain another who's just fallen out with *his* last supplier. You don't go back a week later and push him in a pond, and you certainly don't go back three months later and try to murder his daughter!'

The girl shrugged. Sitting there in his living room, hunched over as if expecting blows, Daniel was conscious of how very slight she was. He knew she was strong too, she had to be, but maybe a lot of her strength was mental rather than physical. Nobody is as strong as a horse. Maybe she was good at pretending to be strong, the way he was good at pretending to be brave. If the pretence was good enough, no one challenged it. You yourself knew it was a sham, but if you never let on maybe no one

172

would guess.

'I can't help that,' Ally said quietly. She had her fingers laced together, gripping tightly. 'I've told you everything that happened, as it happened. Of course no one believes me. I wouldn't believe it myself if I didn't know this man and what he's capable of.'

'Mary knows him too,' Brodie pointed out. 'And she lost almost as much as you did. But she doesn't blame Windham. Not for your business difficulties and not for your father's death.'

'But then, I know him better than Mary does.'

Brodie noted that without pursuing it. 'There's something missing. That argument: are you sure it was about the horses? They couldn't have fallen out over something else?'

'They didn't have anything else in common.'

'Tell me what happened. What they said to one another.'

Even remembering was a pain to Alison Barker. Her voice dropped to a hoarse whisper. 'I'd never seen my Dad so angry. He kept saying, "I used to have a reputation round here. People respected me." I didn't know whether he was going to hit Johnny or have a stroke first. I thought Johnny was going to knock him down. I think they *would* have come to blows if I hadn't come round the corner at the critical moment. Then they backed off like a couple of scrapping dogs, snarling insults and threats at one another. Dad said if he caught Johnny on the place again he'd call the police, and Johnny said "Don't think this is over" and "You're going to pay for this". Then he got in his lorry and drove away, and five days later my father was dead. So tell me: what would you have thought?'

Sorry for her as he was, Daniel still couldn't see it. 'I think I'd have thought he was sick and tired of all the problems crowding in on him, and that he picked a dangerous spot to go on a blinder.'

'OK,' said Brodie, still trying to shape this into a narrative she could believe in. 'Stanley and Windham had a blazing row and ended up trading threats. There's nothing terribly unusual about that in the business world. Believe me: I know. Sometimes it takes mediation to sort out who owes who what, sometimes it takes solicitors. But it's a hell of a way from the threat of fisticuffs to cold-blooded murder. People don't kill one another over things like that.'

Actually that wasn't strictly true. There are really only two reasons people get murdered. One is anger, the other is money. People do die in business disputes, only such murders tend to be either crude and obvious or clever and unsuspected. This fitted neither template.

'You weren't there,' insisted Ally.

But Brodie had got to the bottom of a lot of mysteries she hadn't actually witnessed. It was partly intuition, partly her analytical brain, partly the sort of thought processes that make people good at crosswords, and partly that she knew the comparatively small number of ways that people behaved and was good at judging what they would and wouldn't do in a given set of circumstances. 'Just suppose,' she said slowly, 'that what they were arguing about wasn't just some horses that got sick in transit.'

For once Daniel, who could read her mind like a book, let her down. He frowned. 'What then?'

She scowled disappointedly at him. 'Suppose they were arguing about how Windham was using Barker & Walbrook's horses as a cover for drug running?'

Chapter Fourteen

'I don't think Townes is involved,' said Deacon.

'Despite the German connection?'

Because it was Sunday he and his sergeant

were talking shop in The Belted Galloway instead of the CID offices on the top floor of Battle Alley. In the labyrinth of Deacon's mind this counted as 'Having Sunday Off'. Each man had half a pint of weak shandy in front of him.

'Coincidence,' said Deacon. 'Everyone's parents come from somewhere.'

'My grandmother's Irish,' volunteered Charlie Voss.

Deacon had always taken his red hair as a personal affront. 'Why am I not surprised?'

'If Townes isn't, does that mean Windham is?'

'I don't think it works quite like that. But he does keep popping up, doesn't he? Just when you think you've laid him to rest – the guy had a bit of bad luck, not even so much with the horses as with that damned hysterical girl – up he pops again. And now he's back working for Barker & Walbrook.'

'I suppose that's Walbrook & Barker now,' ruminated Voss.

'That's certainly how Mary Walbrook sees it. It seems fair enough,' said Deacon, 'I doubt there'd still be a business without her grabbing hold of it and refusing to let go.'

'She buys a lot of horses on the continent,' said Voss. 'Whoever carries them will be constantly crossing the Channel. If Windham *is* up to no good, her business would give him a cast-iron reason to bring a big vehicle full of neurotic animals through Dover as often as he needed to. He could be carrying more than horses.'

Deacon had been thinking along the same lines. He thought that meant Charlie Voss was reading his mind, never considered the possibility that he'd learned to read Voss's. 'Get the registration numbers of his lorries and check with Customs if they've given any of them a shakedown recently. Ask them if they had a reason or was it just his turn. Ask them...'

These two men had worked closely together for three years now. They spent hours a day in one another's company. The relationship was a lot like a marriage, and had already lasted longer than some. They knew one another pretty well.

Deacon knew that while Charlie Voss might not make a song and dance about it, he was an astute, intuitive and hard-working police officer who was customarily one, if not two, steps ahead of the game. He knew what it meant that Voss wasn't nodding and reaching for a phone, was just waiting quietly for him to finish. 'You've already done it, haven't you?'

Voss nodded apologetically. 'They've had both his lorries in for a check in the last two months, one a down-to-the-chassis job. They didn't find anything.'

'Did they expect to?'

'No.' Voss didn't sound totally confident of that. 'Well, yes and no. The way it was put to me, they had no reason to suspect him – no tip-offs, no intelligence – they just felt a shade uneasy about him. Just enough to keep an eye on his comings and goings. They hoped to find something but weren't surprised when they didn't.'

'And they emptied that particular lorry and stripped it right down?'

'No false floor, no secret panels, no hidden storage inside the diesel tank. They're as sure as they can be that if he'd been carrying anything apart from horses they'd have found it.'

Deacon gave a glum scowl. 'Maybe he just wasn't carrying anything that day.'

'If there'd been any secret compartments, even empty ones, they'd have found them too. I suppose the driver could always fill his Thermos, but that's not why you take a six-horse transporter to Europe. Easier and safer just to hire a few mules.'

'And he'd been in Germany?'

'He always seems to visit Germany. Well, a lot of good horses are bred there, and a lot of them come here. There's nothing suspicious about him doing regular runs to Germany.'

'There's not much suspicious about him at all, is there?' said Deacon lugubriously. 'Let's be honest: we wouldn't be looking at him at all if it wasn't for that crazy girl.'

'That crazy girl who nearly died of a Scram overdose,' Voss reminded him.

'There is that. But we only have her word for it that she didn't feel like a pick-me-up and buy it from a street-dealer. We'd never have looked at Windham if she hadn't accused him of trying to kill her. But she's levelled accusations at him before, and they were investigated and dismissed as a mixture of grief and malice.'

'Yes,' agreed Voss. 'You don't think we should have investigated Stanley Barker's death a bit more thoroughly?'

Deacon thought he was probably right. There had seemed no reason to treat the incident as suspicious at the time – except for his daughter's protestations, and no one is at their most logical when there's been a death in the family. They had taken what she had to say with rather more than a pinch of salt. That wasn't an unreasonable decision, but it meant Deacon couldn't now look back on the matter of Stanley Barker's midnight swim and state with confidence that nothing had been missed. 'We're going to have to do it again, aren't we?'

'If only for our own peace of mind.'

'Peace of mind be damned,' grunted Deacon. 'If she was right all along, we missed a murder and left a killer at large to try to kill again. This is not a matter of dotting i's and

179

crossing t's. It's what we're paid for.'

'And we earn every penny of it,' Voss said stoutly. 'We're bloody good at what we do, just not quite infallible.'

Deacon speared him with a disapproving eye. 'Have you never heard it said, Charlie Voss, that pride is a sin?'

'I've always thought that lack of pride was a greater one.'

Deacon went on regarding him: not so much with disfavour now, almost – this was worrying – with affection. If he'd realised he was doing it he'd have stopped immediately. Voss recognised the look and said nothing. He'd taken enough stick from his governor in the early months, he thought he'd earned a bit of respect by now.

'OK,' said Deacon. 'Let's suppose, just for the moment, that Stanley Barker's death wasn't as clear-cut as we thought, was neither accident nor suicide. He didn't fall, he didn't jump – he was pushed.' The words verged on the flippant but his tone was utterly serious. 'If Windham was using his lorries to smuggle in drugs, or components for drugs, losing Barker's business would have been a blow to him. Hence the argument that Alison overheard. If he came to the conclusion that he wasn't going to talk Barker round, maybe he thought he'd find it easier to charm Mary Walbrook. She was his partner – with Barker out of the way she'd make the decisions. You could call that a motive for murder.'

'Anything to do with drugs is motive enough for murder,' Voss agreed grimly. 'Because of the sheer amount of money involved. But this happened three months ago. Why are we only seeing Scram appearing now?'

Deacon took a slow draught of his shandy. He thought it was a girl's drink, but since he rarely considered himself off-duty he seldom took enough alcohol to affect his performance. 'Partly because it took time to set up. To establish the factory, secure supplies of the catalyst and perfect the means of sneaking it past Customs. And partly because, when Barker & Walbrook went to the wall, Windham Transport damned near followed. He lost a lot of business, is only now starting to pick it up again. Maybe he couldn't get enough horses to justify keep going to Germany. Maybe there seemed no point putting the stuff on the street until he could be sure of getting regular supplies.'

Voss was slowly nodding. 'Well, he seems to be doing regular business now. And he'll do more if he's carrying for Mary Walbrook again. Also, if he was responsible for Barker's death he'd have had to put everything on hold while it was being looked into. He'd have wanted the dust to settle before he starting taking any chances again.'

181

'You keep saying *he*,' said Deacon. 'But this can't be a one-man operation.'

Voss hadn't thought about that. Now he did he saw Deacon was right. 'It takes someone to get hold of the catalyst – a vet, maybe, or someone working at the pharmaceutical plant. Someone to smuggle it in – say Windham. And someone to turn out the pills. Three of them.'

'Two would be better,' mused Deacon. 'With two of you, if something goes wrong you both know who's to blame. With three, you never know for certain. The vet would be familiar with pharmaceuticals. Maybe he provided the instructions and Windham knocks the things up when he's at home.'

Voss chuckled. 'You make it sound like a flat-pack sideboard.'

Deacon glowered at him. 'Less levity, more detecting, Charlie Voss. What do you think – is it time I interviewed this man?'

'Brodie went to see him a few days ago,' said Voss helpfully.

As soon as it was out he knew it was a mistake. Voss had heard it from Daniel: it didn't occur to him that Brodie might not have told Deacon. What *did* they talk about on their long evenings in? Somehow Voss couldn't imagine Deacon passing them the same way he and Helen Choi passed theirs.

'She did what?' The restraint in the superintendent's voice was like the inertia that stops avalanches falling on Swiss villages, right up to the moment that they do.

It was too late for anything but the truth. 'She made up some story about wanting to import a pony from Germany. To establish whether Windham Transport is a genuine business or just a front.'

It was a valid question: Deacon wished he'd thought to ask it. But what he wished above all else was that Brodie Farrell would stop behaving as if what he did for a living was some kind of a game – anyone could have a go, a talented amateur could always beat a jaded professional, first to collect three *Spot The Blagger* cards wins a *Get Out Of The Morgue Free* token.

'And?'

'He wanted her custom. Offered her a good deal – which was rather awkward since she didn't actually have a pony. So she put him off. But she had no doubt that he's open for business.'

Deacon was pondering. 'Does that necessarily mean transporting horses is his *only* business?'

'If you've found a way of packing drugs into your vehicle that a good sniffer dog can't crack, I suppose it doesn't matter *what* you're carrying as well as long as you're carrying enough to justify your journeys. So the more business you get, the better. It would be worth undercutting your competitors to be sure you always had horses to move in the right part of the world.'

'It would, wouldn't it? Do you know, I still think I want a word with Mr Windham.' Deacon curled his upper lip. 'Actually, I want a word with Brodie too.'

'I have to talk to Jack about this,' said Brodie. Through the windows of her eyes her mind was racing visibly. 'He's been worried sick about the arrival of this new drug from Germany. Scram – the thing Alison took.'

'I didn't take it,' said Ally through clenched teeth.

'Whatever,' said Brodie dismissively. 'He's been trying to find how it's coming in. I wonder if he's thought of a horse-transporter.'

'I dare say he has,' ventured Daniel. 'I don't expect HM Customs & Excise have failed to notice the smuggling potential of a large lorry with a live cargo.'

'No.' A shade reluctantly, Brodie had to concede the point. Anything she could think of – probably anything Deacon could think of – the likelihood was that Customs had thought of months before, and the smugglers a month before that. But there was a body of coincidence building up that she could no more ignore than Deacon could, hammering out the same arguments with Voss half a mile away in The Belted

Galloway. 'So he's being cleverer than that. How? What could he be doing that would be cleverer than hiding drugs in the bodywork of a horse lorry?'

'Having nothing to do with drugs at all,' said Daniel firmly.

'Well yes,' agreed Brodie, 'and that may still be the answer. But somebody's bringing this stuff in, they seem to have some connection to this area, they seem to have contacts in Germany and also with the veterinary trade. It might not be Windham, but it could be. It would explain some things.'

Alison didn't much like Brodie Farrell. She wasn't alone in that. Women tended to find her a bit too competitive, a bit too successful for comfort. She was outspoken and she didn't much care what people thought of her, and she didn't even try to hide the fact. On top of that she was what men called *a looker* – not pretty, no one had ever thought of her as pretty, she went straight from gawky adolescence to stunning – and were drawn as wasps to a honey-trap. Women didn't like that about her either.

What Alison didn't like most was how Brodie became the centre of attention in any gathering she joined. It happened automatically, didn't seem to be an effect she planned or worked for; she didn't seem to be terribly aware of it at all. But Alison was, and it annoyed her more than she could have explained without sounding childish. All that had sustained her these last months, hovering on the brink of the abyss, was a sense of drama. She knew a day would come when she would be proved right and the doubters wrong. There was a certain satisfaction in that, even if she wasn't there to enjoy it.

But doubt is one thing, being upstaged another. The moment Brodie walked on Alison felt herself relegated to the part of a supporting actress.

Nor was her resentment in any way soothed by knowing that Brodie's support was key to finally being taken seriously. Daniel had given her a hearing mostly out of kindness. Kindness was not a significant motive for Brodie, and her opinion was worth more because of it. If Brodie Farrell was persuaded, could Detective Superintendent Deacon be far behind?

So Alison needed Brodie on her side. But she didn't have to like it. 'What things?' she asked guardedly.

'The fight you walked in on, between Windham and your father. Why were they *so* angry? Everyone I've talked to reckons the odd sick or injured horse is par for the course. So maybe your father was bothered that it kept being *him* having to explain to a client, maybe he thought Windham could do better – but why were they *so* angry they almost came to blows?'

Shock dropped through Alison's expression like bricks off a hod. 'You think he found out? My God! You think that's why Johnny killed him?'

'It's a possibility,' said Brodie, dipping her gaze with uncustomary tact.

'I never thought of anything beyond the horses!' gasped Ally. 'But you're right, aren't you? Johnny was using our horses as a cover to bring in drugs. But while he was doing that he let his standards slip and the horses got sick. And Dad didn't believe it was just bad luck, not time after time, and he kept chipping away at it until he got to the truth. And that was it. Drugs. Johnny asked him to keep it to himself and Dad refused. And Johnny killed him.'

Alison had a vested interest in that version of events. It made her disinclined to look far beyond it. But Daniel had seen the reticence in Brodie's eyes, and asking himself what it was about had come up with an alternative scenario. For a moment he wondered if they should even mention it, or leave the girl with the consolation of her beliefs.

He decided it was little kindness to leave her in a bubble that would be burst, without ceremony or much sympathy, the first time she talked to Deacon about it. Better to put it on the table now and let her get used to the idea in her own time.

'There's something else they could have

been arguing about,' he said quietly.

Her thin face was all avid attention, as if he was showing her a glimpse of the Holy Grail. 'What?'

'The cut.'

She didn't understand. 'What cut?'

Brodie sighed. 'Well, there were dead horses to be paid for. They could have been arguing about whether that came out of Windham's share of the profits or your father's.'

Chapter Fifteen

There's one thing about being good with horses: it tends to make you bad with people. Different rules apply. If a horse kicks you, you don't offer to discuss the matter, look for common ground and try to negotiate a means of avoiding confrontation in the future. You retaliate, instantly, so in the small and chaotic space that is a horse's brain it associates its own action with an undesirable result and minds its manners next time.

It should be noted that not all horsemen, and particularly horsewomen, subscribe to this view. They believe that a horse is entitled to an equal say with its owner and should not be constrained to do anything it doesn't want to. They believe that negotiation will accomplish more in the long run.

And indeed it will. It'll accomplish everything the horse wants: long days in the field and an owner who only visits at meal-times, juggling buckets and elbow-crutches with stoic aplomb. Horses are a lot like teenage boys: they're big and strong, they have a childish sense of humour, and given the chance they always argue. They're nicest to be with, and also happiest, when the lines of responsibility are clearly drawn so they know what's expected of them.

Alison Barker had loved her horses dearly, and had got the best out of them, and given them a future in which they would always be valuable to someone, but she hadn't done it by letting them trample her. Now she didn't let anyone trample her. Instead of blanching as Brodie's meaning hit her – and indeed there was nothing subtle about it – she struck out with her fists.

Brodie never saw it coming. She reeled under the first blow, would still have been there for the second but that Daniel flung himself at the girl, wrapping his arms around her, pinning her elbows to her sides. 'Enough!' he commanded crisply in her ear; and by degrees her struggles ceased until she was just standing against his chest, the violence contained, only the hatred still radiating from her.

Brodie was almost too shocked to complain. It's not often a grown woman takes a sock in the eye; unless her nearest and dearest is that way inclined. She pressed the heel of her hand over it and stared, one-eyed and open-mouthed, at her assailant.

'Now, everybody settle down,' Daniel said sharply. He pointed a spare finger at Brodie. 'You too. Honest to God, Brodie, you asked for that. Which doesn't mean' – he gave the girl in his arms a shake without releasing her – '*you* had any right to deliver it. Not in my house. You want to scrap, go outside. But at some point you'll still have to sit down and talk about this, and it might as well be now.'

Ally's whole body was stiff with resentment. 'Why the hell would I want to talk to someone who thinks my father was a drug-runner?'

'Might have been,' gritted Brodie. '*Might* have been a drug-runner.'

'And you.' The girl spun in the compass of Daniel's arms, staring fiercely into his face. 'Is that what you think too? It is, isn't it? That's what you meant. You bastards! You say you're my friends, you want to help me, and all the time that's what you're thinking! You didn't know him, either of you. How *dare* you think that?'

Now her attention was on him Daniel thought the danger of fisticuffs was probably over. At least, he was prepared to risk his front teeth in a way that he wasn't prepared to risk Brodie's. He released Ally and stepped back, spreading his hands. 'A lot of weird things have been happening. But they aren't really weird. Somehow, to someone, they make sense. We're just trying to work out who they make sense to and how.

'And Brodie's right: one of the possibilities we have to consider is that your father and Johnny Windham fell out when a drugs operation they were both involved in went sour. You want people to believe you? Well, your story makes a lot more sense if there was more at stake than a few horses. A man might certainly be annoyed with someone who was bad-mouthing him to their mutual acquaintances, might even seek an injunction to shut her up, but he wouldn't dream of killing her. But he just might go that far if he thought she was going to draw attention to a nice little sideline he'd set up importing illegal drugs.'

'Johnny Windham will do anything that's in his own interests and he thinks he can get away with,' Ally said tersely. 'I'd believe anything of him. What I'll *never* believe is that my father was involved.' Her gaze was sharp, astute. 'How much of this is just a pretty theory and how much do you actually know?'

'If you'll stay in your corner for five

minutes I'll tell you.' Brodie repeated every-thing – there was no reason not to – that Deacon had told her. The German veterin-ary tranquillizer. The factory that was combining it with common pharmaceuticals to produce the powerful party-drug that had already killed two and put four, herself included, in Intensive Care. The fear that this was just the tip of the iceberg: that now the factory was up and running Scram would any day explode onto the streets of southern England leaving devastation in its wake.

'Why doesn't he shut down the factory?' asked Ally, as if that simple solution might not have occurred to anyone.

'If he knew where it was,' said Brodie heavily, 'I'm sure he would.'

'What do you mean by a factory? Literally, a big industrial building with smoke coming out of a chimney?'

Daniel shook his head. 'It might be just a room in someone's house. Or an outbuild-ing somewhere. A power supply, water, privacy. You could do it in a flat as long as you didn't get too many visitors.'

Brodie was watching him oddly. 'How do you know?'

'It's chemistry, isn't it? A lot of good science is done in chemists' kitchens.'

'Well, in this case some bad science is being done there too.'

'The point is,' said Daniel, 'there are too many places where this stuff could be manufactured. Jack can't search every house within a ten mile radius of Dimmock.'

'Of course he can't. Which is why he's so desperate to find one person who's involved in this. One person will do. Once he has a way in he'll get at the truth.'

'Johnny Windham.' There was no missing the cat-like satisfaction in Ally Barker's voice. 'As I keep saying.'

'And it may turn out you were right,' nodded Brodie. 'In any event, Jack'll need to take a good hard look now at everything Windham's ever done or been suspected of, right down to fiddling his income tax and jumping red lights.'

Ally nodded. It was happening – what she'd hung on this long for. 'Tell him.'

As if telepathy was a new service offered by the mobile phone companies, Brodie's warbled in her handbag – no one who knew her was surprised that it played 'The Ride of the Valkyries' – and it was Deacon. 'Where are you? Something's come up. I need to see you.'

'Funny you should mention that,' replied Brodie. 'I'm at Daniel's. Something's come up at this end too. Shall we come to you or...?'

'Stay where you are,' said Deacon, 'I'll be there in five minutes.'

It quickly became apparent that the two leashes of bloodhounds had converged on the same scent. If that's a reasonable analogy; if it wasn't more like one leash of bloodhounds and a Saluki accompanied by a Jack Russell. Over a fresh pot of coffee, which contained rather more stimulant than the shandy Deacon had left undrunk in The Belted Galloway, they compared notes.

Everyone listened carefully to everyone else, but Alison listened to Deacon like Moses taking down the Ten Commandments. When he'd finished she said, 'Superintendent – are you saying now that I might have been right?'

'Honest answer, Miss Barker? I don't know. I want to take a fresh look at the whole business.'

'Well, hallelujah!' she declared. 'You mean, maybe I'm not insane after all?'

'I wouldn't go that far, Miss Barker,' he said gruffly.

'Neither would I,' muttered Brodie, still comforting her eye.

Deacon was looking oddly at her. 'Yes. What happened to...?'

'What we were wondering,' Daniel interrupted hurriedly, 'was if Windham could be using his lorries to smuggle in this German tranquillizer. If he was doing it when he was supposed to be looking after horses for

Barker & Walbrook. If Alison's father found out, and that's why they fought and he took his business elsewhere.'

'Or if they were in it together,' Brodie said stubbornly, keeping her good eye on Alison and her distance from her.

'Or if Dad figured out what he was up to and Johnny killed him because of it,' added Ally, her voice rising as if to meet a challenge.

Deacon blinked and looked to Daniel for an explanation, and Daniel rolled his eyes theatrically. 'We've covered a fair bit of ground in the last half hour,' he murmured.

Deacon shook his head to clear it and tried to get back to what was, for him, the point. 'Charlie says you went to see Windham.' He was looking at Brodie.

'That's right,' said Brodie after a moment, 'though I don't know how he knew.'

'Er – me,' said Daniel, raising a finger as if asking to be excused. 'I didn't know it was a secret.'

'It isn't,' glowered Brodie. 'I was planning on putting an announcement in *The Sentinel*.'

'Sorry,' mumbled Daniel.

Deacon squinted at the ceiling. 'I think I liked it better when you two weren't talking. Daniel, shut up. Brodie, tell me about Windham – what you said, what he said.'

So she did.

'Did you think he had anything to hide?'

'At the time, no, I didn't. Talking about it since, I'm not sure. He wanted to fetch my pony from Germany, that's for sure. But it could be that what he really wanted was an excuse to make another run.'

'Because he has something to bring in that's even more profitable than transporting horses,' said Deacon.

'That's what we were thinking, yes.'

'Customs couldn't find anything.'

'If Customs could find everything that was smuggled in we wouldn't have a drugs problem.'

'Mules,' said Daniel pensively.

Brodie frowned at him. 'What?'

'People who carry drugs through Customs. Not the drug-runners themselves – people they've hired. Poor people and stupid people. They hide small quantities inside their trainers and their children's toys and souvenirs for their mothers, and sometimes inside themselves, and some of them get caught but most of them get through, and at the other end all the small quantities are put together to make quite a large quantity. And that's what the drug-runners call them. Mules.'

'Yes,' agreed Deacon. 'So?'

'I was just wondering if there was any way of using a horse as a mule. They're a capacious animal. If a human mule can carry a commercially significant quantity of drugs in his digestive system, how much more could you pack into a horse?'

Brodie's eyes flared wide with understanding, then flicked to Alison. 'You're the expert here. Is he talking nonsense?'

'I don't know,' said the girl, nonplussed. 'I just don't know.'

Deacon was struggling with the practicalities. 'How do you persuade a horse to swallow a condom full of drugs? And how do you stop it throwing up at deeply inconvenient moments?'

'They don't throw up,' said Ally. 'They can't – they haven't the mechanism. Anything that goes down their throats will come out the opposite end.'

'When?' asked Brodie.

Ally shrugged. 'I've never put a stopwatch on it.'

'Within the next three days, anyway.'

'Oh yes. Horses are the perfect vegetarian – they eat nothing *but* roughage. It goes straight through them, and doesn't look that different when it comes out the other end.' She looked puzzled. 'Why three days?'

'Because Windham reckons to keep everything he brings in from Europe in his own yard for three days. Till a vet passes them fit to go to their new homes, he said. But maybe that isn't the only reason.'

'OK,' said Deacon tersely. 'So this is a

serious possibility? Miss Barker, you know more about horses than the rest of us put together. *Could* you get them to swallow a package on demand?'

She gave it some thought. 'I don't know if I could, but I think it could be done. Ostlers used to shove medicine down horses' throats with something they called a balling iron. These days we tube them – pass a plastic tube up a nostril and down into the stomach. And yes, anything that can go down that tube will go into the stomach. Or for something a bit bulkier than that, a bit of sedative might relax the muscles enough to put it straight down the throat. I don't think it would pose a massive problem to a vet.'

'But where would you find a vet willing to risk his licence to help a drug-smuggler?' asked Daniel.

'The same place you'd find one willing to divert quantities of a large animal tranquillizer from clinical trials to a Scram factory,' said Brodie. 'We knew there was likely to be a vet involved somewhere. Once the money's big enough there's always someone ready to risk his reputation.'

'Slow down,' growled Deacon, 'I want to get this straight in my head. So somewhere in Germany a vet is fiddling his paperwork so that he's ending up with a surplus of the tranquillizer he's supposed to be trialling. And someone in England, probably in or around Dimmock, has the facilities to combine that drug with a bunch of other commoner chemicals in order to produce the next big thing on the party scene. All they need is a way to get the German tranquillizer past Customs in Dover.'

Brodie took up the hypothesis. 'And somebody looked at a horse and saw a barrel on legs. He knew a lot of them came to England, and he wondered what Daniel did: could you get packets of drugs into a horse's digestive system?'

Ally too was getting the hang of this new sport, beach volleyball with theories. She threw a punch of her own as one sailed past her. 'Only instead of just having me to ask, this guy had a vet – a large animal vet at that – on the payroll. So he asked him, and it turned out the answer was yes. All they needed was a form of packaging that would go either up a horse's nose or down its throat, and the patience to wait for it to reappear.'

'And a steady supply of horses being brought from Europe,' added Brodie.

'Do you suppose there are drugs in all the horses he brings in?' asked Daniel.

Deacon shook his head. 'Why take the risk when one horse can carry enough to keep the south coast party scene popping for a month? One horse per load would be plenty. He finds an excuse to have his vet look at the selected animal...'

'If anyone asked he could say it looked a bit colicky,' offered Ally.

'OK,' said Deacon, 'so while he's ostensibly checking it out he whacks a bit of sedative into it and shoves the chemical, packed into something like a rubber sausage, into its gut. Then all Windham has to do is make sure it reaches his yard before nature takes its course.'

'Every so often,' Daniel said quietly, 'someone who's carrying drugs inside them dies when a package ruptures.'

Shock further hollowed Alison's thin cheeks. *'That's* what happened to our horses?'

'Maybe. If someone dies on an aeroplane they conduct an autopsy. If a horse dies in transit, I imagine they call the knackers. It was only because it happened a number of times that people began to wonder if it was more than just bad luck.'

'And Dad guessed what he was doing,' whispered Ally.

Deacon nodded pensively. 'The other possibility, I'm afraid...'

Daniel shook his yellow head in warning. 'Don't even go there.'

Deacon didn't understand. Then he saw Brodie soothing what was clearly going to be a black eye, and he did. 'Ah. No.'

'And now he's working for Mary! We have

to warn her,' Ally said urgently. 'Before it all happens again.'

'No,' said Deacon sharply. 'I mean it, Miss Barker – nothing we've said leaves this room until I say it can.'

'But she's in danger! If we can guess what he's up to, if Dad did, she will too. Maybe not at once but soon enough. Then he'll have to shut her up too.'

'I promise you,' said Deacon, 'I won't let Mary Walbrook come to any harm. But the problem with this is not going to be catching those involved, it's going to be proving it. We need a chain of evidence. We need a horse with the drugs still in it, that got into it while it was in Windham's hands.'

Brodie rather liked the idea of a sting. 'What would you need?'

Deacon thought for a moment. 'First and foremost I'd need a horse. One that's currently in Germany and can be shipped here through Dover. I'd need to be able to prove it was clean when Windham collected it – witness statements from reliable parties saying the animal was in their care for a week beforehand and ate nothing but hay and oats.'

'So when it arrives in Dover and you have it seized,' said Daniel, 'and someone with a peg on his nose goes through its droppings and finds these rubber sausages stuffed with chemicals, only his mother will believe

Johnny Windham didn't put them there.'

Deacon nodded. 'So now I have to find a suitable horse – quickly, because Miss Barker is worried about Miss Walbrook, and discreetly because if Windham gets suspicious he'll carry the horse, all right, he just won't put anything in it.' He blew out his cheeks in a gusty sigh. He thought he had a mountain to climb.

Brodie was trying hard to keep a straight face. 'What you need, Jack, is a reputable finding agent. Speak to her nicely, promise to meet her expenses, and if you're very lucky she'll do it for you and Johnny Windham will never suspect that you're involved.'

Deacon frowned. 'What are you telling me? You know of a suitable horse?'

'Well – yes and no. Right now there is no horse, but Windham thinks there is. Give me twenty-four hours and I'll give you your mule.'

'*How?*'

'Jack, trust me – this is what I do. I have a buyer, I have the transport waiting, I can even tell you the animal's name.'

'Who's the buyer?' asked Deacon.

'What animal?' asked Ally.

Brodie flashed her most winning smile at Daniel. 'He is. And it's a pony called The Saracen's Daughter.'

Chapter Sixteen

She started with Dieter Townes first thing the next morning. She gave him fifteen minutes' notice, phoning ahead to tell him to stay in the yard because she needed him to help with her inquiries. To her that sounded sufficiently official to command obedience without actually containing a claim to be something she was not. Only on the drive to Cheyne Warren did it occur to her that it was a bit like sticking a note through someone's door saying *Fly – all is discovered.* At least if she found him at the stables it suggested he had nothing much in his life to be ashamed of.

He was mucking out when Brodie got there. He looked up at the sound of her car, and neither hurried anxiously to meet her nor stood quaking, just waited calmly for her to come over. 'And just what are these inquiries you need my help with, Mrs Farrell?' he asked coolly.

She flashed him her most engaging smile. 'Sorry about that, Mr Townes. I hope I didn't alarm you. But it is important, and it's important to be discreet – it may end up being a police matter. You won't be involved in that, but I do need some technical advice.'

'Try me.'

'I need a pony,' she said. Though she paused, he realised it wasn't that simple and kept waiting. 'I need it to be in Germany now but available to ship to England immediately. I need it to be an Exmoor pony, and I need to be able to pass it off as a daughter of a stallion called The Saracen. Where do I start looking?'

Townes gave it some thought, then shook his head. 'I don't think you can do it. It used to be possible to pass one horse off as another if you really wanted to but now they've all got passports that record their breeding. We might find you an Exmoor mare in Germany but I can't see how you'd get away with lying about her sire.' He eyed her disapprovingly. 'Or why you'd want to, for that matter.'

'I can't tell you any more,' said Brodie, 'except that I'm working with the police on this and it's not going to backfire on either of us. Especially if I can't make it work. I couldn't find a pony of unknown breeding and fib?'

'You could find any number of ponies of unknown breeding, and that's what it would say on their passports. But none of them will be Exmoors. There just aren't that many true Exmoors around, and their breeding should be a matter of record. Why does it have to be an Exmoor?'

'Because I said it was,' she confessed rue-fully. 'It was just a story – I never thought I'd have to produce the damn pony.'

'You've told someone you know of an Exmoor mare by The Saracen, and it's in Germany but you can acquire it for them.' It was an accurate enough assessment: Brodie nodded. 'And you don't, and you can't, and you're trying to lie your way out of trouble. Mrs Farrell, I can see exactly how this would end up as a police matter.'

She understood his misgivings, wished she could allay them. But she was worried that an incautious word might find its way to Windham Transport. 'Would talking to Detective Superintendent Deacon set your mind at rest?'

She fully expected him to say 'No, of course not', that he trusted her. He said, 'Yes.'

It was a brief and guarded phone call, but after it Townes set himself to helping her. 'Is it the animal that's important? Or the bloodline?'

Brodie wasn't sure what he was asking. 'I need a pony, that's all. But I cited this particular bloodline when I was describing it. If I produce something different, some-body might get suspicious and what we're trying to achieve by all this will go down the tubes.'

'There might be a way to use any pony mare you can get your hands on and it wouldn't matter what it said on her passport. Because it wouldn't be her bloodline that was significant but that of the foal she was carrying.'

Brodie was confused. 'But surely the foal will have the same bloodline as its mother. If I can't find an Exmoor to pass off as The Saracen's Daughter, how can I pass off the foal as The Saracen's grandchild?'

'Surrogacy,' said Dieter Townes, and gave her a lesson in the economics of horse-breeding. A mare carries a foal for eleven months. She may breed every year, she may not. When she's pregnant she's not doing much else, which is a problem if she's a competition mare. And a foal which is the progeny of both a mare and a stallion which have proved themselves in competition is worth much more than the foal of untried parents.

'What the owners of top mares do is harvest their eggs and transplant the resultant embryos into surrogate mothers – mares which have no genetic connection with the foal they're going to deliver. The benefits are that the best mares can now, like the best stallions, produce many more offspring than nature intended, with minimal risk to themselves and minimal disruption to their athletic careers.'

He kept looking at her until Brodie indicated that she was with him so far. 'OK. Suppose you'd managed to find The Saracen's Daughter, but her owner wasn't willing to part with her. What he might sell you is an embryo of hers implanted in a healthy but unremarkable pony mare. She'd carry it to term and deliver it as normal, and never know it wasn't hers; but genetically it would be the offspring of The Saracen's Daughter and whatever Exmoor stallion had been chosen to sire it.'

Already Brodie could see the advantages, both for breeders and for her. 'So all we need is a healthy pony mare? We don't need it to say anything in particular on its passport?'

'Exactly,' said Townes. 'Whoever this is that you don't want to get suspicious, you tell him that you weren't able to purchase The Saracen's Daughter but you have an embryo of hers in a surrogate mare and she's the one you're bringing back from Germany. What do you think? In all the circumstances – which you know and I don't – would that be a plausible tale?'

Brodie thought all round it before she answered. But she couldn't see a problem. The paperwork would refer to the pony she bought – any bog-standard pony mare that she could pick up cheap in Germany. The main thing was to have a credible story. So far as she could make out, Townes had provided her with exactly that.

'Do you know, Mr Townes,' she said, 'I do believe it would.'

An evening spent on the Internet and she had most of what she was going to need to make this work. She found a dealer near Essen who could provide her with a fit pony mare ready to travel. Her breeding wasn't entirely clear but there was probably a bit of Haflinger in her somewhere. She was eight years old and called Gretl.

The dealer, whose name was Mannheim, was prepared to isolate the pony immediately and vouch for everything that would be fed or otherwise administered to her for a week before Windham came for her. A member of Dimmock CID would fly over three days before Gretl's departure to ensure the continuity of evidence that would take the case to court. Brodie didn't go into the reasons for these unusual measures or why the English police were interested in a German pony, and beyond seeking her assurance that Gretl would be unharmed Herr Mannheim didn't ask questions.

Before any of these arrangements were made she asked if Mannheim had had any dealings with Windham Transport, and he said he hadn't.

Brodie organised for a vet to take a barium

X-ray of the pony before her journey started. With that, the statement from the man feeding it and the testimony of a British police officer who'd had it under observation throughout the relevant period, Brodie believed a court would accept that any substance present in the pony's guts on arrival at Dover must have been put there by or with the connivance of the carrier. From her days in a solicitor's office she knew that courts would sometimes tie themselves in knots rather than accept the patently obvious, but she thought those three bits of evidence together would make it hard for the most cautious of jurors to do anything but believe.

The only thing she had to leave to chance was whether Windham would select Gretl as a mule. He might have six or eight animals on the lorry, of which probably only one would be used. All she could do was make the little mare as attractive a target as possible.

Once her plans were laid she phoned Johnny Windham. She told him the story of the surrogacy, and provided him with Gretl's details and Mannheim's number so that final arrangements could be made.

'He tells me she's an easy pony to handle. I suppose, to be a surrogate she'd have to be. She's obliging with the vet so she shouldn't give you any problems. She's rather bigger than an Exmoor, he said – about 140 centimetres, which probably makes more sense to you than it did to me, and built like a tank. She's not a valuable pony herself but she'll do my client's job for him.' Which was true enough.

She asked when Windham could collect the pony and when she could expect delivery.

Windham consulted his diary. 'Essen? That's about four hundred kilometres to Calais. I'll have a lorry in the area next week. If she's confirmed in foal and ready to leave, why don't I pick her up on Tuesday morning? We'll be on our way home by then, I'll have her at my yard that night. I'll keep her for the usual three days, just to make sure she isn't incubating anything nasty, and deliver her on Saturday. Where will you be keeping her?'

Brodie was ready with that too. 'Appletree Farm, Cheyne Warren.'

Windham nodded. 'I know the place. Eleven o'clock suit you?'

'Perfect,' said Brodie. If he'd said midnight she wouldn't have argued: if all went to plan not one of them, not her nor the pony nor Windham himself, would be there.

She told Deacon the arrangements that she'd made, noting with quiet satisfaction that he didn't query any of them or wish she'd done something different, just jotted them down.

'Who are you sending to Essen?' she asked.

'Jill Meadows,' he said. 'She can pass herself off as a groom and Windham shouldn't even notice her. I'll need to arrange a car for her – once the pony's on the lorry I want her to follow it. I want her to be able to say that the lorry left the Calais road at such-and-such a time and went into a yard at this address, and emerged an hour later and drove non-stop to the ferry. When the address turns out to be a vet, or a dealer's yard where a vet just happened to be present, that'll be another nail in their coffin.' He raised his voice, shouted for Charlie Voss. 'I'm going to need a Eurostar ticket to Essen for Meadows, and a car for her when she gets there.'

Voss was taking notes. 'When?'

'The pony's being collected on Tuesday morning. We want her at Mannheim's yard sometime on Friday.'

'Fine,' said Voss.

'Fine,' said Deacon.

'Fine,' nodded Brodie, 'only make it two tickets.'

A good part of everything she said was chosen for effect. She loved the way people's eyes came round to her as if drawn by magnets, widening with alarm, and the careful way they picked their words as if she might be dangerous when provoked.

Voss said, 'Yes?' uncertainly, and Deacon said, 'What?' and made it sound like steel-capped boots.

'Of course I have to be there,' said Brodie, as if it was the most obvious thing in the world. 'I set this all up. If something comes unstuck at the last minute, somebody's going to have to fix it on the wing. Can Jill Meadows do that? Can you do it, from here? Jack, I don't know if *I* could do it from here. I need to be on the spot. If Jill can pass as a girl groom, I'm sure I can.'

'Of course you can,' growled Deacon, 'if we bury you in the midden for three days first. Brodie, *I* could pass as a girl groom before you could.'

She didn't take that as an insult. 'It doesn't matter what I look like because Windham mustn't see me. We've met, remember? I'll keep out of sight while he's in the yard. Jill can chew on a bit of straw and tell me what's happening. Then we'll follow him at a distance.'

'What's this *we* nonsense?' demanded Deacon. 'You're not a police officer. You're not one in this country so you're certainly not one abroad. You're a private citizen. You're here to be protected and served.'

'And as a private citizen,' she replied smoothly, 'I'm free to travel to Germany whenever my business requires it. This pony is my responsibility, remember – I promised Herr Mannheim I'd take care of it. If it comes to some harm it's my reputation at stake.'

Deacon gave in with a bad grace. 'As long as you're not wanted by Interpol I suppose you're free to go anywhere you want. OK, Charlie, make it two tickets. God knows how I'll get the expenses approved.'

'By pointing out that I was the one who made it possible for you to wrap up a major drugs operation,' Brodie said tartly. 'You're talking as if this was a holiday!'

He sniffed at her. She flounced at him. Charlie Voss went and booked the tickets.

Chapter Seventeen

They dressed to be inconspicuous in a working stable-yard. Meadows wore faded jeans, a sweatshirt over a checked shirt and wellingtons, and carried a video camera in a battered backpack. Brodie wore designer jeans, a suede jacket and a pair of fringed leather boots from a brief and now inexplicable sortie into line-dancing.

The liaison officer from the local force who met them at Essen station introduced himself in near-perfect English as Hardy Schroeder. Meadows produced the documents she'd been furnished with to enable her to do what she was here for.

Schroeder looked Brodie up and down in

a manner that was only kept from being offensive by the merriment in his eyes. 'And this must be your friend The Singing Cowgirl?'

Brodie offered him an elegant hand. 'Brodie Farrell,' she said sweetly. 'If this happens, I'm the one you'll have to thank.' She'd been expecting a big Aryan blond but they must all have gone to work in the movies. Schroeder was a dark-haired man of about thirty, of average height and build, entirely unmemorable. She put two and two together and, although he said nothing to confirm it, decided he worked with the German equivalent of the Drugs Squad, where being unmemorable was a survival strategy.

He had the car waiting outside. He handed Meadows the keys. 'This is now the property of the English police force. You are booked onto the Dover ferry for Tuesday afternoon. Your licence and insurance are in order. Please remember to drive on the right.'

'Aren't you coming with us?'

Schroeder nodded. 'I'll take you to Mr Mannheim's stables. Then on Tuesday I'll travel with you as far as the border. If anything happens before then, it's my business. Afterwards it's yours.'

Brodie's expectations were confounded again when they reached Mannheim's yard. All she knew of the horse world were Dieter Townes and Johnny Windham and Alison

Barker and Mary Walbrook, creating the impression that attractive athleticism and lasting good looks came with the territory. Talking to Erich Mannheim on the phone had done nothing to disabuse her. The guttural accent made it hard to judge his age, but beneath it was a sort of solemn sexiness that made her look forward to meeting him. And it doesn't take two grown women to watch one pony for a weekend. She told herself a little harmless flirting would pass the time nicely.

Herr Mannheim was sixty if he was a day, no taller than Daniel but twice as far round, surrounded by a gaggle of grandchildren. He greeted them courteously, had some of the larger children take their bags and showed them to a room over the stables where they would be sleeping. Then he took them to meet Gretl.

Even to Brodie's inexpert eye she was a plain pony. She was an interesting colour – something between clotted cream and custard – and had a nice friendly eye, but apart from that there was little to recommend her. Except, just possibly, to someone wanting to smuggle drugs inside her. She was quiet and easy to handle, broad without being big, and of minimal value. If a package ruptured in transit, a modest cheque would cover the loss. If the other animals Windham was collecting this trip were sports horses

worth thousands of pounds with knowledge-
able owners waiting for them, Gretl would
be his mule of choice.

Assuming he was doing what they thought
he was doing. There was no hard evidence. *If*
he was, there was a good chance that this
was how he was doing it, and other things
followed from that – including the possibility
that Stanley Barker's death was neither accident nor suicide and his daughter had
survived a murder attempt. But that basic
premise, that Johnny Windham was using his
business to smuggle drugs from Germany
into England, could yet be disproved. If all
this time, effort and expense was for
nothing, Jack Deacon would not be a happy
bunny. Fat, solemn, polite Herr Mannheim
was looking a better prospect all the time.

The weekend stretched ahead. Brodie
found herself missing Paddy. She'd gone to
her father for the weekend. Brodie had
explained that she needed to travel to
Germany on business but not the precise
nature of that business: if she'd known it
involved ponies the child would have stowed
away in her mother's luggage. Now Brodie
leaned on half-doors and rails and watched
the animals eating and working, and lent an
unpractised hand at grooming some of the
quieter ones, and was surprised at the big
achy space that was the absence of her
daughter.

Meadows made a point of checking Gretl every couple of hours, watching her fed twice a day, and even got up in the middle of the night to check that she was still in her stable – not because it was necessary but so that she could tell a court she had. Brodie knew she went out after midnight because there were bunk beds in the grooms' flat and Meadows had the top one. Brodie thought about offering to do one of the late checks for her, but it was cold outside and her bed was warm.

In reflective moments Brodie worried – not much but a little – that she was getting selfish as she got older. The woman she was today bore no resemblance to who she was the day John Farrell said he wanted a divorce. The upheaval had made her reappraise her life in every conceivable way, and she'd emerged from it stronger, tougher, meaner probably, but ready to cope with life's vicissitudes as she never was when she was kinder and more caring. She'd done the nice-girl-becomes-devoted-wife bit, and where it got her was the divorce court. Now she was much more her own person than she was ever bred to be: Paddy came first, herself second, her friends third, and after that she didn't much care what people thought of her.

The weekend passed. On Monday Brodie and Meadows accompanied Gretl to the surgery of Mannheim's vet, where the X-ray showed all normal on the intestinal front. Meadows took it into custody as part of the chain of evidence.

Then it was Tuesday morning. Hardy Schroeder arrived at the yard at seven and the three of them went over the plan together. They hid the silver car round the back of the house, and after that retired to Herr Mannheim's sitting room from where they could see anything coming up from the road.

The dealer furnished them with the promised statement that nothing had been administered to the pony other than feed. Brodie thought he must have had an idea what they were doing but he was polite enough not to ask. Perhaps it suited him better not to know for sure.

At twenty past nine the familiar red and white lorry with the name of Windham Transport emblazoned on the side turned into the yard. Meadows got it on her camera through the gap in the curtains. 'I need a shot of the driver,' she said tensely.

Brodie didn't dare go with her for fear of being spotted. 'Be careful.'

'You think?' The detective constable left the house via the kitchen garden.

Five minutes later she was back. She showed Brodie what she'd shot. 'That's him, isn't it? Windham himself.' She'd had only a brief glimpse of him in the yard at Peyton Parvo.

Brodie had spent almost an hour in his company. She nodded. 'That's Johnny Windham, all right. Which is interesting. He didn't tell me he'd be driving himself.'

'Maybe he wasn't planning to until you provided him with a suitable mule,' suggested Meadows. 'And he's on his own. Mannheim's girls helped him load. They put Gretl in the end stall. As far as I could see the lorry's full. If he picks up anything else it'll have to travel in the cab with him.'

Which was just what Brodie wanted to hear. Everything that was happening was consistent with what they believed was going on. 'Then he'll meet with his vet friend next.' She felt a quiver of satisfaction that it was all coming together. Of course she was anxious too, and would be until the pony was safely in Deacon's hands and whichever of his officers had been annoying him most was wearing rubber gloves and an expression of terminal distaste.

But one way or another, they were going to find out if Windham was just doing his job or had a particular interest in Brodie's unremarkable little pony. It wouldn't quite exonerate him if he didn't take advantage of the opportunity it presented, but it would suggest that Alison Barker was the one who was up to no good.

But if Windham took the bait the whole complicated exercise would have been justified. Deacon would owe her big-time. Even apart from that, no one with a child can afford to be disinterested in the drugs culture. Capping one pipeline, jailing one smuggler, would keep a lot of other people's children safe. All she could hope was that someone would do the same for her when Paddy was a vulnerable age.

When the ramp of the horse-box was up Windham disappeared for a couple of minutes into Erich Mannheim's office. Then he climbed into his cab and drove away. The first phase of the operation was complete.

Meadows drove the car, with Schroeder beside her to help with directions. Brodie made herself at home on the back seat.

In the course of setting this up Brodie had spoken to a horse vet – to check that what Alison Barker told her was feasible was in fact feasible, and to ask how long such a procedure would take and what facilities would be necessary. She was told that it would require nothing you couldn't carry in the back of a car and could be done in minutes without unloading the pony as long as she was accessible. For instance, the last one onto the box.

So Windham's vet could meet him at a lay-by anywhere along the road, drop the ramp and get to work on the pony. In the unlikely event of someone asking, Windham would say he thought it might be unwell and arranged for a vet to see it. Fifteen minutes later he'd be back on the road, with nothing to show for his detour except a somewhat hung-over Gretl.

And there would *be* nothing to show for the next day or so. Customs at Dover could strip his lorry to the chassis without finding anything incriminating.

Meadows hung back as far as she dared. Once they hit the autobahn at Duisberg she was able to keep the lorry in view from quarter of a mile back, too far for Windham to notice he was being followed.

The road headed for the Channel ferry almost as a crow would fly it. The names on the signs were familiar ones: Eindhoven, Antwerpen, Brugge, Calais. After fifty kilometres they reached the Dutch border. Reluctantly, Schroeder had them drop him off. 'Let me know how it works out.'

'We will,' promised Meadows, and then they were on their way again. Brodie checked the map. Another eighty kilometres – an hour at this rate – would take them into Belgium. She began to feel terribly uneasy. She couldn't see why, if he was going to do what she needed him to do, Windham would leave it to the last minute.

But halfway across Belgium the big lorry

took the slip road off the motorway. Brodie heaved an audible sigh of relief. Jill Meadows flicked her a tight grin. 'Looks like we're in business.'

On the roads they now found themselves following she had to close the distance to keep the lorry in sight. It was a balancing act between losing it and being spotted. A couple of times it got so far ahead they began to fear it had made its surreptitious stop all unseen. When she speeded up, at least once she found herself pulling up behind it at a junction.

'He's heading for someone's yard,' guessed Brodie. 'If he was just pulling off the road he could have found somewhere much closer to the motorway.'

Meadows nodded but said nothing. She was concentrating on the pursuit, grateful for the flat landscape that enabled her to see the high-sided vehicle at a distance across the fields.

And it was across a couple of fields that they saw the lorry slow down and then turn into a driveway. The drive was lined with white post-and-rail fencing and there were horses in the paddocks on either side.

'Keep going,' hissed Brodie; and Meadows cast her a barbed glance and said, 'Really? You don't think I should follow him into the yard, then?'

She found a belt of trees three hundred

metres further on and parked there, shielded from sight. 'Stay in the car,' she told Brodie. 'I need to find out where we are, get some kind of an address for this place. Don't worry, I'll be back before the lorry leaves.' She took her backpack with the camera in it.

For twenty minutes Brodie stayed with the car, watching the end of the drive which was all that she could see from here, listening for the lorry's engine, feeling her nerves wind tighter and tighter until she knew that the first sign of action would jolt her to the core.

Then Meadows was back, appearing silently from among the trees because she hadn't wanted to be seen on the road. 'He's on the move,' she said shortly, starting the car.

'Did you manage to get him on film?' asked Brodie.

Meadows shook her head. 'I couldn't get close enough. But I got a shot of the lorry in the yard. It should be enough.' Brodie could hear it in her voice that she wasn't as confident as she would have liked to be.

Between the trees they saw the red lorry appear at the foot of the drive and turn left, heading back the way it had come. Meadows allowed it to get a head start before following.

'Calais next stop,' said Brodie to reassure her.

'From your mouth to God's ear,' gritted Meadows, and Brodie laughed out loud because for a moment she sounded just like Deacon.

But almost as soon as they returned to the motorway Windham pulled off again, this time into a service stop. He parked in the commercial lot and walked across the concourse.

'Do we follow him?' asked Brodie.

Meadows shook her head. 'We watch the lorry.'

Where he'd left it, hard against the garage wall, they had a clear view of the cab. Even if Windham suspected he was being followed he could not have sneaked back and driven off without being seen. And indeed, after a few minutes he reappeared with a paper under his arm and a fast-food carton in his hand, and got back into the cab. There he stayed for another fifteen minutes, eating his lunch and reading his paper. Then he started the engine and pulled back onto the road.

Meadows let him regain his lead before following.

What neither of the women saw was that, parked beside the garage immediately behind the large red lorry, was a small white lorry which let the silver car get out of sight before it too drove out onto the motorway.

Chapter Eighteen

At quarter to five Meadows phoned home. 'We're on the ferry, sir. So's Windham, and so's the pony.'

'You have them in view?' asked Deacon anxiously.

'Well, no. The lorry's on the cargo deck. But it's not going anywhere. He won't be able to move until everything off-loads in Dover.'

Deacon looked for the flaw in that but couldn't see one. 'Fair enough. Customs are standing by. They'll pull him over as soon as he clears the ramp and impound his load. They've organised lairage and there's a vet on call to hurry things along. I suppose we *are* sure there's something in there to find?'

'I don't know why he'd have stopped near Antwerp otherwise. There was no room on the lorry for another horse. And he was in there just about the time we were told it would take. I can't vouch for it, sir, I didn't see him shove something down that pony's throat. But he's doing everything we anticipated he'd do, which probably means he's up to what we think he's up to.'

'He hasn't made you?'

'I don't see how he could have. And surely if he had he wouldn't have boarded the ferry. It's too late to change his mind now. We have him.'

Deacon and Voss were in position half an hour before the ferry was due to dock. Cross-channel ferries are not known for running early, and even if this one raced in on a following wind Customs were ready. They didn't need Dimmock's senior detective telling them how to do their job. But Deacon was bad at delegating even to his own officers. He started every day with the suspicion that the sun might not rise if he wasn't awake to supervise it.

So he sent Voss to watch the foot-passengers disembarking – just in case, he said. He didn't expect Windham to abandon his lorry and come ashore as part of a Lacemakers' Guild day-trip to Bruges, but just in case that instinct for self-preservation which is keen in all living things and honed to a fine edge in drug-smugglers should knee him in the groin and tell him to drop everything and get out. Deacon himself took up a position at the ramp from where he could see the vehicles being ushered off the ship.

He saw Windham's lorry emerge from the gloom of the cargo deck, the tall red vehicle unmistakable long before the name emblazoned across its white flashes could be read. There were still lorries all around it.

Even if he'd wanted to make a dash for it – and there are good reasons why *The Italian Job* was filmed with Minis rather than horseboxes – it was a physical impossibility. When the Customs officer stepped out in front of him he had only two choices: stop, or run the man down and then stop. He stopped.

It was not, after all, the first time he'd been in this position. He'd got away with it before, must confidently have expected to get away with it again. He must have thought that all he stood to lose was time. And indeed, as things stood at this moment, whatever Deacon believed and however well the jigsaw seemed to fit together, that might be all he stood to lose. Daniel's leap of intuition might have been wrong.

Jack Deacon allowed himself a little inward grin. He wasn't one of the world's great philosophers, but actually he knew himself better than most people gave him credit for. If this worked it would be a successful police operation. If it didn't it would be because Daniel Hood was mistaken.

Soon after the red lorry was pulled aside a silver car came up the ramp and followed it into the Customs shed. Deacon hurried to meet it.

He told himself afterwards that it wouldn't have made any difference if he'd stayed where he was, watching everything that came off that ferry. If he'd even noticed the white van, which among so many he might not have done, he wouldn't have asked himself what it was carrying or where it was going. So far as he knew, so far as anyone involved in the investigation knew, it was a red lorry they were after, not a white van.

And there it was, surrounded by Customs officers by the time he got there. One of them was talking to the driver. Brodie and Jill Meadows abandoned rather than parked their car and came over to watch the action. They all arrived beside the lorry in more or less the same moment.

After the Customs officers had inspected his documents they asked Windham to drop the ramp. He climbed down with just a hint of exasperation in his manner. 'You do know I've got a lorry full of horses?'

'We'll take care of them,' promised the officer.

Windham shrugged and went to the back of his lorry. The ramp was secured by a complicated system of bolts that slid up and sideways. He manoeuvred them out of their keepers and lowered the ramp, and pulled aside the two gates that enclosed the last stall.

And the stall was empty.

Brodie stared at it open-mouthed. She knew that Gretl had been there: she'd seen the video footage of the pony being loaded. Onto this lorry, into that stall. Now there was just some straw on the floor and a hay-net.

Windham noticed her standing among the on-lookers. 'Mrs Farrell?' He managed to sound surprised. 'I wasn't expecting to see you here. But I was going to call you. I'm afraid I had to leave your pony behind. She wasn't very well. I was a bit uneasy about her coming through Belgium, so I tracked down a local vet and took her to his place. He's holding onto her for a few days. It's probably nothing serious but I couldn't risk travelling her any further. As soon as I'm done here we'll phone him, ask how she is. All right?'

By eight o'clock the last of Daniel's students had packed away their maths books and headed for home, their footsteps chiming on the shingle beach, their laughter drifting back to him on the wind. He sighed and shut the door.

He was a good teacher. He was good at breaking down the terror barrier that is all that stands between most people and the ability to do everyday maths. He took students who couldn't do long division and got them through their GCSEs. But what he couldn't seem to do was share with them the beauty of the subject.

To Daniel, mathematics was like a gallery full of Old Masters, a riot of colour and meaning, a treat for the intellect, a world of possibilities that got his blood flowing and his ears singing. But he could never explain that well enough that his students believed him, and were inspired to struggle on through the murky complexities until the glorious dawn burst upon them. He believed that it was his fault, that he was failing them. He didn't know how he could call himself a teacher if he couldn't get his students to see what was, to him, as plain as day.

But then, they didn't come to him for a life-altering experience. They came because they needed to pass maths in order to study what really interested them, and as soon as they reached the required standard they would throw their books in the back of a cupboard and never open them again. That wasn't failure. He'd done what they needed him to do. So what if they were left un-moved by the wonders of fractal geometry? Even at his most buoyant, Daniel never felt that his own life had been such a resounding success he should encourage others to emulate it. Most people, especially teen-agers, had more important things to think about than the square root of minus one. They had friends to meet, careers to choose, partners to find, families to build. They had lives to lead that would quickly reveal his for what it was: half Greek tragedy, half

Whitehall farce. They didn't need his pity or his regrets. They probably thought he needed theirs.

In fact, he reflected, they would be wrong. He liked his life. Most of it, for most of the time, which was probably all that most people could say. Maybe it was childish but he got a real buzz out of fractal geometry. Sometimes he wished he knew a bit less about maths and a bit more about people, so that when he was alone he could be sure it was from choice. But one thing he knew for sure was that the worst forms of loneliness have nothing to do with being alone.

When the sound of laughter had faded he went downstairs and tapped on Alison's door. His odd little house had been more upside-down than ever since the rebuild. He'd taken the opportunity to incorporate the ground-floor boathouse into the living accommodation, which gave him two extra rooms. But he liked living above the heads of those walking on the beach, so he used the new space as a study and a spare room. It meant guests traipsing upstairs if they wanted a bath, but fortunately there weren't many of them and they never stayed long.

There was no reply from inside. He tapped a little louder and then opened the door a crack. 'Ally?'

She was there. She was asleep. Daniel

listened to her breathing for a moment but it was perfectly normal, even and relaxed. He left her rolled up in her duvet like a hibernating dormouse, turned off the bedside light and shut the door.

Which left him with an evening with no commitments in it. He had things he should be doing. Boring, everyday things like housework and laundry and defrosting the fridge, all the things that tended to get neglected when Brodie was around and there were more interesting demands on his time. She had come to fill his life, to an extent he could hardly explain and in ways that would have surprised her had he tried. His ear was always half-cocked for the sound of her heels on his iron staircase. His world had been much simpler before she came into it, but he never wanted it back.

But a glance out of the window told him what he already knew instinctively: it was a clear night. And a clear night sky always took precedence over housework. Daniel hated dirt and wouldn't live in squalor, but he knew from experience he could clean the house from top to bottom in an hour once the stars had clouded over. He took the telescope out of its corner and set it up on the gallery, his fingers working on autopilot, too accustomed to the job to need the guidance of his eyes. Instead he looked around the sky, locating the objects of his current interest. He'd been taking some measurements of the Cepheid variables. It wasn't cutting-edge astronomy, there were no Nobel Prizes to be won doing it, but it was a harmless way to pass a happy hour on a cloudless night.

He was comparing Mira Ceti, midway through its forty-seven week period, to a couple of sixth magnitude stars close by when he heard footsteps on the shingle below and someone called his name. He groped for his glasses – it was easier to use the telescope without them and there was more than enough magnification to compensate – and waited for the imprint of the stars to fade from his retinae. 'Up here.'

A man was halfway up the steps. There was just enough backwash from the street lamps on the Promenade to pick out the clipboard in his hand. 'I've got a delivery for you. I'm going to need a signature, and also somewhere to put it.' He spoke good colloquial English with a European accent.

A white van was parked at the top of the beach. Daniel frowned. He wasn't expecting anything. 'What is it?'

'A pony. Forgive me,' added the driver, 'but this does not appear to be a farm.'

'No,' said Daniel, stupidly, aware something had gone wrong and trying to work out what it was, 'it's a beach. You weren't supposed to bring it *here*.'

'You are Daniel Hood?'

'Yes.'

'Then it's your pony.'

Daniel couldn't argue with that. He'd agreed, however reluctantly, to let Brodie name him as her client which meant that, technically, the carrier was right. It was no use trying to explain to the man that (a) he was supposed to be an Englishman called Windham and (b) he was never meant to get this far – he should have been arrested by Customs at Dover. Daniel didn't know what it meant that that hadn't happened: a change of plan Brodie hadn't thought to mention to him or a major cockup that she wasn't even aware of yet. Either way, the man with the clipboard seemed blissfully unaware he should have been talking to his lawyer by now.

Daniel tried to think. 'A stable's been rented for it in Cheyne Warren. Can you take it there?'

The man shook his head regretfully. 'I cannot take it any further – I am out of hours. I must unload it. It's a nice quiet pony – you could tie it to the railing until morning.' He turned and began crunching up the beach to his van.

'I'm not tying it to my house!' exclaimed Daniel indignantly. 'It's a pony, for God's sake – it needs feeding, watering. Hang on a minute, will you? There must be someone we can call to sort this out. Your boss?' He trotted up the shingle in pursuit, determined the man wasn't dumping a pony on him when he had nowhere to put it, no way of moving it and twelve hours of darkness ahead.

The man shrugged without breaking his stride. 'You can call my boss on the cab phone. All I know is, I cannot take it any further when I'm out of hours. This is where I was told to bring it. You should not have said to bring it here if you wanted it somewhere else.'

'I didn't,' insisted Daniel. 'There's been some kind of a mix-up. For one thing, Mr Windham was supposed to keep it at his place for three days – quarantine or something. I think you must have misunderstood your instructions. Look, get him on the phone, will you, and let me talk to him.'

'Very well.' The phone was on a curly cord: he lifted it down and dialled. Then he held it out for Daniel to hear. 'We must wait a moment – the number is engaged.' An idea occurred to him and his face brightened. 'Would you like to see your pony while we wait?'

'We're not unpacking it.' Daniel was fairly sure that wasn't the right word.

'You can see it from the groom's door.' The driver opened a small door in the side of the lorry and stood back.

There was a lamp on inside. A smell like flowers and sweat – and more pleasant than that probably sounds – spilled out along with the light. Daniel found himself studying an animal the same colour as the hay it was eating, with curious dark eyes and warm breath that hung on the air.

He found himself smiling. 'Isn't she pretty?' he said – proving, if any proof were needed, that he had Nelson's eye for a horse. He reached up an uncertain hand and the pony bathed it in her breath.

What happened then was hard to explain. It was so quick, so unexpected, that he pretty well missed it. The world stopped for a second, like a skipped heartbeat, then flipped over, and then began settling gently around him like snowfall. For some reason he was sitting on the kerb beside the white van, with his head bowed and slow drops like dark tears falling in his lap. He thought, 'Blood...' but couldn't organise his brain enough to take the next step and work out what that meant.

It wouldn't have made much difference if he had. He was sitting on the kerb because he couldn't stand, and he still couldn't have stood if the man had been armed with a Kalashnikov rather than a brass-handled walking stick. His consciousness was fading as slowly but inexorably as a winter sunset.

Before he passed out entirely the driver

lifted him to his feet and pushed him through the little door in the side of the van. Daniel's body was as slack as a length of well-chewed string: when the man released him he sprawled in the straw. The driver picked up his feet and pushed them inside. Then he closed the door, got back in his cab and drove off.

Chapter Nineteen

People whose experience of the world comes largely through a television screen must think that human consciousness is a little like an electric lightbulb. Turn off the power and you're asleep; and when somebody flicks the switch again, instantly you're awake. Awake, hell – five minutes later you're off shooting Liberty Valance.

In fact it's not like that. Human consciousness is not a power circuit such as an electrician would recognise. There is no switch. The traditional way of taking it offline is to inflict the kind of blunt trauma that causes brain damage. With a brass-handled walking stick, for instance.

And while brains can be surprisingly resilient and survive, even recover from, damage that would scramble a computer irreparably, they don't just shrug it off and get back to work as if nothing had happened. There's a half-lit wasteland between unconsciousness and being fully aware in which the mind wanders, stumbling and confused, as it tries to work out where the world went.

That wasteland was where Daniel found himself now: with enough self-awareness to know that something bad had happened but insufficient command of his senses to work out what.

The first faculty to firm up was his hearing. He could hear an engine close by – so close it rumbled up at him through the very floor. Not a car engine, too rough and deep, but still more like that than anything else. Also, the floor was too close and shaking too much. It was on the move, and he was lying on it.

Nor was he alone. He could hear someone else moving softly nearby. An unhurried rustling sound, the occasional dull thud, and a slow rhythmic grinding that was almost soporific. Nothing threatening but all of it alien. By degrees his aching brain put it together. The pony: standing in straw, occasionally shifting its weight from one foot to another, chewing away at its hay-net with the methodical application of an animal that likes to spend sixteen hours a day eating.

The image of the pony coalescing pixel by

pixel in his mind somehow kick-started his vision – encouraged his eyes to report in. There was light in here, and colours, even if most of them were shades of brown. Shapes were less distinct, at least until his groping fingers located his glasses lying in the straw beside him and returned them to where they could do some good.

Then the rumbling little world around him gained some dimensions that helped him identify it. It was a horse-box, en route to God knows where. He and the blonde pony were the only passengers.

At that point he remembered the man with the clipboard. 'Do you want a look at your pony?' 'Isn't she pretty?' Then... He didn't know what had happened then. He knew something had taken him down – not so much pain, which takes longer to cut in than consciousness takes to fade, more the terrible sick feeling of something dreadfully amiss. Confusion, alarm. The slow falling. He didn't remember how he got in here but he could guess. He'd made the classic mistake of turning his back on someone he should have watched like a hawk, and his reward had been the reward for trusting souls since the year dot: a brisk clip behind the ear with a blunt instrument.

And now he'd been kidnapped? He couldn't imagine why. That might have been the concussion but he didn't actually think so. He assumed this development was connected with Brodie's trip to Germany, but even if the man in the cab *was* a drug-runner there was nothing Daniel could tell him. Not with a gun pressed to his temple, not under torture. A spasm of primitive fear wound through his gut like a parasite. Having no useful information wouldn't save him if no one believed him. It hadn't before.

Which made getting out of here a matter of some urgency. With the light on, and his glasses on, and some of his scattered wits returning to the roost he was able to make a reasonable assessment of his situation. The good news was that he wasn't restrained in any way. The less good news was that it was hardly necessary: he was enclosed in a box, travelling at perhaps fifty miles an hour, secured by doors that opened from the outside and constructed with the containment of a ton of agitated horseflesh in mind. He wasn't going to get free by setting his shoulder – even his good shoulder – against the door and heaving.

Nor was he going to climb out over the back ramp and drop to the road as the van slowed for a bend. He'd seen horse trailers with the top shutters pinned back to aid the circulation of air, with a broad gap between the top of the ramp and the roof. But this wasn't a trailer but a box, and the ramp closed up to the roof. There were ventilators along the eaves on both sides but he wasn't getting out that way either.

He gave the roof a closer look. It occurred to him that might be the weak spot in a horse-box, particularly a rather elderly little one. It was the one part that was never built to withstand the weight or determined assault of a horse. He thought it might be timber, in which case there was the possibility of a rotten spot; but it was metal, folded down and secured with rivets.

So if he couldn't get out he'd have to get someone to let him out. He sat down in the straw again, keeping a cautious distance from the pony, to think about it. It was night: even had he the means to write messages on scraps of paper he could poke through the ventilators it would be morning, and him and the van long gone, before anyone found one. What else? Smoke-signals? He couldn't risk starting a fire in here – plus, not being a smoker, he hadn't a lighter on him.

He was discouraged but not yet despairing. He did have on him the most potent weapon that a man can carry, the lethal weapon by whose deft use puny humans have turned animals that were stronger and faster than them, with sharp claws and massive jaws or thundering hooves and great spreading horns, into expensive wallpaper – his human brain. He could think. There would be a way out of this. As his mind cleared, he would find it. He sat in the straw and tried to tease out some options.

The box journeyed into the night. He had no sense of the direction they had taken. Daniel's head ached and he wasn't sure how much time was passing. He owned a watch but he didn't have it on.

If someone chanced by the netting-shed they'd realise something was wrong. He'd left his telescope on the gallery and the door unlocked. But what chance was there of that? Brodie was on her way back from Germany – she might call him when she got home but if it was late she might well wait until morning.

Brodie? Think it was too late to disturb him and tell him about her day? No, he thought with a wry smile, there was every chance that she would either call at his house or try to phone him. And she'd expect him to wait up for her, so if she got no reply she'd want to know why. So sometime tonight he would be missed. It wasn't a lot to look forward to but it was something.

And there was more. Something had already gone wrong with her plan or this pony wouldn't be amiably chomping hay beside him as they rumbled through the darkness into the South Downs. It would be standing in a Customs shed somewhere, surrounded by policemen, while someone stood by with a sieve. What that meant to

242

Daniel was that even now Brodie could be trying to report the cockup to him, anxious to find someone to blame before everyone else involved blamed her.

Knowing he was missing was one thing, finding him another. But then, she didn't have to find him. Deacon would be looking for the pony, using all the facilities at his command, and when he found it he would find Daniel as well. There were things about Jack Deacon that Daniel didn't like, and more things that he didn't understand, but he knew he was a good detective. He would find both of them. Though how quickly, and in what condition, he was unwilling to speculate.

Incredibly in the circumstances, Daniel found himself yawning, his head nodding on his chest. He blamed the concussion, but tension was probably at least equally responsible. Finally he decided there was no reason to fight it. He'd searched his prison and found no way out. Coming back to his predicament fresh might help. Feeling the cold, like a small frightened animal he burrowed into the straw in the corner of the box furthest from the pony's feet and let the tiredness take him.

'It isn't possible,' Brodie stated blankly, too amazed to know how foolish she sounded. 'We had him in sight the whole way.'

'Well, obviously you didn't,' barked Deacon, 'or the damn pony would still be on the box.'

'They must have left it in the yard in Belgium,' ventured Jill Meadows.

'Why?' demanded Deacon. 'The whole point of carrying the pony was to stuff it with drugs. Why in God's name would he take it somewhere for that to be done but then leave it there?'

'Maybe it all went wrong,' hazarded Brodie. 'Maybe the sedative was too strong, or a package ruptured. Maybe it died and he had to leave without it.'

Maybe it was that simple, thought Deacon. It wouldn't be the first time he'd seen good work scuppered by bad luck.

'What does he say?' asked Meadows. 'Where does Windham say it is?'

'I haven't asked him,' growled Deacon. 'I'm not sure I'm going to.'

Brodie's brow gathered in a puzzled frown. 'Why on earth not?' She might have put it stronger than that, but she'd known this man long enough to know that he didn't make a lot of mistakes, and the ones he did make weren't stupid ones. Whether or not she could see it, he would have a reason.

'Because if I do he'll know we're onto him. If I question him about the pony, he'll know we've been watching him and he'll know why. I don't think I want to tell him that. If I

don't, maybe he'll have another go at bringing home the bacon. Maybe – just maybe –
we'll be luckier then. If he realises he's been
rumbled but I haven't the evidence to hold
him, he'll walk and either set up a new
system or get someone else to run the old
one. Either way, we'll be back at square one.'

Brodie thought about it. 'But surely he
knows we're wise to him now. Is there anything more to lose?'

'Possibly. It depends on why he left the
pony behind. If he dumped it because he
realised we were following it, then yes, we're
blown, we might as well turn the heat up and
hope he'll bubble. But if he left it behind
because it was sick, he might be thinking the
reception committee was just the luck of the
draw. If they get him back on the road as
quickly as possible, he might think that's his
shakedown for this month and arrange
another shipment as soon as he can.'

Brodie grimaced. 'He saw me. He *can't*
think that was a coincidence.'

'Why not? You have a reason to be here –
to meet the pony. OK, he was surprised, but
if he didn't already suspect he'd been set up
that wouldn't tell him. He has no reason to
connect you and me, after all. If you tell him
it's all part of the service, he may well
believe you.'

She nodded slowly. It was a toss-of-the
coin thing: heads or tails, it might as easily

be one as the other. She was glad it wasn't her call. 'What are you going to do?'

Deacon hadn't decided; but he knew he had to, and he had to do it now. If he was going to let Windham run, every minute's delay made it likelier he'd smell a rat. Which didn't matter if he already knew what was going on; but it was possible that he didn't. However he weighed the odds, Deacon came back to that. Heads or tails, and no way of predicting which.

He called the Customs shed. 'Let him go. Apologise. Sincerely. Tell him his name came out of the hat, there's a bit of a push on from head office, help him load his horses and get him on his way.' Then he called Voss. 'Follow him. Let's see what he does next.'

To Brodie it seemed obvious. 'He's going home. Even if he'd got the pony with him, that's where he'd be going now. He has no reason not to, and every reason to do what he said he'd do. He's not going to risk blowing his cover by getting inventive.'

Knowing she was right did not incline Deacon to be generous. 'This could have been avoided,' he said bitterly. 'Three days you were watching that pony. And you still managed to lose it.'

Meadows said nothing. There wasn't much she could say: it was true. He'd trusted his newest DC with an important task and she'd let him down. She doubted he'd trust her with another.

But Brodie wasn't apt to take criticism lying down, even when it was justified. And this wasn't. 'We did our best, Jack. We stayed as close to it as we could without being seen. I'm sorry it went pear-shaped, but short of dressing up as a pantomime horse and travelling with it we did everything in our power to make this work. I don't think anyone else could have done better. Including you.'

Meadows was watching her open-mouthed. She'd never heard anyone speak to Deacon like that. She was wondering where to hide if he went ballistic.

Instead he just grunted, 'But the bottom line is, we've no idea where the damn pony is, or even if it's alive or dead. And I'm the one who has to explain to God why we've nothing to show for a week's work, a left-hand-drive car and a Eurostar ticket to Germany.' He didn't mean God, of course – he meant Superintendent Fuller, who had to approve his expenses.

Brodie had her mouth open to correct him – 'Two Eurostar tickets...' On second thoughts she shut it again.

When the van stopped, instantly Daniel was awake. He wasn't sure what it meant but he knew it meant something. The engine stopped and he heard the sound of the cab door. Then nothing. He waited, the nerves drawing tighter under his skin and in his belly. He heard the breath snatching in his throat and tried to steady it. He tried to ready himself for whatever was coming.

The groom's door in the side of the van opened and the man stood framed in it, darkness behind him, his face lit by the interior lamp. He had a walking stick in his hand. Daniel's heart gave a little hopeful flutter. He was no kind of an athlete, never had been, was always the last child left sitting on the bench in PE, but there was a chance – he put it no higher than that – that even he could outrun a lame man.

Then he looked again at the stick and understood. It had a brass handle in the shape of a horse's head. A heavy brass handle. It wasn't an aid, it was a weapon.

In his other hand he had a length of rope. 'Turn round.'

Daniel shook his head. 'No.' His voice was shaking too.

The man sighed. 'Understand one thing,' he said. 'All my working life I have handled horses. They weigh perhaps 600 kilos each, and much of the time they don't want to do what I need them to. They're strong and they're fast and when they're frightened they'll fight, with their teeth and their hooves. Any one of them is capable of killing a man. But in the end, they all do what I want them to.' He didn't wave the stick in a menacing fashion. He didn't have to. The menace was implicit. Daniel bit his lip. Then he turned around.

Chapter Twenty

'I don't want to hurt you,' said the man with the accent. 'It's late, I've had a long drive, I just want to get some answers and then go to bed. Yes?'

Mostly for the sake of his self-esteem, Daniel made himself consider before answering. 'Yes. Probably.'

The man nodded amiably. He wasn't a big man – bigger than Daniel, but still not big in the way Jack Deacon was big. He was, however, formidably functional: compact and hard-muscled. It never occurred to Daniel that he could win a fight with anybody; it occurred to him to wonder if he could survive a fight with this man. He might find out. But it would be better to keep any sparring on an intellectual level. Daniel had always been better at thinking than doing.

'Good,' said the man. 'Now. This pony belongs to you?'

'Yes,' agreed Daniel. As far as he understood it that was in fact the legal position.

'It was bought for you in Germany by Mrs Brodie Farrell.' He said it carefully, as if he'd learned the name by rote.

There was no point denying what he plainly knew. 'Acting as my agent,' said Daniel. 'That's what she does – she finds things.'

'But the pony was for you not for her.'

'It's my name on the bill of sale.'

'Yes.' The man gave a little sigh which Daniel didn't understand. 'So why did you want this pony? It's a very ordinary pony.'

'It's carrying an embryo transplant.' He was proud of himself for remembering that. 'From a bloodline we thought was lost.'

'So I was told,' nodded the man. 'What bloodline?'

Panic flicked Daniel's gut from the inside. He tried desperately to wing it. 'The stallion,' he said with a confidence he didn't feel. 'It was a very important stallion in its day. But we thought the bloodline had died out. Then Mrs Farrell heard of a last daughter still alive in Germany. I bought an embryo transplant, and this pony is carrying it.' He looked at the man unblinking for so long that his eyes began to burn.

'Please,' asked the man firmly, 'what is the name of this stallion?'

It was no good: Daniel didn't know. He'd been told, but he'd never thought it would matter and he couldn't remember.

Again the little sigh, half sad, half disappointed. 'Of what breed was this stallion,
then, that it was so important to preserve his
bloodline?'

It was there, just at the back of his mind.
He nearly got it. 'Ox-bow?'

The man was nodding gently. 'This isn't
your business, is it, Mr Hood? You know as
much about ponies as I know about nuclear
physics.'

'Funnily enough,' said Daniel, 'I know
more about nuclear physics. But you're
right, I don't know much about ponies. I
still own this one.'

For a few moments the man just watched
him. Then he said, 'If you know nothing
about ponies, Mr Hood, I wonder what you
know about mules.'

It may have been word association, but
something seemed to kick him in the belly.
He caught his breath. 'Also nothing. Except
that one of their parents is a donkey...'

'No,' said the man carefully, 'I think you
know more than that. I think that the reason
you're interested in this pony is the same
reason I'm interested in it. I think you know
very well that what it's carrying is not an
embryo transplant.'

Daniel despised lying, but even if he
hadn't he'd have been monumentally bad at
it. His face registered every thought that
passed through his head. He could have

denied this, but he couldn't have denied it convincingly. He said nothing.

'So,' said the man. 'You worked it out. Now I need to know who else knows.'

'The police,' Daniel said. 'The police know.'

The man chuckled. 'Well, maybe they do and maybe they don't. Either way, it suits you for me to think so. But why should I believe you?'

Daniel shrugged. It was a little more lopsided than usual because his hands were lashed to the breast-bar behind his back. They were still in the horse-box, the pony an interested observer. 'You said it: I know nothing about horses. I only got involved because Dimmock police were trying to work out how the drugs were coming in and...'

He saw too late where he was going with this, tried to keep Brodie out of it. 'Someone thought of a way to test what was being done and who was doing it. All they needed was a name for the paperwork. It seemed simple enough. The general feeling was that even I could manage that.'

The man nodded. 'Mrs Farrell.'

'It's a CID operation,' said Daniel stubbornly.

'Mrs Farrell came up with the story and booked the transport.'

'Detective Superintendent Jack Deacon is

in charge,' insisted Daniel. 'Don't think you can scare her off without taking him on.'

'I'm not interested in scaring anyone off,' said the man negligently. 'Tell me how much they know, and how much they just think they know.'

Daniel saw no reason not to. The time for discretion had gone. 'They thought they knew it all. But they needed the pony to prove it. They expected to have it by now. If you've still got it, I imagine they're surer than ever that you're doing what they thought you were doing but they've lost the evidence.'

The man considered. 'So if we say nothing and do nothing they can prove nothing.'

'I suppose.' There was something bizarre about talking this candidly with a man that far on the wrong side of the law. It shouldn't be this polite. But events had progressed beyond the point where either man stood to gain anything by subterfuge. Laying their cards on the table was the only sensible alternative. Nothing that Daniel could either learn, guard or impart now would significantly impact on the outcome. That was good, because it meant Windham's friend with the brass-headed walking-stick had no reason to see him as a threat. But it was also strange. He felt at a gut level that he should be fighting this man, intellectually if not with his fists. He was involved in a vile trade and

Daniel had nothing but contempt for him. All his instincts said they shouldn't have been chatting amiably about how Deacon's case was coming together.

Perhaps similar thoughts were passing through the other man's mind as he watched Daniel with sombre eyes. Or perhaps not. 'There is of course the question of what to do about you.'

Daniel was quite proud of his casual little shrug. Though he didn't believe he was in any real danger, there was an anxious knot in the pit of his stomach that couldn't help wondering. 'They know by now that I'm missing. They'll have guessed why. Someone will have seen this van parked outside my house. You won't get it out of the country. The best thing you can do now is leave it here – wherever *here* is – with me and the pony inside. By the time we're found, you could be halfway home.'

The man was nodding slowly, seemed more than half convinced. 'The problem with that is you can identify me. I needed to talk to you – but now I have, I need you to stay silent.' An odd, almost playful expression stole across his face. 'Mr Hood, can I trust you to stay silent?'

Ethics or not, Daniel would have lied like a trooper if he thought he'd be believed. But it was a trap. 'No. But what can I tell the police that would help them find you? You're an average-looking man with a foreign accent. That's going to be a real help to the guys watching the Channel ports.'

The man chuckled. 'This is true. But if I *am* caught, you can identify me.'

'If you're caught, I'll be the least of your problems. If you're caught it's because they've already worked out who you are and circulated a picture of you. Nothing I can tell them will make any difference.'

He believed that. He believed that, logically, there was no more reason for this man to harm him than there had been for him to take a beating rather than answer his questions. Logically, there was no reason he shouldn't walk away from this. But at the back of his mind was what the world had taught him: that not everyone thinks logically.

This was the vet. He hadn't said as much, but he'd talked about handling big excitable horses and anyway it made sense. Deacon reckoned Windham had one partner and one only, and he had to be the one who had access to the German tranquillizer. If Windham had needed help to evade the authorities on his journey back from Essen, where else would he seek it? And the good thing about *that* was that vets are scientists, and scientists have the inside track when it comes to thinking logically.

Daniel tried to appeal to that pragmatic

side of him. 'Look, you've only got two options, yes? – to kill me or leave me alive. If the police have your picture, killing me won't make you safe. It'll get you another ten years.'

'It is true,' admitted the man, 'murder always ups the ante. Is that the expression?' he asked. 'Ups the ante?'

Daniel nodded.

The man did the regretful little sigh again. 'But only the first murder. All subsequent ones come for free.'

It was gone nine o'clock before Brodie thought of Daniel. She knew he'd be waiting to hear from her. She thought he'd be starting to worry and that she ought to call him, tell him what had happened. But he didn't answer, and when she glanced outside she saw the stars that were the reason why.

Half an hour later she tried again. This time, after a long delay, someone picked up. But it wasn't Daniel, it was Alison Barker.

At first Brodie could get no sense out of her. She sounded both vague and distressed. 'Put Daniel on,' Brodie said, a couple of times. 'Let me talk to Daniel.'

'I can't find him,' whined the girl.

'Try the gallery. He'll be out with the telescope.'

'He isn't there. I looked.'

The cats of unease were walking up and

down Brodie's spine with their claws out. 'Alison, are you all right? You sound... Are you all right?'

'Yes. It's just, I can't ... think. I took... My head's all woolly.'

The cats were right. 'Alison, listen to me. This is important. What did you take?'

'Pills,' mumbled the girl, faintly annoyed. 'I don't know what they're called. Listen. I can't find Daniel. Do you know where he is?'

'Are you sure he isn't outside? Look again.'

It was a couple of minutes before the girl came back. 'There's no one there. Only the telescope.'

Now the alarm bells were ringing carillons in Brodie's head. That telescope was a valuable piece of equipment; more than that, it was Daniel's baby. He might have gone for a walk, he might have gone to the shop, but he wouldn't have done either leaving his telescope unprotected outside. 'Stay where you are, Ally, I'm coming over. Don't go to sleep.'

When Brodie reached the shore Daniel's front door was still unlocked, the telescope still pointing skyward on the gallery, and Alison had – despite her instructions – lapsed once again into unconsciousness, curled up on the living room sofa. Brodie shook her vigorously, at first without response.

'Ally! Ally, wake up. You have to wake up and tell me what it is you've taken.'

She was on the point of calling an ambulance when her efforts finally bore fruit. Alison Barker opened a bleary eye that slid over Brodie a couple of times before connecting. 'Hello.' She sounded like a punch-drunk boxer.

'What did you take? Ally!' she shouted as the girl went to nod off again. 'You have to concentrate. Tell me what you took.'

Alison waved a vacant hand at the stairs. 'Pills. Sleeping pills. I couldn't sleep so I took...'

It would be quicker to go and look than wait for her to explain. Brodie found the bottle on the bedside table in the spare room. It was almost full, and the label was for a prescription medicine. She hadn't been out cruising for drugs, she'd just taken a sleeping pill and not had time to sleep it off. Brodie returned upstairs, reassured on that score at least.

Alison was drowsing again. Brodie shook her shoulder firmly. 'Will you get your head together? I need you to tell me about Daniel. When did you see him last? How long has he been gone? Ally! Something's happened to him, and God help us but you're the only one who might know what!'

Rather than hang around Battle Alley

scowling at people who'd done him no harm, Deacon went home. He scowled at the cat instead, and the cat scowled back.

A little after ten the phone rang. It was Brodie, and she was worried. 'Jack, something's happened to Daniel.'

The last thing on Deacon's mind right now was Daniel Hood. He stared at the phone stupidly for a moment before answering. 'What sort of something?'

'I don't know. Alison took a sleeping pill and went to bed soon after seven. At that point he had pupils with him. I tried to phone him about nine but there was no reply. Half an hour later I got Alison, still groggy from the sleeping pill and scared because she was alone. Jack, he'd left the door unlocked and his telescope outside.'

Deacon sucked in a breath. 'No,' he agreed, 'that's not normal. And Alison's checked the house?'

'So have I. I'm there now. There's no sign of him. He hasn't left a note, and his wallet's in the kitchen.'

'Any signs of a struggle?'

'None that I can see.'

Deacon wanted his bed. He wanted to finish this day so he could start another in the hope it would be better. 'I'll be round in five minutes.'

There were no signs of violence that he could see either. He crossed the Promenade to the Victorian terrace opposite, some of them houses, some of them shops with flats over them. He started at The Singing Kettle. The café was closed now, but it would have been open until nine and Mr and Mrs Miskimmin lived on the premises.

Mrs Miskimmin had spent most of the evening baking for the next day, but her husband had been in the café and saw a vehicle parked close to the netting-sheds. He hadn't seen anyone get in or out, but it was there for a few minutes. Then it drove away.

'What kind of vehicle?' asked Deacon.

'A van of some sort. I couldn't tell you what make. White, high sided – a bit bigger than a Transit.'

Deacon considered. 'Could it have been a horse-box?'

The café owner shrugged. 'I suppose.'

'Were there any markings on it? A company logo, anything like that?'

'I don't think so. Or if there was I didn't notice. But then, it was already dark.'

'What time was this?'

'About eight o'clock maybe, or a little later? Mr Deacon, what's going on?'

Deacon didn't answer him. 'Did you see Hood at any time during the evening?'

Miskimmin nodded. 'He was out on the balcony with that telescope of his. It's a clear night,' he added with a tolerant grin. 'He's always out there if it's a clear night.'

'Before or after you saw the van?'

'Before.'

'And after?' He wanted to be sure.

Miskimmin shook his head thoughtfully. 'No.' He asked again, determined on a reply. 'What's happened? Is Daniel all right?'

Deacon had noticed this before: that people who had no reason to care whether Daniel Hood was alive or dead found themselves doing so. It wasn't that he had a lot of friends, more that a lot of people who were mere acquaintances somehow recognised him as a decent human being and enjoyed his amiable presence just enough to miss him. He added a little value to a lot of lives. When the time came there wouldn't be a crowd at his funeral – just Brodie, and Paddy, and Brodie's neighbour Marta; and probably Deacon too because there was every chance he'd be looking for a murderer, someone whose patience Daniel had finally pushed to breaking point. But half the town would notice he was gone and be sorry.

Deacon didn't understand that, and not understanding troubled and annoyed him. But then, Deacon was a good man rather than a likeable one. People who knew him well mostly admired him. But an awful lot of people didn't want to know him that well.

He said honestly, 'I don't know, Mr

Miskimmin. We can't find him.'

'Maybe he went off in the van.'

Deacon nodded grimly. 'Maybe he did.'

Chapter Twenty-One

'It's true, then.' Daniel's voice was not much more than a shocked whisper. 'Stanley Barker *was* murdered. Alison was right. Everybody told her she was letting emotion cloud her judgement. But she was right all along. He didn't jump and he didn't fall – he was pushed.' His chin came up like a challenge. 'By you?'

'Of course not,' said the vet. 'I wasn't even in this country at the time.'

But Daniel couldn't stop thinking. Worse, he couldn't stop doing it aloud. 'But Johnny Windham had an alibi. He was abroad when Stanley died – the police asked him to prove it and he did.' He looked up, his eyes widening. 'There's someone else.'

For a moment, before he managed to mask it with annoyance, the vet looked troubled. He was an intelligent man – far more intelligent than Windham, which was why until now he'd done all the thinking and Windham had taken all the risks – and not given to painting himself into corners.

What he'd said hadn't been careless or un-thinking, verbal wallpaper to fill a gap. He'd said it because, if you need someone to do what he's told and not get stroppy and argue with you, and not start to wonder if he could take you in a fair fight, there's a lot to recommend putting the fear of God into him.

What he hadn't expected was that Daniel would pick the threat apart to see what it would tell him. 'Mr Hood, you're asking too many questions,' he observed. 'It's not a healthy thing to do.'

Somehow Daniel managed to laugh out loud. 'You mean, you might have to kill me twice?'

The man laughed too. Even people who found him in their way could sometimes hardly resist Daniel's quite unconscious charm. 'No. I mean, who knows what may happen in the next few hours?'

'So you're going to kill me, but not yet.'

The man gave a non-committal sniff. 'I'm merely suggesting that we try to remain civil while we wait, and not anticipate the balance of necessities.'

Daniel swallowed hard. 'So what are we waiting for?' As soon as it was out he realised this was not a sensible thing to have said.

'I'm waiting for nature to take its course with this pony's digestive system,' the vet said calmly. 'Until then, this is a good place to be. It's quiet, no one will come, we will not be disturbed. If I leave here I must take the animal with me and risk your friend the policeman spotting me. Afterwards, I can walk away with all I need in a plastic bag.'

Daniel didn't want to be reduced to begging, but ultimately he valued his life above his dignity. 'At which point, I can't do you much harm,' he said in a low voice.

The man shrugged. A chill like meltwater ran down Daniel's spine. That was how much someone's life meant to these people: a shrug of the shoulders. If pressed, perhaps he would toss a coin. 'I'll tell you what, Mr Hood. I'll think about it.'

Deacon knew now he'd done the wrong thing about Windham. If he'd held onto him he could have asked him about the white van. He had a fair idea that the missing pony was in it, and it seemed likely that Daniel was in it too.

He should have considered the possibility of another vehicle. He knew Windham wasn't in this alone. That they could rustle up a second horse-box to break their trail should not have come as a surprise. In all likelihood it was on the same damn ferry. That would be the smart thing to do. While Customs were watching for the Windham Transport lorry they were hardly likely to pull in a second horse-box. A white van with a nondescript pony on board would have been less likely to attract attention on that sailing than any other.

But that meant Windham had boarded the ferry knowing he would be stopped. The operation had been blown long before Calais. Deacon shoved his hands deep in his pockets and glared at Brodie. 'He made you.'

'What? No way!' Her dark eyes flashed dramatically.

'He must have done.'

'It's not possible, Jack,' Brodie insisted. 'We were so careful.'

'Maybe he spotted the car,' said Meadows in a low voice. 'I tried to keep my distance, but it's a long journey – maybe he saw it just once too often.'

It wasn't impossible. But she hadn't taken any chances, or made any mistakes, that she shouldn't have. 'It wasn't your fault,' said Brodie stoutly. 'I suppose, if you've the makings of a fortune with you, you're probably pretty paranoid. Maybe he did notice the car and it was just enough to make him wonder, and wondering was enough to make him dump the evidence.'

Then she shook her head. 'But he was never out of our sight. And if he suspected he was being followed, why leave the motorway at all? He could have stuck to his schedule and picked up the catalyst another day.'

'He didn't spot you until after he'd met with his vet friend,' growled Deacon.

'But that was the last place he could have off-loaded the pony,' insisted Brodie.

'He didn't stop at all between there and Calais?'

'He went into a service station for a coffee and a paper. Then he drove on.'

'And you had the lorry in view throughout?'

'Yes.' Then Brodie's eyes narrowed. 'And no. We had the front of the lorry in sight. We could see Windham in the cab. The back was sandwiched between other vehicles and the garage wall.' She grimaced. 'I suppose, if there was someone else to do it, the pony could have been taken off Windham's lorry and put onto another one without us seeing.' Understanding how easily an expensive surveillance had been compromised made her feel very small.

Deacon was spitting tacks. 'So all he had to do was phone his mate from his cab to say he might have company. His mate met him at the service station and while you were watching Windham he off-loaded the pony onto another horse-box. It wasn't exactly *The Great Escape*, was it? My Aunt Martha could have pulled it off!'

Brodie didn't know what to say. She'd thought they'd done a good job; only it turned out Windham had done a better one and now the pony was missing and the drugs were missing and Daniel was missing, and she didn't know where to start looking for any of them. The only thing she was sure of was that they weren't at Windham's yard. He hadn't made enough mistakes to give them reason to hope he'd made that one.

'What will you do?' she asked in a low voice. 'Pull Windham in? Give him the third degree, make him tell us where they've taken Daniel?'

Exasperated as he was, Deacon could find it in him to be sorry for her. This odd-couple relationship she had with Daniel, he might not understand it but he knew how important it was to her. If Hood got hurt because she'd made mistakes she wouldn't forgive herself. He wished he had an answer for her.

'I could, but it wouldn't achieve anything. He knew we were onto him before Daniel was lifted. He knew he was being watched: it was the perfect alibi. I can pull him in but I can't make anything stick and he knows it. He'll just sit there smiling, inviting me to try. Time's on his side, not ours. Once he has the catalyst from inside it his mate can shoot the damn pony, and Daniel too, and torch the van, and we wouldn't know him if he walked down Battle Alley in broad daylight.'

Brodie knew – the conclusion was unavoidable – that Daniel was in danger. But Deacon saying that made it real. Tears welled in her eyes and she could do nothing to stop them.

Seeing them made Deacon feel like shit. He knew there was no kindness in his soul. Most of the time he either didn't notice or didn't care, but just occasionally he hurt someone he didn't mean to and then he felt like shit.

It was too late to bite his tongue, and she wasn't stupid enough to believe him if he back-tracked now. An apology was all that was left. 'I'm sorry. I'm tired, I'm bad-tempered – what do I know? Maybe he just wanted to find out what Daniel knows. It's his name on the paperwork, maybe they had him down as the brains of the operation. In which case, by now they know different. Maybe they've chucked him out on top of the Downs somewhere and he's walking back to civilisation.'

Brodie appreciated him trying, however unconvincingly. She managed a watery smile. 'But you don't really think so.'

'I don't know. I want to think so. It's possible.'

'I think you were right the first time.'

He needed some realistic hope to offer her, not platitudes. He groped in his tired mind for the next move. 'If they'd wanted him dead they could have taken him into his house and killed him there, and Alison with him. They didn't. They wanted to talk to him. Obviously we suspect Windham, but do we have the rest of it – the German end, the vet, the factory? Just how badly are they blown? Well, there's nothing Daniel knows that he wouldn't be prepared to tell. He has no one to protect. He probably said this was my idea rather than yours, but apart from that he hasn't any information worth getting hurt over. That's one thing to be grateful for.'

After a moment Brodie nodded.

'So they needed somewhere to talk where they wouldn't be disturbed,' continued Deacon. 'Not Windham's place – he knew he was under surveillance before they arranged this. Somewhere else. Somewhere he could park a horse-box without anybody asking why, and stay for – I don't know how long a horse's gut is! – maybe a day or so.'

What had begun as an attempt to find some reassurance for Brodie was actually raising his own spirits. 'You know, there's time left in the programme. This man isn't going to kill Daniel out of panic – he has no reason to panic. He's somewhere he feels safe enough to sit and wait, and he knows he's going to be there for maybe another day. He knows we're watching Windham, but so does Windham – he's not going to lead us anywhere. As long as he can keep

Daniel secure – and let's face it, he's not the Incredible Hulk – he doesn't need to do anything else.'

Brodie could see that. 'But the time will come when he has to make some kind of a decision. He can take his package and run, and leave Daniel to be found. But Daniel's a witness against him – the only one who can tie him into this business. Why would he risk leaving him alive?' Her voice was desolate. She was desperate for an answer but she didn't think there was one.

'I don't think he will,' Deacon replied honestly. 'But that point could be twenty-four hours away. He won't kill him before he's ready to leave. You never know what the future holds and he'll want to keep his options open. If we catch up with him he can use a live hostage in a way that he couldn't use a corpse.' He'd done it again, and again he kicked himself at the flicker of pain that crossed her face. 'Brodie, we have a whole day to find them in. Don't tell me I can't find two men, a horse and a horse-box with twenty-four hours to look.'

He wasn't making this up. Policemen aren't used to having time on their side: in a situation like this, a day's grace was an unexpected luxury. But if he'd been talking to Voss rather than Brodie he'd have acknowledged that even one district of a small and over-populated island is dauntingly large when it comes to making a thorough search.

An experienced team would take a day to search one house thoroughly enough to be sure nothing had escaped their scrutiny. To search every wood, every barn, every garage or factory building that could hide a small horse-box was an impossible ambition – even if they confined themselves to a ten-mile radius of Dimmock, and there was no reason to suppose the box had travelled no further than that. It could be travelling still. Twenty-four hours was enough time to conduct a proper search only if they knew where to start searching.

Despite his efforts to shield her, Brodie was thinking pretty much the same thing. But at least she was thinking. 'They'll have taken him somewhere they feel safe. Somewhere Windham knows but thinks we'll never find. But what about Ally? She's spent all her life with people like Johnny Windham, going the places they go. If he knows a secret hideaway, maybe she knows it too.'

Deacon turned and looked at the girl who was once again asleep on the sofa. 'You want to ask her?' he said doubtfully.

'With Daniel's life on the line? Damn right I will.'

First she went into the bathroom and turned the shower on. With the regulator turned right down the water was icy. She went back into the living room and fixed Deacon with a determined eye. 'It might be better if you're not here for this bit. Do you want to nip out and buy some triple-roasted Colombian coffee?'

He knew that what she was protecting him from was not the sight of Alison Barker in a wet T-shirt but the elevated eyebrows and disapproving looks of his superiors. As a civilian and a woman, she could get away with things that he, as a detective super-intendent and a man, could not. But Deacon was always interested to learn just how much he could get away with. 'Daniel's decaf'll do.' He helped her lift the sleepy mumbling girl and steer her into the bathroom.

Brodie was taller than Alison Barker, and when she was this determined she was strong. But even she still couldn't hold the girl at arm's length. Without a second's thought she kicked off her shoes and shed her jacket, and otherwise fully clothed she stepped into the bath and under the pound-ing water dragging Ally with her.

The chill of it flayed her, making her gasp. It had a similar effect on Alison. From soporific and barely able to stand, the girl in her arms turned wildcat in an instant, kicking and writhing and swearing in a high, shocked monotone. Brodie hung on, forcing her head under the icy blast, yelling in her ear. 'Wake up, damn you! Wake up and listen to me. Daniel's in danger, and it might not be your fault but you're the reason it's happened, and even if you weren't you'd be the only person who can help him. Wash that cotton-wool out of your head. I need you to think!'

Daniel lived alone: there weren't enough towels in the airing cupboard to dry both of them. Brodie stripped and shrugged herself into his dressing gown. Then she sat Ally on the side of the bath, flooding the floor, and toweled her vigorously through her pyjamas. While she toweled she explained.

'Where would they take him? It must be somewhere Windham knows – the other guy's a foreigner. Windham phoned him and told him where to find Daniel, and he also said where to take him. Come on, Ally – think. Private, big enough to take a horse-box, no nosy neighbours. Preferably no one within shouting distance. It can't be any-where we'd know about, which rules out his place and yours. But this is your world – chances are, any place Windham knows, you know too. Try to think. If you had a horse and a hostage, and you didn't want anyone finding either of them for twenty-four hours, where would you go?'

Alison was shaking with the cold. But she was awake enough now to know what was being asked of her, and to understand that it was important. Her pinched face was rigid with the effort of thinking.

Suddenly it cleared. She looked up through the rat-tails of her hair with a burst of intelligence like sunrise in her eyes. 'There is a place. I don't know what it's called. I don't know how to find it. But I know where to start.'

Chapter Twenty-Two

Detective Sergeant Voss was on his way back from Windham's yard on the edge of Romney Marsh. Deacon turned him round. 'Change of plan,' he growled. 'Discretion just stopped being an option. Pick him up and bring him in.'

'On my own?' Voss didn't mind the occasional black eye. But he was worried that, in a straight fight, Windham might win and get away.

'I haven't time to send up reinforcements,' snarled Deacon. 'Just get on with it. Are you a man or a mouse?'

'Yes,' Voss answered firmly. 'So why exactly are we ditching everything we've done so far and going at him like a bull in a china shop?' The miles between them notwithstanding, he winced when he realised he'd said that out loud. It was the sort of thing he thought a lot but didn't usually say to Detective Superintendent Deacon.

Deacon didn't usually waste time explaining himself to junior officers. Voss was different. He was certainly Deacon's junior but also his partner. They worked best when they worked together. Though he'd have died rather than admit it, Deacon had considerable respect for his sergeant. He wasn't just a good policeman, he had a good mind. Right now Deacon needed the help of good minds. So he brought Voss up to date.

'I'm on my way,' said Voss. His voice was altered, quiet and focused. 'I'll have him at Battle Alley in about ninety minutes. If I can get anything out of him before that I'll call you.'

'If he knows the game's up he could turn nasty,' warned Deacon.

'With any luck at all,' said Voss.

Deacon put his phone away with a grin that was unexpected enough for Brodie to notice. 'What?'

'I think Charlie Voss has been working for me too long.'

While he'd been making phone calls, Brodie had had Alison Barker poring over a road map, trying to work out where she lost her virginity.

'It's getting to be a long time ago,' she muttered. 'I was fifteen. The last thing on my mind was the grid reference!'

Brodie understood that. 'So tell me how it happened.' Ally's eyebrows rocketed. 'I mean,' she elaborated, 'where you were going, where you'd been. How long you'd been on the road. We can narrow it down from there.'

The girl nodded. 'We'd been to the Bath & West. Horse Show,' she added, remembering she wasn't talking to someone from her world now. 'We were there for two days. My dad had to get back to meet a client, I stayed with the horses. We dropped someone off in Winchester and after that it was just Johnny and me.'

Despite everything that had happened since, the memory made her smile. 'I thought it was my lucky day, driving through the night beside Johnny Windham and nobody else awake. What did I know? I was fifteen.

'After the sun came up he said he was going to have to take a break and did I mind? *Mind?* I'd have spent all day sitting on the hard shoulder with him. But he said he knew a place where we could get out and stretch our legs. Five minutes off the main road, he said, though I think it was a bit more. There was a gate. Big curly thing – it must have been grand once but it was patched with tin and off its hinges. He drove the lorry between some overgrown bushes and there was this house. Huge, but derelict. Gutted –

you could see through from the front windows to the back. Johnny said there was a fire years before and they'd never had the money to rebuild.'

'And that's where it happened,' said Brodie softly.

'Yes,' said the girl crisply, 'that's where it happened. On a horse-rug on the grass, wet with dew, and he said he loved me. And I was fifteen and believed him.'

'And you never told anyone? Mary thought you had a schoolgirl crush on him. What about your father – did he know?'

Ally shook her head. 'At the time I had no reason to tell him. I had a secret lover – what girl wants to share that with her parents? By the time I realised it was over, which was three months after everyone else knew, it seemed childish to complain. I wanted him when I thought it meant something – I wasn't going to scream "Rape!" when I found it didn't. I felt used, and foolish and embarrassed. I just wanted never to see him again – and even that wasn't going to happen unless I was prepared to say why.'

Deacon steered them back onto the subject. 'So we're looking for a derelict mansion not far from the A272. How long after you'd left Winchester?'

Brodie stared at him as if he'd said something gross. Then she realised he was right: for a moment she'd forgotten what had led to this.

Ally blinked, pulling herself back to the present. 'Winchester?'

'You dropped off some of your load in Winchester, yes? How long did you drive after that before Windham turned off?'

She tried to think. 'I don't know. Quite a while – at least an hour, maybe two.'

'Which – one or two? An hour is what, thirty miles in a horse-box? Somewhere around Petworth. Two hours would have taken you to Hayward's Heath. There's a lot of southern England in between, Miss Barker. Try to be more specific.'

'I wasn't watching the dashboard!'

Brodie was doing what she did best: extrapolating from what she knew to what she wanted to know. 'You'd recognise this house if you saw it again?'

'Yes. But isn't that the problem – that we don't know how to find it?'

'I know how to find it.' She was on her feet and halfway to the door. 'Come on, we're taking this to my office. Give me half an hour on the Internet and I'll show you a picture you can recognise.'

'How?'

Brodie paused just long enough in the doorway to throw back a smile of infinite hubris. 'By being very good at what I do, Ally. I find things, yes? Well, this is how I do it. Watch, learn and be impressed.'

In fact it didn't take her half an hour. Her fingers moving almost fast enough to deceive the eye, she flicked from one specialist website to another – National Trust, English Heritage, great houses, lost gems, architectural salvage. After twenty minutes they'd trawled through what was essentially a brick-by-brick survey of the architectural history of the South Downs. A couple of times Ally had sat up straight in her chair only to subside, disappointed, once she'd had a better look.

Finally she let out a squawk. 'That's it!'

Deacon, perching awkwardly on the edge of Brodie's desk, his neck craned to see over her shoulder, almost fell off. 'You're sure?'

The girl looked him full in the face. 'You're a man – you probably don't even remember your first time. I do. It was there.'

He believed her. At least, he believed she thought so. He couldn't be sure she was right, and he couldn't be sure that, even if she was, Windham had also remembered the place when he came to need somewhere to hide a horse-box. But it was their best chance to get ahead of the game. Unless Johnny Windham was overcome by a sudden urge to confess all to Charlie Voss, it was their only chance. 'Where? What's it called?'

Brodie hit the printer button, at the same time reading the details aloud. 'Sparrow Hill. A Regency mansion south of Guildford. Reduced to a shell by a fire shortly after the First World War. A picturesque rather than important site, now largely overgrown' – her voice sharpened – 'by the rhododendrons lining the driveway! That's it, all right, Jack. It's exactly how she described it.'

Deacon was taking down the map reference. 'You drive. I'm going to be on the phone.'

Voss was still twice as far from Sparrow Hill as Deacon was: there was nothing he could do to help. Except that he had Windham with him, and Windham knew things that even Brodie was only guessing. Rather than speeding up, which was why Deacon had called him, he let the car slow to a crawl and then pulled over.

He turned on the interior light and swivelled in his seat to look Windham, handcuffed in the back, full in the eye. 'We've found them.'

Windham gave an elaborate sigh. 'I still don't know who you're talking about.'

'No, I know,' said Voss evenly, 'you don't know anything about a white horse-box. You left the pony in Belgium because it was unwell and as far as you know it's still there. So this'll come as news to you. It isn't. It's in a small white horse-box no great distance from here, with somebody feeding it all the prunes it can take.

'Now, I know that you know who that is. He's a friend of yours and you're working together on this. But we don't need to argue about it just now. Because there's someone else there too, and he's a friend of mine, and if he's been hurt, or if he's going to get hurt, you're the one in custody – you're the one who's going to pay. Not to put too fine a point on it: if Daniel Hood ends up dead, you're looking at a life sentence.'

He paused, waiting for some reaction. There was none. Windham continued to gaze at him impassively.

Voss nodded. 'You've probably heard of life sentences that work out at just a few years and you're thinking it's not too big a risk to take. We nail you for manufacturing and distributing drugs, you're going down anyway – what's the difference?

'The difference is, you kill someone in the process of making and distributing drugs – and not someone who got in the way of a shoot-out or a speeding car but someone who was taken from his house because you thought he had information you needed – and you're no longer looking at eight years, you're looking at twenty. You'll be pushing sixty when you get out.'

For the first time Windham's gaze flickered. He brought it back quickly, defiantly, but Voss had seen. Encouraged, he pressed on. 'You don't want to believe that holiday-camp line either. Any time in prison is hard time. Twenty years of it is like climbing Everest on your hands and knees. Harder men than you have been broken down, bit by bit, until there's nothing left but dust.

'Frankly, I don't much care what happens to you. I don't care if you spend every night of those twenty years face-down on an iron bedstead with a queue of men paying for you in snout and phone-cards. That's not why I want your help. I want it for my sake, and my friend's sake. But the *real politik* of the situation is, you help me and there are things I can do to help you. Less time, and easier time. Don't pass up on that unless you're sure you want to.'

Windham came from that same middle-England background as most people involved with horses: neither aristocratic nor entirely plebian, not rich on inherited wealth nor dependent on benefits. His natural forebears were the yeomen of England, independent farmers, men of substance and self-reliance, men who worked hard for what they had and defended it jealously, even against kings. He did not spring from criminal stock, with an inbred knowledge of and stoicism about the consequences of failure. He didn't grow up knowing where to catch the bus for Durham and Parkhurst. Career criminals do everything they can to avoid prison but don't fear it in the way that essentially law-abiding people do. They know what doing time involves. They know that, left with no choice, they can do it.

In many ways the white-collar criminal, the man who gets into it because he has a talent or an idea that can be exploited more profitably on the wrong side of the law, is harder for the police to deal with. He may have the money, the connections and the education to use the law to shelter him from justice. He never uses the words, 'It's a fair cop, gov.' But if he has a weakness, it's that anything which pricks the bubble of his ego, that undermines his sense of being in control, may tip him into disaster. He won't, as the career blagger would, fall back on sullen silence as his last defence. He will lie like a trooper in the attempt to maintain the image of innocence, and sooner or later he will knit a rope to hang himself. That was Voss's hope: that once panic set in and Windham started talking, whether or not he began with the truth, he wouldn't be able to stop.

And he could see it in Windham's face that he was now considering his options. Wondering if there was any way he could still get out of this scot-free or if it was time to choose between greater and lesser evils.

He decided there was nothing Voss could prove if he didn't help him, no witness against him if he protected the man with the white van. Voss saw the moment when he might have buckled come and go, and the self-confidence that had got him through his life so far wash back into the vacuum. Voss, whose forebears had tilled the soil owned by Windham's, recognised the lift of the head, the supercilious look down the nose, the bored nasal inflection of the voice. 'I'm sorry, Sergeant, you really are barking up the wrong tree. I'd help you if I could but I can't. I don't know any of the people you're talking about.'

Voss hung onto his patience. 'We will prove it, you know. We're going to tie you into this. The only question is what you're going down for – drug trafficking or something worse.'

Windham sighed theatrically. 'Sergeant Voss, I know you think you're doing the right thing. But you've made a mistake. You've listened to the hysterical rantings of the Barker girl and decided that where there's smoke there must be fire. I understand: she's plausible. She's had a rough time and everyone's sorry for her. You're not the first to believe her – I've been investigated before. And cleared. I will be again.'

Voss went on looking at him. 'You're really going to let this happen?' he said at last. 'You're going to let someone die rather than admit you could save him?'

'Sergeant Voss, I keep telling you. I

couldn't help your friend if I wanted to.'

And that was it: the first mistake, that Voss could use to pry open the oyster. 'You keep telling me you *do* want to, Mr Windham. And why wouldn't you? If you're not involved in this, why wouldn't you want to help an innocent bystander? Why wouldn't you do everything in your power to save his life?'

They stared at one another for ten or fifteen seconds, which is a long time to share an enforced intimacy with a hostile individual. The atmosphere in the car around them crackled with electricity.

At the end of those fifteen seconds, Windham blinked.

Chapter Twenty-Three

For a man with no kindness in his soul, Deacon felt a curious impulse to dissemble when Voss called to say the white van was holed up at a place called Sparrow Hill not far from Petworth. Instead of saying, 'Yes, we know, we're on our way there now,' he found himself beating around the bush in a most uncharacteristic manner, so that Brodie gave him a puzzled look that went on just a little too long for someone driving fast at night.

And in the end he had to come clean and never mind Voss's feelings. 'The girl thought it was a possibility. Windham took her there once, years ago. She never knew the name. Brodie found it on the Internet.'

Voss knew better than to ask how. He firmly believed Brodie could find the date of the Second Coming on the Internet. He tried to hide his disappointment. For just a minute there he thought he'd cracked the case. 'If we want him to, Windham will phone his partner and tell him we're on our way. Do we want him to?'

That was a hard one to call. If the man was in his right mind at all he would immediately leave the van, the pony, the contents of its stomach and Daniel, and head across country until he found a busy road where he could start hitching his way back to a Channel port. Five minutes' head start was worth having, in the circumstances. Half an hour was a passport to freedom.

Which was the other side of the coin. If they warned him they wouldn't catch him. Whereas maybe, if Deacon timed this right and large officers in flak jackets sneaked up on him unawares, they could have him in custody almost before he knew he'd been found. But something could go wrong. With his back against the wall and only one shot left in his locker, the status of his hostage could rapidly deteriorate from unenviable to untenable.

Whatever Deacon decided he could be wrong, perhaps disastrously so. It was an uncomfortable position to be in. But he wouldn't have changed places with Daniel.

'Ask him about this man. What he's like; what he's likely to do. Will he cut and run if we give him the chance? Will he hurt Daniel if we don't?'

There was a brief hiatus in which Deacon could just hear voices offset from Voss's phone. Then the sergeant was back. 'He says his name is Kant. He's the vet – the one with access to the tranquillizer. Windham says he's smart – a lot of this was his idea; of course, he would say that – and determined. If he's cornered, we shouldn't count on him coming quietly. If Daniel's still alive...'

The car swerved violently. Deacon didn't dare glance at Brodie. *'If?'*

Voss ploughed on with the sentence, his voice doggedly expressionless. 'If Daniel's still alive, he'll carve him like a Christmas turkey if he thinks it'll back us off long enough for him to get away.'

Deacon didn't ring off but let the hand holding the phone slump into his lap. He stared into the darkness ahead, the road a bright arrow in the headlights. He might have been thinking aloud, he might have been speaking to Brodie. 'We can't let him go.'

She sucked in an unsteady breath. 'He has Daniel. Because I put his name on the paperwork: that's all. That's the only reason he knew who to look for, where to find him. My fault. Again.'

'You couldn't have known. You couldn't have guessed...'

'Maybe not. But we know now.'

Deacon squeezed his eyes shut for a second. He knew what this was doing to her. He knew it was in his power to lift her burden. It was a close call – he'd already recognised that. There were arguments for playing it either way. No one but him would ever know for sure if he'd let his relationship with Brodie Farrell, and hers with Daniel Hood, affect how he did his job.

'You heard what Voss said. This is a dangerous man. A vicious man engaged in a bloody, immoral trade. And we have him cornered. In all likelihood we can take him down today and he'll never hurt anyone else ever again. We can't let him go.'

'You found him once, you'll find him again.' Her voice was a plea. 'You don't even need to let him go – just let him *think* he's getting away. Pick him up again after Daniel's safe.'

'And what if next time he's cornered it's somebody's child he takes hostage?'

'I don't care!' she cried. 'Jack, I don't care! There aren't half a dozen people in the world I care about, and he's got one of them right now. Because I got cocky and careless, and stupid, my best friend's in mortal danger. Maybe he's in pain right now – maybe he's dying right now, Jack, and there's nothing I can do to help him. But there is something *you* can do. You can tell this man he has an hour to run as far as he can if he leaves this very moment. You can tell him you know everything Daniel knows and more; and anyway the biggest threat to him isn't what Daniel might say, it's what Windham might say, and he'll still be in custody whatever happens to Daniel. Tell him that. He'll see there's no point hurting Daniel now. He'll drop everything and run.'

'I can't,' said Deacon dully.

Brodie took her eyes off the road long enough to risk all their lives. Her voice cracked. 'Jack...!'

'Brodie, I can't. You know that. If I do as you ask, maybe it'll help Daniel but only by risking other people's lives. When we reach Sparrow Hill, we'll have to cordon it off and search it. Everyone engaged in that will be in danger. They have the right to expect that I made it as safe as I could. That I didn't warn a dangerous man they were coming. And particularly not because my girlfriend asked me to.'

If her voice had fallen any lower it would have been inaudible. 'I will never ask you anything else,' she said. 'If you do this for me. And also if you don't.'

'I'm sorry.'

He was fourteen years old when Deacon first noticed that people had started walking round him. At first it was other schoolboys, then other rugby players, later it was drunk-and-disorderlies on street corners who took one look at him and sobered up fast. Of course, in 26 years as a police officer he'd been involved in some major punch-ups; but not as many as colleagues who were less well equipped to deal with them and – let's be honest here – got less enjoyment out of them. When you're built like a brick privy even desperate men look for an alternative to taking a swing at you.

So it was the last thing he expected when Brodie, still with one hand on the wheel, snatched for his phone, shouting into it even as she did. 'Charlie! Do it. Tell him...'

But by then Deacon had taken it back, and had it out of her reach in his left hand. His voice was terse, the words clipped. 'Sergeant. Don't let Windham anywhere near a phone. Under no circumstances. Get him to Battle Alley and book him in. I'll see you there when this is all over.'

'Sir,' said Voss, expressionless, and the phone went dead.

Brodie had tried and lost. She concentrated on her driving. Except to say: 'I shan't forget that, Jack.'

'No,' he said gruffly. 'I don't suppose you will.'

Two hours ago, though this turn of events had startled him, as the shock wore off Daniel had felt largely optimistic about his situation. Nothing he knew was worth protecting with his life, and though the man with him was undoubtedly ruthless, he wasn't the sort to overreact out of panic. He'd do what, and no more than, was necessary to protect himself, and Daniel had thought that left him with every chance of walking away from this.

It would have been possible to think so still. Apart from a sharp blow with a blunt instrument and the discomfort of the plastic string – in fact it was baler twine – lashing his wrists, he was still largely unhurt, and the natural human desire to avoid unpalatable conclusions might have persuaded him that his captor did not in fact want to harm him. He'd said as much: it was tempting to believe him. If he had, Daniel would have done nothing to provoke the man to rethink his approach. Nothing to make it harder for him to finish his job and return safely home. He would have kept quiet except to answer, accurately and politely, any questions he was asked, and still until he was told to move.

But Daniel was not a fool. He was in many ways a simple man – in others a strangely complicated one – and his open, honest face often led people to underestimate him. People who knew him a little tended to think him a bit dim. But they were wrong. Daniel Hood was a highly intelligent man, and not just with facts and figures. He was astute, and he always knew the difference between what he wanted to be so and what was likely. It wasn't likely that a professional drug-runner, far from home and with a hugely profitable enterprise to protect, would free someone who could identify him. He was pretending he might solely to encourage good behaviour. In fact, as soon as he had what he was waiting for, Daniel knew the pantomime would be over.

Knowing that was oddly liberating. If this man had purposed his death from the moment he answered his door, nothing Daniel had or hadn't done, or would or wouldn't do, or could have done, was a factor. He hadn't read the situation wrong or made the wrong choices. There were no right choices. All that would have saved him from this was being somewhere else when the white van pulled up at the shore. Sheer luck: and luck alone stood between him and the Grim Reaper now. If he'd been missed, and if he could be found before nature took its course with this pony's digestive system, perhaps he would live. If not he expected to die.

He wasn't afraid of dying. He was afraid of pain, but everything this man had done so far had been efficient, professional: there was good reason to hope he'd do the thing cleanly. Daniel resented being robbed like this – of the chance to grow old, bald and querulous, of the chance to have a comet named after him, of the chance to tell Brodie how he felt about her in a way that she couldn't misunderstand – but the prospect of death was not so much a horror to him as an unknown, a black hole. And Daniel was an astronomer: black holes fascinated him. He was curious to know what was on the other side.

Werner Kant was curious about Daniel. He couldn't seem to pigeon-hole him. They'd spent some time together now, with nothing happening and no suitable subject for small talk, and he was getting bored. He'd given the pony an injection to speed things up a bit, and at intervals there was a sound like a small avalanche from the back of the box and he went to poke through the detritus with a stick. But it wasn't much to occupy the mind of an intelligent man. He found himself wondering about his hostage.

'You're not a policeman,' he hazarded.

'I teach maths,' said Daniel.

That didn't help. 'If you're not a policeman and you know nothing about horses, how did you become involved?'

Daniel had wondered that himself. 'They needed a name for the paperwork, that's all. If they'd said the pony was for Detective Superintendent Deacon, Windham might have got suspicious.'

Kant chuckled. 'It's possible. He's not the sharpest tool in the box, but I think even pretty Johnny would have wondered about that.'

'Is that any way to talk about your employer?'

Kant laughed out loud. 'Johnny Windham? I don't think so. Windham is hired help: he does what he's paid to do.'

'Including taking all the risks.'

'Of course. There's very little point being a criminal mastermind if you're going to take them yourself.'

Daniel blinked, taken aback by his honesty. 'So you're not going to claim it's all an unfortunate misunderstanding.'

'It's a little late for that,' admitted Kant. 'It's a great pity. It was a good idea – almost foolproof. Moving production to England put distance between me and how the tranquillizer I was signing for was being used. I knew a carrier who was greedy and dishonest but reliable enough in his way. It all came together more easily than I expected.' He sighed. 'And now I have to start again. Such is life. What you can do once you can do a second time.'

'The police are onto you. They're looking for you right now.'

'But they aren't looking here. And when my consignment reappears and I deliver it and leave, there will be nothing to tell them if they were even on the right track.'

Daniel caught his breath. He thought he'd come to terms with the idea. But hearing your own death spoken of as a *fait accompli* will always cause a little *frisson* of shock.

The man noticed. 'I'm sorry, that was – tactless. You should forget I said it.'

'Oh yes,' said Daniel, recovering sufficiently for sarcasm, 'that's going to happen.'

The man was watching him with a puzzled half-smile. 'You – confuse me. You are different.'

'Different to who?'

'I think, to most people. Certainly to me.'

'I should bloody well hope so!' exclaimed Daniel indignantly. 'You're a drug baron! You killed Stanley Barker, and you're going to kill me. For money. As epitaphs go, there are worse ones than *He was different to the man who killed him.*'

'You are angry,' observed Kant sagely.

'Of course I'm angry,' yelled Daniel. 'You intend to kill me, and you have no right.'

'No. But I have a need.'

'*Need?* Need is when you've no food for your children. You're a vet, aren't you? You

295

have a good career. How can you possibly claim need?' He paused then, frowning. 'How did that happen? That you went from easing suffering to supplying recreational drugs for a living?'

Kant shrugged. 'Opportunities presented. The returns are remarkable. If you'd had the idea, you'd have done the same.'

Daniel gave a scornful laugh. 'No.'

'There is a demand, I meet it. I believe in the market economy.'

'You kill people! You ruin their lives, and you kill them.'

'Stupid people.'

'Children, some of them. One family in my town lost two sons to your garbage. One was fifteen, the other was seventeen. Maybe they were stupid, but they were young enough to have an excuse. What's yours? You wanted a new car, better holidays? Is there nothing in the world precious enough to put your own selfish desires on hold for?'

The vast majority of murders are committed in anger. But this was not an emotional man. His profession – both his professions – required him not to be. Unemotional, and unimaginative. When the moment came Kant would kill him without compunction or regret, but Daniel had little to fear from him in the meantime. He wouldn't cripple him first with an irate fist or boot.

And, being an unimaginative man, he answered as if the question were not rhetorical but an attempt to elicit information. 'Very little. Does that surprise you?'

'It shouldn't, should it?' said Daniel softly. 'But somehow it manages to. It doesn't matter how much proof I see to the contrary, I go on believing that people are basically decent and inside every thug there's a misunderstood philanthropist trying to get out.'

The man had to work out what he meant. Daniel could see him translating in his head. Then he beamed. 'Mr Hood, you're an optimist! How quaint.'

Daniel answered with a wry smile of his own. 'It's an uphill struggle at times. But I'd rather be an optimist who's sometimes disappointed than a pessimist who never is.'

'And a philosopher.'

'And I'd rather be one of those than a man who grows fat on the blood of other people's children.'

At that a flicker of displeasure crossed the other man's face. He still wasn't moved to violence; rather he seemed a little hurt. As if they'd been having a civilised conversation and Daniel had spoiled it. It wasn't that he cared what Daniel thought, just that it seemed rude to express it that way. 'I think it's time you were quiet for a little while now,' he said disapprovingly.

'I think, if you have your way, I'm going to

be quiet for a very long time,' said Daniel, reckless with the death of hope. 'I don't feel inclined to oblige you.'

The man nodded, taking his point. He opened the door in the side of the box and dropped down to the ground outside. Daniel waited. He'd thought he could hardly make his situation any worse. Now he was forced to wonder.

The man returned with a loaded syringe in his hand. 'You know what this is?'

Daniel couldn't take his eyes off it. 'I can guess.'

'You understand, this isn't the finished product, it's the raw material. I need to perform a standing castration on a colt, this is what I use. It's a good product for horses. It keeps them sedated without interfering with their vital functions – cardio-vascular system, balance and so on. It stops them falling on me while I operate,' he explained in layman's terms.

'For use by people as a recreational drug, of course, we have to vastly reduce the potency. Even a tiny amount of it at this strength would have catastrophic effects. I don't just mean it would kill you, although of course it would. I mean it would fry your brain. I don't know what that would feel like. No one has ever been able to say. But you're going to find out if you give me any trouble. Do you understand?'

Daniel had thought he was past fear. He was mistaken. He had to force an answer out; and then try again because it was just a strangled whisper the first time. 'Yes. Yes.'

'Good. So now we wait quietly, yes?'

'Yes.'

Chapter Twenty-Four

It was in Deacon's voice as he spoke that he knew he was in for a fight over this. 'Brodie, I need you to stop the car.'

She glanced at him, dismissive, didn't so much as slow down. 'Why,' she asked waspishly, 'are you feeling sick?'

'I'm going to drop you off here. You and Alison. I'll pick you up again, or have you picked up, inside half an hour.'

'No,' said Brodie, and kept driving.

'I mean it,' he said tersely. 'This is a police operation. There are armed response units on their way, which means if he doesn't come quietly there could be shooting. I don't want either of you in the line of fire.'

'I know what you're doing,' she retorted through clenched teeth.

'I told you...'

'...the official version,' she interrupted acidly. 'What you'll put in your report. What they want to read at Division, and what somebody'll pat you on the back for. The Correct Way to Proceed in the Circumstances. But not the reason.'

He shook his head, bemused. 'I don't know what you mean. What do you want me to say?'

'That you don't want me to watch you sacrifice Daniel to the greater good.'

She could have spiked him with her Come Dancing stilettos without making him catch his breath like that. 'I don't *want* any of this! I'm stuck with it because it's my case so I get the blame when it all goes pear-shaped. I'll do everything I can to get Daniel out of there safely, the same way I would with any other hostage. For what it's worth, most hostage situations end peacefully. Most hostage-takers eventually accept that they're only making things worse for themselves and give up. But I don't want to be handling a tricky situation with part of my mind on where you are and what you're up to. Let me do my job, Brodie. Stay here, and let me get on with what I'm paid to do.'

'No,' she said baldly. 'I'm coming with you, Jack. I'm going to be right there. I can't make you fight for Daniel, but by God I'll see if you don't. If you let him die because that way you get to tie up all the loose ends, and his death will be on someone else's record and someone else's conscience, you and me are through. I'll have lost a friend, and you'll have gained an enemy.'

On the back seat Ally Barker had the distinct impression they thought they were alone. They were arguing with a passion that even married couples don't use in public. They frightened her. After three months of the keenest loneliness she had dared to put her trust in these people, only to find they had no confidence in one another. It was like listening to your parents row, and knowing they were going too far – any second now one of them was going to say something unforgivable and the only possible outcome would be divorce. She wanted to knock their heads together. She wanted to scream just to remind them she was there.

'Is that what you think?' Deacon's voice was rough with resentment. 'Dear God, is it? You think it doesn't matter to me whether Daniel comes through this? Because he's your friend, and I'm jealous of the part of your life that he has access to and I don't. That with him out of the way I no longer have to worry about the spectre at the feast. That's what you meant by tying up loose ends?'

'Brodie, Daniel Hood's a pious little prat sometimes. He's sanctimonious and he's arrogant and he irritates the hell out of me more often than not. And somewhere along the line he became my friend too. It's the only reason I haven't decked him a dozen times. I can't explain it and I don't know how it happened, only that it did. There's something about the little sod that – I don't know, I can't find the words – touches people. He gets involved in their lives. You think he's just watching from the sidelines, but he isn't – he's changing things. Changing people.'

She went to answer him but he wouldn't let her. He had a point to make, and it was important, and she was going to hear him out. 'But even if he didn't – if we'd never met, if I'd never felt the urge to shove his telescope where no stars shine – I still wouldn't be using him as a tethered goat to shoot a tiger. Not for fear of your temper tantrums but because that's not what we do. We don't make trades. We don't put a value on this person's life or that person's suffering and weigh up whether it's worth more than what we can get for it. It's my job to protect Daniel to the best of my ability. And everyone else.'

'And right enough,' he acknowledged, 'that's where a conflict can arise. It isn't a question of who's involved, it isn't even a question of numbers. It's not about Daniel at all. It's about the man holding him, and the fact I have a good chance to take him off the street – him and his whole damned setup. There's a drugs factory out there and if I get him, maybe I can close it down.

'If numbers were the issue I'd have to tell you that that would be a good deal. We'd save a lot of lives that way. But it's not even a consideration. The only decision I have to make is whether to take a dangerous man or let him run. And that's no contest.'

Brodie was upset and afraid. This was Daniel they were talking about, and the fact that he mightn't be around tomorrow, and that thought paralysed her brain and stopped her from seeing the sense, the wisdom, the morality even, of what Deacon was saying.

'That's a convenient argument, isn't it?' she spat. '"It wasn't my fault, I was only following orders". Where have I heard that one before? You can dress it up any way you like, Jack, and you'll probably convince people who don't know you as well as I do, but I know what's going on here. Yes, it's a difficult decision, but not for you. You've hated Daniel's guts from the day you met. No – from the day you told him to jump and he didn't ask how high. From that day to this, a part of you has been waiting for a chance to make him pay.

'It's about Daniel, all right. And not Daniel and me but Daniel and you. He's smarter than you are, and he's a better man than you are, and you resent him like hell. And this is your time. You have his life in your hands. The only problem is that he's not here to beg for it.'

Deacon had been a police officer most of his adult life. He'd never thought of being anything else. It was important work and he was good at it, and if the downside was that every so often someone used you as a punchbag, that was a price he would pay. He'd been shot at, he'd been cut, he'd been thumped and kicked until there was no part of his body that hadn't been black and blue at one time or another. But he'd never been stabbed in the heart until now.

He had trouble finding a voice – any voice, much less one his colleagues would have recognised. 'You're upset. I know that. It's why I don't want you there while we deal with this. But afterwards we need to talk. If you really think I'm so jealous of Daniel that I'm prepared to gamble with his life and hope to lose, maybe we *should* call it a day. Because you have no idea who I am, and you shouldn't be sleeping with strangers.'

Ally held up a tentative hand and mumbled, 'You guys do know I'm here, don't you?' And Brodie snarled, 'Shut up,' and Deacon grated, 'Don't take it out on the girl.'

The lights of a petrol station hovered in the darkness like a spaceship. Deacon tried the voice of authority, that had bluff young policemen cowering under desks. 'Pull in here.' He waited for her to do as he said. He was still waiting as the lights twinkled and vanished in the mirror.

He pursed his lips. 'All right. I'm not going to wrestle you for it. When we get there, if you're still determined to obstruct me in the pursuance of my duty I will arrest you. Count on it.'

'You don't scare me,' sneered Brodie.

'I'm not trying to scare you. I'm trying to get you to see sense.'

'By which you mean, see it your way.'

He hung onto his temper by his scuffed and often bruise-blackened fingernails. 'Brodie, I'm just about past caring how this looks to you. But you will do what I require of you. I have the power to make you.'

She didn't doubt that he meant it. Later she would regret forcing him onto this path, but right now all she cared about was Daniel. She had always insisted there was no conflict between her feelings for these two men, but all three of them had known that one day there would be a choice to be made. And none of them, herself included, could have predicted the outcome.

'Do what you have to,' she said through gritted teeth. 'And so will I.'

No one who knew him well would have been surprised to learn that Daniel Hood, tied up in a horse-box, helpless as a beast on its way to the slaughterhouse, was seeking consolation in mathematics. Unable to

305

move enough to ease his muscles, his back was a slab of pain from the nape of his neck to the back of his knees. The blood flow congested by the baler-twine around his wrists had made his hands swell until the plastic cut into the flesh. Also, he had a headache. In such circumstances almost no one else in the entire world would have been thinking about the First Law of Thermodynamics.

To Daniel, the First Law of Thermodynamics held out the hope of something beyond the void in the same way that heaven serves believers. He'd been an atheist since he was old enough to vest his faith in logic and build a personal philosophy out of facts mortared together by probabilities, but the more he read and the more he thought, the less he felt constrained to accept that everything ended when the heart stopped.

The laws of thermodynamics are about the first thing a budding scientist learns, and the first of them is the law of the conservation of energy – that it can be transmuted but neither created nor destroyed. He reasoned that, since a personality undoubtedly exists despite having no physical structure, it must be a form of energy, in which case there was every chance that what the world knew as Daniel Hood would continue in some guise beyond the black hole and he'd get a chance to see what lay on the other side. He hoped so. Whatever it was, it had to be more inter-esting than nothing.

From the other end of the box came a soft rumble as the mare lifted her tail and, with a beatific expression, made another deposit in the straw behind her. Resignedly Kant took up his stick again and walked down the unoccupied half of the box, not really hopeful, just going through the motions.

This time it was different. Daniel saw him stiffen then lean sharply forward. He threw the stick away and pulled a long plastic glove from his pocket, and continued the search by hand. He picked up a wisp of straw from the floor of the box and cleaned them off, then he held them out triumphantly for Daniel's inspection – three black rubber cylinders with rounded ends, just small enough to pass through the pony but big enough to contain a significant volume of liquid. In Windham's kitchen or some similarly ad hoc facility, this catalyst would be combined with a few domestic chemicals and emerge as Scram in quantities so vast it could be sold cheap to teenagers and still make a fortune for everyone involved.

'Mission accomplished,' Kant announced with vibrant satisfaction.

'That's all of them?' For obvious reasons Daniel was hoping the answer would be *Nein*, or even nine.

But no. 'All.'

'You counted them out and you counted them all back again?'

In times of war it's things like that which betray spies. You can speak a perfectly fluent, colloquial version of someone's language but something like that won't make sense unless you were part of that society at the particular time it arose from. Daniel found himself trying to explain. 'It was a reporter. In the Falklands. He couldn't say how many planes...' He gave up. 'Now what?'

The man's face went still. Of course, he understood why Daniel couldn't share his enthusiasm at a job well done. 'Now I deliver these and go home.'

'That wasn't what I meant.'

'No.'

In some ways life is harder on the strong. They have more to defend, more to lose. There were things Daniel would die to protect but his image wasn't one of them. 'I'm not a threat to you. I can't get out of here until someone finds me and frees me. By the time I'm talking to policemen – and they're shouting at me for knowing nothing they can possibly use – you'll be safe. I know my life's of no value to you, but it is to me. I don't want to die for no good reason.'

Kant watched him with calm unflinching eyes. A vet resolves a lot of suffering and also ends a lot of lives: perhaps there wasn't the barrier in his mind that stops the average man-in-the-street, even when he's very angry, from killing. At the same time, he was an intelligent man under no particular pressure to make a split-second decision on which his own safety might depend. There was just a chance that an appeal to reason would succeed.

Daniel saw it in his eyes first, and held his breath because he could have been wrong. But then the smile appeared on his lips too and the man nodded. 'All right.'

Dead on cue a tiny electronic orchestra struck up with 'Colonel Bogie'.

And the other reason you don't take civilians on sharp-end police operations is that they don't know the basics – the things so fundamental you don't think to remind people – things like turning off the ringer on their mobile phones when they're part of a surveillance.

It was Alison's, buried in the pocket of her coat where she hadn't given it a moment's thought. In a busy street, even in a crowded room, it might have been barely audible. In the silence of a rural estate late at night, so far from the nearest traffic that they'd left the cars quarter of a mile away and crept up on foot, it filled the air.

They'd met up with the armed response vehicle and a contingent of officers from the local division at the gates of Sparrow Hill.

Deacon had engaged in a quick briefing with their inspector before deploying into the estate itself. He expected to find the van in the courtyard behind the house, mainly because the stable block would seem the obvious place to head with a horse-box, but he wasn't putting money on it. The driver might have figured out that an aerial search would find it harder to spot him under trees than among buildings, or he might have been smart enough to realise that would only apply in daylight. Either way, Deacon wasn't making any assumptions. They would search the park as they advanced on the house.

He left Brodie and Alison in his car with an injunction to stay there and no confidence at all that they would obey. In fact, he walked away quickly so that he wouldn't see when they didn't. There wasn't time for a confrontation, a shouting match could blow their cover instantly, and in spite of what he'd said he had no intentions of arresting either of them. Better not to know, then, that he was being defied.

Brodie gave him a minute's head start then got out of the car. 'Are you coming?'

Ally gestured nervously in the direction of Deacon's departure. 'But Mr Deacon said...'

'Yes he did,' agreed Brodie. Her voice was like iron. She shut the car door quietly and

310

began walking up the drive. After a moment, torn and nervous, Alison followed.

In the darkness, unable to use a torch for fear of giving themselves away, it was difficult to be sure they weren't overtaking the cordon. But as her eyes adjusted Brodie found she could see the movement of dark figures against the dark background and she took care to stay behind the advance. Anxious as she was to find Daniel, she didn't want to be the one who found Werner Kant.

The van was in the stable-yard. As soon as the advance guard had a clear view under the gate-house they could see it. A small door in the side was open, spilling light onto the cobbles and silhouetting the single figure standing beside it. Deacon didn't think it was Daniel. With the light behind it the face was obscure and the conditions made it hard to judge scale. In any group of men Daniel was usually the shortest, but here there were no reference points.

But if it had been Daniel standing out in the yard with nobody near him, he wouldn't have been standing there long – he'd have been running for dear life.

The firearms officers and the men armed with nothing but training and bloody-mindedness had been manoeuvred into position by means of whispered phone calls and were waiting his word to go. Deacon made them wait, watching to see if anyone else appeared. It only took one man to drive the horse-box but that didn't mean he was alone. Also, he wanted to locate Daniel before the action started. If he was in the van the guys with the guns needed to know.

And that was when 'Colonel Bogie' rang out in the stillness of the night.

Chapter Twenty-Five

'Ah,' said Kant softly. 'We seem to have been discovered. I wonder how that happened.'

'Don't look at me,' Daniel said quickly. 'I don't know where we are, and I've no way of telling anyone if I did.'

'Nevertheless, we are no longer alone.'

'Poachers?' hazarded Daniel, without much hope.

'I think we should assume it's the police.'

'Does this' – he didn't know how to put it – 'change anything?'

Kant considered, but not for long. 'I think it might, yes.'

An hour ago, when he thought it was inevitable, Daniel had been able to face death with something approaching composure. Not exactly reconciled, not exactly unafraid, but giving a good enough performance to satisfy the critics.

But then, for just a moment, he'd thought he'd dodged the bullet, and with that had come the realisation that appearance isn't everything, that a good performance may convince the audience but the actor will always know it's not the real thing. Of course he was afraid, even if he didn't dare admit it. The keenest astronomer in the world would sooner observe a black hole than dive into one. Now the void loomed again and his courage was all used up. His voice came out a plaint 'Please...'

There was a note almost of kindness in Kant's tone as he climbed into the box. 'Mr Hood, you misunderstand me. Your death will not serve me now. What I need from you is a distraction. Let us look on the bright side. You may survive.'

Threats come in different forms. Daniel had heard a few of them in his time. That was one of the worst. 'What are you going to do?'

Perhaps nothing had changed. Perhaps this was what Kant had had in mind all along. His hand went straight to the right pocket and came out with a cigarette lighter.

'No,' whispered Daniel. 'Oh dear God, no. Don't do this.'

A man who could call setting fire to someone a distraction had probably heard a lot of entreaties in his time, and paid scant heed to any of them. He bent over and began gathering straw from the floor into a pile. 'Try not to be alarmed,' he said as he worked. 'Look, I'll put it well away from you. There'll be plenty of time for them to get you out. But while they're doing that, they're not chasing me.'

'You can't...' Daniel's voice cracked and he had to start again. 'You can't start a fire in here! It'll be an inferno in seconds! If you're going to kill me, at least make it quick. I've *been* burnt. I don't – I can't...' He ran out of words. And for all that they were achieving, there was no point struggling for more.

Kant paused in what he was doing and for a moment eyed his captive with something akin to compassion. But practicality – what he'd called the balance of necessities – intervened. He shook his head. 'I'm sorry. Naturally you are afraid. But whoever it is out there won't let you burn. In just a few minutes now you will be free. And so shall I.'

'And what if it isn't the police?' In his agitation Daniel was actually stammering. 'What if it's a couple of teenagers using this place as a Lovers' Lane? You think they're going to risk their lives to get me out? I'm going to die in here! I'm going to burn and I'm going to die!'

'Ah.' The man hadn't thought of that. He

thought about it now, but only briefly. He couldn't know for sure it was the police closing in on him until it was too late, and he wasn't prepared to gamble with his safety. He shrugged dismissively. 'What are the odds? No, you'll be fine.' And he bent and lit the fire.

And the pony snorted and, white-eyed, backed to the limit of its tether. And Daniel let out a wail like a terrified child.

There aren't many retiring violets in the police force, but even among colleagues Jack Deacon's temper was notorious. It's why the whole of Battle Alley, with the exception of the loyal DS Voss and (usually) Superintendent Fuller, referred to him as "The Grizzly". In spite of that, or perhaps because of it, people tended not to notice that his language was not particularly colourful. When he swore it wasn't cutting-edge obscenity but the slightly old-fashioned oaths of his London childhood that he fell back on, and they were just quaint enough these days to have an odd gentility about them.

But there was nothing genteel about what exploded from his lips when his carefully manoeuvred cordon revealed its position with a few jolly bars of military music. Even these tough police officers listened with interest in case there were some in there they hadn't heard before – but only after they were sure it wasn't their mobile sounding off.

Alison Barker might not be a professional stalker like Deacon, or even a semi-pro like Brodie, but she knew instantly the magnitude of what she'd done. It took her possibly three seconds to find the phone and shut it up. After that she stared at the dim pale circle in the darkness that was Brodie's face and was too appalled even to apologise.

Brodie didn't do a lot of swearing either: partly because she had a young daughter and children soak the stuff up like blotting paper, and partly because she didn't have to. She could get all the venom imaginable into a few quite ordinary words. 'You stupid girl,' she hissed, just loud enough for Ally to hear, and Ally burst into tears.

When Deacon had established that none of his borrowed officers was responsible, he spun and found exactly what he was expecting – Brodie on his heels. 'Was that you?'

'It was us,' she agreed with a kind of terse contrition. 'What do you think – any chance he didn't hear?'

Deacon weighed up the distance from where they were to the van in the courtyard, and also the deep silence broken only by his own furious heavy breathing. 'What do *you* think?'

'Sir?' It was one of the firearms officers.

He'd noticed a change in the quality of the light coming from the open door of the horse-box. It was growing stronger, and it was flickering.

For the merest second Brodie tried to tell herself it was an optical illusion. Or the light had been on long enough to weaken the battery, hence the flickering; or just long enough to warm up and brighten. But even as she ran through the options she knew she was fooling herself. She knew what kind of light flickered as it strengthened. 'It's on fire!'

Then they heard the cry, desolate as the night, and it might have been fear or it might have been agony but either way they knew, every one of them, that its author needed help right now. And it didn't matter that they broke their cover at a run, and it didn't matter that for a second the bright rectangle of the doorway framed a leaping figure that landed in the dark and ran. Seconds counted, fractions of a second counted, and every one of them had held a cigarette stub too long or touched a casserole fresh from the oven and knew what a burn felt like. It was no longer a question of containing a dangerous situation. A man was alive inside a burning box, and nothing else mattered until either he was out or he was dead.

In the same way that you tell children never to run with scissors, firearms officers are strongly advised not to run with weapons drawn. However John Wayne makes it look, you can't fire an accurate shot on the move. At a run, you'd be lucky to hit a barn wall from the inside. But, like children, there are times when the urgency of the situation makes it impossible to obey. This was one of those times.

Even so, the guns slowed them down, so that Deacon and Brodie reached the courtyard first. For a big man, Deacon could move fast when he had to. And Brodie, who took a positive pride in never unduly exerting herself, had all the incentive necessary.

They came together, breathless, both ripping off their coats, a couple of metres from the van, with a clear view of leaping flames through the open door. The fire seemed to fill it. Smoke was pouring out of the high-level ventilators, and the vehicle rocked with the thunderous panic of the animal inside.

Deacon grabbed Brodie's arm as she went to climb up. 'You can't go in there!'

'Daniel's in there!'

'What if he can't walk?'

The urgency of the situation notwithstanding, Brodie could see the sense in that. If need be, Deacon could lift Daniel bodily and throw him onto the cobbles in a way that she couldn't. She nodded quickly. 'Be careful.'

'*That* boat has sailed,' grunted Deacon, grabbing both sides of the doorframe and swinging himself up.

Inside, conditions were marginally better than he'd expected. The fire had started – had *been* started – opposite the groom's door precisely in order to be visible and alarming. It would spread, there was too much straw and wood in here for it not to, but it hadn't spread yet.

The frantic pony was in the far stall and Daniel in the nearer, his hands lashed to the breast-bar. His face was white with fear, the eyes stretched behind the thick lenses. 'Jack...'

It was a moment's work to free him. Deacon used his penknife to cut the baler-twine. As his hands came free Daniel's knees gave way and he dropped to the rubber floor, gasping in the smoke and fumes.

Deacon fisted a hand in his clothes and yanked him upright. 'On your feet, little man. You're not hurt, it's just shock – fight it. I don't propose to carry you while you can run.'

Daniel hit the ground like an inept diver, knocking the wind out of himself, and an instant later Deacon landed beside him. They helped one another to their feet and then others were there too, Brodie among them, clutching their arms and dragging them clear. They staggered back from the burning van, the flames filling their eyes, the smoke gnawing at their lungs, their muscles turned to string by the awareness of how narrowly they had escaped.

And then a shriek ripped through their brains like shrapnel, and the horror surged back that there was still a living soul in there, trapped and burning. Daniel spun on the spot, staring back into the flames. He retraced a couple of steps, then stopped. He looked from Brodie to Deacon in terrible distress. His voice cracked. 'We can't leave it in there!'

Brodie took his hand. 'I don't think we have any choice,' she said softly.

'Jack...?'

Deacon shrugged roughly. 'I nearly didn't go in for you, I'm sure as hell not going back for a horse.'

'We can try! We have to try...'

'No,' said Deacon firmly, 'we don't. It's an animal. Nobody's risking their life for an animal.'

'It's too dangerous,' Brodie agreed. 'Any-one who went in there now would likely be kicked to death by a panic-stricken pony. And he'd never get her out. They won't – the fear confuses them, they're too scared to leave a burning building. Isn't that right?' She turned to Alison for support.

The rosy glow of the flames was reflected in the streaks of tears on Ally's thin face.

She'd thought her stupidity had cost a good man his life. Now he was here, singed but safe beside her; but relief was tempered by the knowledge of what was happening, what was going to happen, just a few metres away, before her very eyes unless she screwed them tight shut. And what she didn't see she would hear: the screams of terror and then of agony as the flames consumed the box and its occupant. She whispered, 'Can't we put the fire out?'

'Sure we can,' snarled Deacon. 'With the fire extinguishers my guys carry in their free hands. Look, if we'd brought the cars up there might have been a chance. But it'll take ten minutes to get them, and that's too long to leave that animal to suffer. The kindest thing we can do now is get someone close enough to shoot it.' He strode away, looking for someone with a gun.

Daniel shook his head in despair. 'I'm going to try. I know it's stupid, but I have to at least try.'

'You're going to get yourself killed!' cried Brodie, aghast. 'Jack risked his neck to get you out of there, and you want to go back in? Are you *mad?*'

'Maybe.' He nodded. 'Maybe. But Brodie – I know what she's going through.'

She had no answer to that. He didn't mean it as a reproach, but it slid in under her ribs like one.

Ally said, 'I'll help.'

Daniel stared at her. Then he shook his head again. 'It's too dangerous.'

'Too dangerous for me but not for you? At least I can handle a horse! Listen,' she said urgently, her hands fisted in his clothes, demanding his attention. 'I don't know if we can do this. But if we can't do it together, you sure as hell can't do it alone.'

Without waiting for an answer she was struggling out of her coat. But she didn't throw it down, she tucked it under her arm. 'Listen to me. We need to get the back ramp down. Let me do the slide-bolts – they're tricky if you haven't seen them before. Inside the ramp there'll be some kind of a gate, maybe double ones that fold back to form a chute. The pony's on the left, yes?'

Daniel nodded, surprised that she knew.

'You always travel a single in the offside stall,' she explained briefly. 'Until they reached the Channel, that was the left-hand side. So we go up the right side and duck under the breast-bar. I'll use my coat as a blindfold and untie her. There won't be room to turn her, she'll have to back off. Daniel, you'll need to keep the fire off both of us for as long as you can. If we can calm her down, it won't take half a minute. If we can't we won't be able to do it at all.'

For just a second longer he didn't move. 'Why are you doing this?'

'The same reason you helped me,' she said. 'Because I can.'

'I don't want you to die paying me back.'

'I don't intend to,' she retorted, half laughing, half crying. 'If this isn't going to work you won't see me for sparks.'

He tried to grin back, couldn't. Sick with anticipation, he nodded. 'All right.'

When they reached the rear of the box Brodie was there too. Daniel shook his head. 'Not you.'

'Why not?' she demanded, ready to be offended.

'Because of Paddy.'

She accepted that. 'I'll do the gates, and wait for you here.'

They weren't the only people round the box, but everyone else was watching the flames at the front, and listening to the screams and desperate kicking of the pony inside, and cringing. Perhaps no one else realised there was a bigger door at the back. Certainly no one saw them move towards it. Someone would have stopped them if they had.

Ally was right: Daniel would never have worked out the slide-bolts for himself. She touched the metal cautiously but there was no heat in it yet, which was a good sign. Then she gripped and yanked, and the ramp came down. Even before it touched the cobbles, without further instruction Brodie was reaching for the gates. As she dragged the first one aside Daniel was doing the same with the second.

Just for a second, God knows how, he'd forgotten what it was they were trying to rescue. The flying hooves that had been hammering on the gate didn't stop when the gate was moved – they hammered on Daniel instead, driving into his ribs with enough force to bowl him down the ramp.

'Careful!' yelled Ally.

'Uh-huh,' grunted a winded Daniel.

Then they were inside. Daniel tried to tell himself the situation wasn't as bad as it looked from the courtyard, that the fire which had flared up quickly in the nest of dry straw prepared for it was now growing more slowly as it had to find its own fuel. But there was no doubt that it was growing. Another interesting point was that this was a van, not a trailer. Somewhere, possibly under their feet, was a fuel tank. Daniel had no idea if the van ran on petrol or diesel, but he knew that when fuel tanks explode they go not with a whimper but a bang. Halfway through the box he hesitated.

Ally crashed into him from behind, driving him forward. 'Keep moving!' she yelled. 'We haven't time to think about this.' So he did.

Trying to get away the pony had stretched her rope to a bar like iron. She'd been loaded by professionals: it was fastened with a quick-release knot, but it couldn't release under pressure like that. Ally tugged and tugged at the end and nothing happened. 'She needs to take a step forward.'

Daniel looked at the fire in the front of the box, licking up the timber-lined sides and curling back under the roof, and his eye was white-rimmed like the pony's. 'She's not going to do that!'

'She has to. Or she's dead.'

She flung her coat over Gretl's head and tied the sleeves under her chin, a bit like a baby's bonnet. Daniel couldn't see how blinding the poor creature would help, but it did. Some of the panic went out of her. Her cries turned to desperate gasping snorts, and she stood shaking, stamping her feet; but she stood. Alison, as if unaware of the flames climbing over her, stroked her face and her neck where the butterscotch coat curled with dripping sweat, and spoke gently to her.

Daniel was doing the best he could to fight the fire with his sweater. It wasn't much of a weapon and the fire was winning. 'Now,' he gasped. 'Ally, it has to be now. There is no more time.'

But all Ally said was, 'Shhh.'

All Brodie could see from the rear ramp was the flickering of a fire occulted by its own smoke and by figures moving through it. She couldn't hear their voices over the wild trampling of the pony. She kept her word and stood at the gate, and counted the seconds and the tenths of seconds, and still they didn't come.

Finally she could bear it no longer. She shouted into the burning box, with as much authority as she could muster with her voice quaking, 'You have to come out now, Daniel. You did your best – you have to come out now. Grab Ally and leave. Now! Daniel – please!'

Someone grabbed her elbow tight enough to hurt and it was Deacon who'd hurried to the back of the box, drawn by her yells. Lit by the red and yellow flames his face was gargoyle-twisted with incomprehension. 'They're in there? *You let them go inside?*'

She knew he was going to follow them. She didn't want him to. She thought she was losing Daniel, and that would be unbearable. But what if she lost Deacon too, trying to save him? She hung onto his arm with all her strength. But his strength was the greater, and he cast her off.

His foot was already on the ramp when something changed: the quality of the light coming from the box. A patch of darkness appeared in the middle of it, and grew, and took on the shape of figures. Three of them. Out of hell walked – one of them backwards – a man, a girl and a pony.

Chapter Twenty-Six

Someone found a tank of rainwater in the courtyard and, dunking a coat in it, laid it over the animal's back. It wasn't until later that Deacon discovered the coat was his.

Daniel pulled up his shirt gingerly to examine the brace of semicircular imprints on his middle. 'How do you know if you've cracked a rib?'

'You can't breathe well enough to talk about it,' said Brodie briskly.

'Is everybody all right?' asked Deacon, moving round the little clusters of people. 'Is anyone hurt? Do we need an ambulance? Daniel?'

'I'm fine,' said Daniel – adding, *sotto voce* and with a sidelong glance at Brodie, 'Apparently.'

'Miss Barker?'

'Me too.'

'What about the pony? Do we need a vet?'

'Yes. I don't think she's burnt, at least not seriously, but she'll be in shock – she'll need fluids. We'll need transport for her too.'

He nodded and made the calls. He also summoned a fire engine, though he doubted it would arrive in time to save the van which was now ablaze from breast-bar to breaching. Only once help was on its way did he get round to checking what he thought he already knew. 'I don't suppose anybody got a shot into the bastard who did this?'

A chorus of shaking heads all round. No one had fired at all. The only glimpse anyone had had of him was the leaping figure silhouetted against the flames. After that there was no time to look for him.

'Daniel. You spent a couple of hours with this guy Kant. What can you tell me about him?'

'He's the vet, the one with access to the tranquillizer. We were right about how they were doing it. He put the packages into the pony in Belgium, and they'd just come out the other end when you people announced your arrival with a marching band.'

Ally blushed, her cheeks bright as the flames. 'That was me. Sorry.'

'Don't worry, you redeemed yourself.' Daniel grinned, and she beamed back.

Deacon dragged them back to the matter at hand. 'So he got what he was waiting for and he left. Where would he go?'

'To the factory, I think. He was still intending to deliver the stuff. But that was before you guys showed up. Maybe by now he's on his way home by the shortest route.'

Deacon thought about what Kant had already done, about what Windham had

said about him. 'And leave the job un-
finished? When he's got a rare and valuable
chemical in his pocket? When to bring in
another consignment he'd have to face
Customs again? I don't think so. He'll do
what he said – make for the factory. This
could be their last batch of Scram for a
while: they're not going to waste it.' He
turned expectantly towards Daniel.

'You're going to ask me where the factory
is, aren't you?' guessed Daniel ruefully. 'I'm
sorry, I don't know. He didn't volunteer the
information, and I was too scared to press
him.'

Deacon gave a gruff little chuckle. 'Don't
worry about it. I would have been too.'

Daniel appreciated his kindness, unexpected as it was, but he didn't believe him
for a moment. 'He said if I stopped annoying him he'd let me go. I don't know if he
meant it. He might have done, because he
didn't tell me anything that you wouldn't
already know or could guess. Except...' And
then he stopped.

'What?' asked Deacon.

Watching him, Brodie knew he was struggling with something. Her voice was soft.
'What is it, Daniel?'

On reflection he didn't see why he
shouldn't come straight out with it. It was,
after all, what the girl had thought all along,
and been told wasn't possible. Told, in

essence, to go away and come to terms with the fact that she hadn't lost her father, he'd left her. In time she'd be glad to know that he'd had no choice. 'He said – he gave me to understand – that they killed Stanley Barker.'

Ally took a breath so sharp it sounded like ice cracking.

Deacon pursed his lips reflectively. 'Did he indeed? That was supposed to have been investigated.'

'It was important to them that it looked like an accident,' Brodie said simply.

Deacon sniffed. 'It seems we owe you an apology, Miss Barker. So it was Windham after all? How the hell did he manufacture an alibi that put him on another landmass?'

Daniel shook his head, sprinkling ashes of burnt straw like dandruff. 'I don't think he did. At least, that's what the vet – Kant? – said. He said it wasn't him either. Which means someone else is involved.'

So Voss had been right and he had been wrong. With Kant extracting supplies of the tranquillizer in Germany and Windham transporting it to England, they'd needed a third man to make the pills. Deacon caught himself pretending to have thought so all along: the scowl was for his childishness. 'I suppose, if we find the factory we find the third man. But now we've lost Kant, where do we look for the factory?'

'Windham knows,' suggested Brodie in a low voice.

Deacon chuckled darkly. 'What, you think I'm going to take him behind the bicycle sheds and find out? It doesn't work that way, Brodie. Even playing by *my* rules it doesn't work that way.'

'He told you about Kant. And about this place.'

'He told us what he had to when the alternative was becoming an accessory to murder. He wasn't turning Queen's Evidence – the only one he was trying to help was himself. Now Daniel's safe he'll clam up again.'

'He's already an accessory to murder,' said Ally tightly. It was the first thing she'd managed to say since Daniel's revelation. 'My dad's. If this other guy killed him, why wouldn't he say so?'

'Because he doesn't have to,' Brodie said patiently. 'He can prove that *he* didn't kill your father. He can afford to wait and see how much the police have or manage to get. Of course he's implicated – we know it, and he knows we know it. It may come down to what can be proved. He may claim he was just driving the lorry: where he drove it, and what was in it, was down to Kant. That he never knew what he was carrying.'

'Nobody's going to believe that!' exclaimed Alison in amazement.

'No, they're not,' agreed Deacon. 'But proving the extent of his involvement may be difficult if that's how he plays it. His story may be that he was peripheral to the operation, he wasn't trusted with all the details. That he doesn't know who else was involved, or where the factory is, or anything except that he was told to hold onto particular animals for two or three days and then someone he didn't know came and mucked out their stables for him. Of course the jury won't believe him. But they'll ask me to prove that he was in it up to his neck, and I'm not sure that I can.'

'You mean they've beaten us?' Brodie was staring him straight in the face. 'You mean, after all we've done, all we've been through – all right, all Daniel's been through – they've achieved exactly what they set out to achieve: they've smuggled another consignment of tranquillizer in from Germany and right now it's on its way to their factory to be turned into Scram, and nothing we've done has stopped them or even slowed them up?'

'Welcome to my world,' sighed Deacon wearily. 'We've got a word for operations like this.'

'What word?'

He shook his head. 'It's not a good out-loud word.'

She let it pass. 'Roadblocks?'

'He's not on the road. He's travelling across country, with everything he needs in his coat pocket. If it takes him two days to reach the factory, that's no problem to him. He'll do everything necessary to stay out of sight – not exactly hindered by the fact that there's still nine hours of darkness ahead.'

'Bloodhounds, then?'

'Went out with deerstalker hats and really big magnifying glasses.'

'There must be *something* we can do!'

'There is. I can wrap up here and start interviewing Windham. Miss Barker, I'd like you to stay with the pony until the vet arrives, but after that the three of you can go home. Take my car, someone'll give me a lift.' Then he looked around him. The fire was already dying back, letting in the chill of the night. 'Has anybody seen my coat?'

The on-call vet agreed with Alison's assessment. Brodie was the tallest: he had her hold the bottle above her head as he ran liquid into the pony's veins. There was some singeing to the coat but no burns to the skin. He administered a sedative, got a warm rug onto her and loaded her – with surprisingly little resistance, in view of what had happened last time she was on a box – into the trailer that arrived soon after he did. The driver asked Deacon for a destination.

For a moment Deacon was nonplussed.

He'd have known what to do with a car which had been used to smuggle drugs, but you can hardly book a pony into a police garage. 'Brodie, where were you going to have this thing delivered?'

'Appletree Farm, in Cheyne Warren,' she replied. 'But I don't know if he'll be able to take it tonight. Windham was supposed to keep it for three days first. Dieter may not have a stable ready.'

Deacon chucked his head and snorted, a bit like an irritable horse himself. 'Which kind of raises another point, doesn't it? If Windham has horses in his yard, do we need to make arrangements for them now we've arrested him? Or does he have a wife or a partner to look after them?' He was looking at Ally.

She shook her head. 'He lives alone. But he's abroad with the lorry a lot – he has a couple of local girls coming in to feed and exercise.'

'OK. So we could take the pony there.'

'There won't be anyone there in the middle of the night. I could go with her and get her settled in – put down a bed and make up a meal that'd hold her until the girls show up around eight – but I imagine the yard's locked up.'

Which wasn't what Deacon wanted to hear. 'Well, I can't put it in the Evidence Locker until morning. Will somebody offer me a sensible alternative?'

So Ally did. 'Why don't we take it to Peyton Parvo? I expect Mary's in, but if she isn't I have a set of keys – I can do everything that's necessary.'

It was as good a solution as Deacon could have hoped for. 'Do it.' He thought a little longer. 'I don't suppose it's in any danger now? I shouldn't post a guard on it for fear of someone turning up to...' He wasn't quite sure what, let the sentence hang around until it faded.

Ally smiled. 'What, silence it? Stop it attending an identity parade, prevent it from taking the witness box? I don't think so, Mr Deacon. It's only a pony. It stopped being of any value to anyone the moment it took a million dollar dump.'

He was watching her with half a smile on his lips. He'd misjudged Alison Barker in a number of different ways, but this casual indifference wasn't fooling him. 'Only a pony? So why did you risk your neck for it?'

She hadn't really an answer. 'It was Daniel's idea.'

'It was Daniel's idea that you risk your neck in a burning horse-box while he watched?'

'Don't be silly!'

'So it was Daniel's idea to risk *his* neck in a burning horse-box, and your idea to help him.'

She couldn't argue with that. 'I suppose.'

He shook his head, and if there was disbelief in his gaze there was also respect. 'What is it with women and horses? I know that was a cheap one, but even a better one wouldn't have been worth as much as a family car. You wouldn't have risked being burnt to save a car!'

The girl laughed out loud. 'Of course not. A horse is a living creature. It has a value quite apart from what someone might be prepared to pay for it. An animal's life is cheap, but not to the animal – it's the only one it has. If you want them, you owe it to them – or perhaps not even to them but to whoever's keeping score – that there's some-thing in it for them. You look after them. You treat them decently. You don't watch them burn if there's something you can do about it.'

Deacon went on regarding her for a moment – dirty, soot-stained, her hair tangled in her face. 'Your father teach you that?' She nodded. 'I'd have liked your father.'

She nodded. 'A lot of people did. He was a decent man, a man with a lot of friends. Right up to the moment that he was found face-down in a pond, at which point all the people who'd liked him, all his friends, and all the professionals whose job it was to find out what happened to him, decided he was actually a bit of a coward who'd commit suicide rather than deal with failure. A lot of people let him down, Mr Deacon. The police among them.'

He wasn't a man who took criticism graciously, least of all from members of the public who – this was the irony – he would have given his life to protect. Brodie held her breath.

But Deacon didn't jump down Ally's throat. 'Yes. But we're not done yet.'

Alison travelled with the pony while Brodie drove Deacon's car. Daniel sat so quietly beside her she wondered what he was thinking. Then she realised he wasn't thinking – he was asleep.

He woke with a start as they left the main road and headed into the Three Downs. 'Are you all right?' asked Brodie.

For a second he seemed not to know where he was. Then he let out a ragged sigh. 'Fine.'

'Really?'

He smiled at her. His smile, coming out of a frankly homely face, still did things to the backs of her knees. 'I think so. It got a bit hairy for a while there, but it's over now.'

'He didn't hurt you?'

'He knocked me out. I've still got wool where my brain ought to be. But no – for a drug-smuggler and accessory to murder, he was a civilised man.'

Brodie thought a little while. Then she said, 'You do know what you did back there?'

'Oh yes,' said Daniel tiredly. 'I've got the singed eyebrows to prove it.'

'Seriously. You walked *into* a fire.'

He shook his yellow head. 'That wasn't the clever part. The clever part was walking back out again.'

She stopped the car and put on the interior light so she could look at him properly. 'I'm not sure either was particularly clever. Clever isn't the issue. The point is, you managed to do it. Six months ago you couldn't have done. Six months ago you couldn't have toasted marshmallows over a bonfire.'

He shrugged his narrow shoulders awkwardly. 'With marshmallows you have a choice. When someone – something – something alive is in pain, you don't. You do what has to be done. That's all it was.'

But Brodie knew better. 'Six months ago you couldn't have done what you did tonight if it had been *me* trapped in a burning trailer! You'd have wanted to, you'd have tried to, but you couldn't have done it. I don't think you realise how much better you are these days. How much stronger.'

He hadn't given it any thought. Now he did he had to concede she was right, and a faint smugness crept into his smile. 'Maybe

I'll end up working as a fireman.'

'Fireman be damned. Maybe you'll end up working as a teacher.'

For the first time in two years it was possible to contemplate. He enjoyed his tutoring and it paid the bills, but it wasn't what he'd wanted to do since childhood, what he'd trained for, what he'd been good at. Last time he tried to return to the class-room the panic attacks had unmanned him. Now there seemed a chance that next time he tried it might go better.

It was gone midnight when the horse-box turned into Barker & Walbrook's yard in Peyton Parvo. There were no lights showing. Alison disappeared around a corner and a moment later three big lamps high on the walls came on orange and started brightening first to pink and then to white. She returned to the car. 'Stay here a minute. I'll let Mary know what's happening, then I'll sort out a stable.'

Another minute and a light came on in the flat above the office. The visitors waited while Mary Walbrook climbed into her working clothes and then she and Ally set to with bales of straw and feed buckets and hay-nets. In no time Gretl was installed in her stable, a little drowsy from the sedative but essentially unharmed by either her long journey or her close shave.

In a fit of largesse Brodie wrote a cheque

for the transport. She thought she'd be able to claim it back from Deacon, but if not it was probably the least she could do to make up for the wasted effort of, so it seemed, half the police on the South Coast. It had been an expensive debacle, always one bee short of a sting.

When the trailer had left, the four of them stood at the stable door watching Gretl eat.

'Let me get this right,' said Mary. 'They were smuggling drugs *inside* her?'

Daniel nodded. 'In rubber canisters about so big.' He spread the fingers of one hand.

'How many?'

'Three. At least, three came out the other end, and he seemed satisfied with that.'

'He?'

'Kant. The vet who was working with Windham.'

The woman shook her head bemusedly. 'I never heard the like of it. I wonder how long *that* had been going on?'

'As long as we were getting sick and dead horses from Johnny Windham,' Ally said bitterly.

Understanding dawned. 'You think *that's* why...'

'Some of the canisters leaked,' said the girl shortly, 'and some of them split open. When the horse got a trickle of tranquillizer into its gut it got sick. When it got the whole load it died.'

'But the vet blamed a virus.' Mary thought about that. 'Of course, they always blame a virus if they don't know what's going on. And we never suspected...'

'*You* never suspected,' said Alison. 'Dad did. That's why they killed him.'

Mary put an arm around her shoulders. 'Alison, you know what the police said...'

'Actually,' said Brodie, 'Ally's right. She was right all along, only no one was willing to listen. It seems Stanley got suspicious about the sick horses and either he worked it out or he was so close to doing that they had to shut him up. Kant as good as said so.'

Mary Walbrook stared hard at Daniel. 'Is that true? He told you they killed Stanley?'

Daniel nodded. 'Not in so many words. But that was his meaning, yes. He wanted me to know.'

'*Why?*'

'To scare the living daylights out of me,' said Daniel honestly. 'Got to say, it worked.'

But Mary was looking at Alison. 'Ally – I don't know how to apologise. I thought it was just the grief talking. I thought you were looking for a conspiracy because the truth hurt too much. I am desperately sorry. You had the right to expect better from me.'

The girl linked an arm through hers, hugging it. 'It's all right. It was a reasonable thing to think. You were kind to me, and maybe that mattered more than believing me.'

'But the rest of it... They tried to *kill* you. And still we kept telling you – *I* kept telling you – you were making it up.' Her voice was hollow with regret. 'I can't imagine how that must have made you feel.'

The girl chuckled. 'Pretty crappy. But it's over now. I suppose.' She looked questioningly at Brodie. 'Or will it all start again as soon as the dust has settled?'

Brodie pulled a face. 'I can tell you what you want to hear, or I can tell you the truth.'

'The truth.'

'Yes, it'll happen again. Someone else will produce the same drug by the same means and smuggle it in the same way. There are enough horses travelling between Britain and Europe, and more than enough profit in the equation, that someone will try to make it work where Kant and Windham failed. Maybe the German authorities will be able to tighten up access to the tranquillizer, but it's a legitimate drug – you can't expect them to take it off the market because some acid-heads in England are getting high on the stuff.'

'So what did we achieve?' asked Alison softly.

'It'll be someone else. Not Kant and not Windham. Kant'll be on the run, because if he goes home the police will be waiting for him. He won't be able to practice, and if he can't practice he can't get hold of the tranquillizer. We've put him out of business. And we've put Windham behind bars. That's what you set out to do, and you've done it.'

'For taking a backhander to look the other way.' She sounded at once angry and disconsolate. 'It isn't enough.'

'No, it isn't,' agreed Brodie. 'It won't be enough for Jack either. He doesn't want to promise you something he's not sure he can deliver, but he'll do everything in his power – and probably some things beyond his powers – to bring Windham to justice. For drug-smuggling, and for complicity in your father's murder. Even if he didn't push him in the pond, he had common cause with whoever did and Jack'll prove it.'

The girl nodded and looked away. 'So I may never know who killed my father. I know why – we all know why now, no one's going to go on thinking it was the act of a coward, and that's worth having. But if it wasn't Windham and it wasn't Kant then it was the third man, and we don't know who that is. What if we never know? The chances are that, when somebody finds a fresh supply of that tranquillizer and sets about manufacturing Scram again, it'll be him. The man who murdered my father. And it's probably someone I know.'

Brodie wished she could tell her she was wrong. But she couldn't.

She caught Daniel yawning. She'd had a long day but his had been even more trying. 'Come on, it's time I got you home. Ally, are you coming or are you going to stay here?'

'I'll stay here, bring Mary up to date on all the details. If that's OK?'

'Of course,' said Mary Walbrook. 'Listen, this changes things. If your father died trying to protect this business, you're entitled to more than if he'd given up on it. We're going to have to talk that through, with solicitors if you want. I never wanted to deprive you of anything that was fairly yours.'

'I know that,' said Alison Barker quietly. 'I always knew it. Don't worry: you're not losing equity, you're gaining a partner.'

Brodie took Daniel by the shoulders and steered him towards the car. 'Come on, PyroMan, before your spark goes out.'

He was asleep before she reached the road.

Twenty minutes later, as the lights of Dimmock hove into sight over the last swell of the Downs, he was awake again. Brodie was aware of him stirring beside her, lifting his head as if it was heavy, hauling himself out of his slump. 'Nearly home,' she said.

Under the fringe of bright hair his forehead was creased. His lips formed a sort of question mark. 'Brodie,' he said uncertainly, 'stop the car.'

'Feeling sick?' she asked sympathetically,

doing as he asked. 'It's just reaction.'

But he made no move to get out, just sat there knitting his brows, puzzling away in the depths of his intelligent light grey eyes. He shook his head slowly. 'Something's wrong.'

'What sort of something?'

'I'm not sure.'

'OK.' Brodie Farrell wasn't the most patient woman on the planet so it wasn't simple kindness keeping the sarcasm from her voice. She was giving him room to do what he did best – think – and keeping an open mind while he did it.

Perhaps it was that open-mindedness, that state of receptivity that she reserved for Daniel and almost no one else, that occasionally allowed what he was thinking to resonate in her own brain and give the impression to outsiders that she was psychic. It irritated the hell out of Deacon when they did this.

She said slowly, 'We should have brought Ally with us.'

Daniel was nodding, carefully. 'I think so too. But why?'

'Because she isn't safe where she is?'

That was what Daniel's gut was trying to tell him. He struggled to understand. 'Why should anyone hurt Ally now? Now everything she believed has been shown to be true? She was a danger to them while she was trying to get the police to investigate her father's death, but she isn't any more. With Windham behind bars and Kant on the run, the only one who could threaten her now is the third man. And he'd be crazy to stick his head above the parapet when none of us knows who or where he is. Ally should be safer now than she's been for months.'

'But she isn't, is she?' said Brodie softly. 'We're not imagining this – if we both feel this way it's for a reason. Something we've seen or heard is ringing alarm-bells in both your brain and mine.'

'What are we going to do?'

Brodie gave a weary sigh and cranked the steering-wheel round. 'What do you think? We're going back.'

Chapter Twenty-Seven

Brodie found herself driving faster and faster, even though she didn't understand why. It was enough that some part of her brain had worked it out, at least as far as knowing what needed to be done. They could work on the reason together as she drove.

'Something doesn't fit,' she insisted. 'Somebody said something or did something that should have meant something to us. To *us* – both of us, we were both there. And neither of us picked it up.'

'Not the vet, then,' said Daniel, flinching as she took a corner fast enough to leave some of Deacon's tyre-rubber behind. 'Alison herself?'

'Or Mary.'

'Mary?' Daniel echoed doubtfully. 'What could she know that we don't?'

They thought about it. That was important: they thought about it and didn't dismiss it out of hand. But everything they knew about Mary Walbrook painted her as a largely benign and in any event peripheral figure in the drama. Alison Barker's father's partner, her last remaining friend, who'd visited the girl in hospital and seemed worried about her and...

And given the impression that nothing Ally said should be entirely trusted.

Brodie said slowly, 'Mary Walbrook was there or thereabouts all the time this was going on. Maybe Windham deceived her too.'

Daniel looked straight ahead, down the track of the lights. 'That's possible,' he said carefully.

There were, of course, other possibilities. Brodie said, 'Or maybe she was in on it with him.'

Though he rather liked the woman, Daniel tried to put that out of his mind and made himself concentrate on what they knew or could reasonably infer. 'This has been going on for several months at least. From when Barker & Walbrook first started having problems with horses Windham was bringing them from Europe. But she and Barker were partners for fifteen years. Why would she turn her back on that to go in with Windham?'

To Brodie the answer was so obvious she was embarrassed having to spell it out. She wouldn't have had to for anyone else she knew. But to Daniel, loyalty was something so precious he couldn't imagine anyone casually throwing it aside.

'The money of course,' she said. 'There was the potential to make a great deal of it. I mean, a real, genuine, never-work-again fortune. And then, Stanley Barker was a fat man in his fifties, and Johnny Windham is a fit man in his thirties.'

Daniel stared at her. 'You think they're lovers?'

Brodie shrugged. 'Why not? They're two attractive people – unless you have problems with their morals, and obviously they wouldn't have with one another's. It would explain why Windham gave up Kant but wouldn't give up the third man. The third man isn't a man, he's a woman. Mary Walbrook.'

Daniel hadn't got past the thought of

them as lovers. 'She's older than him.'

Brodie laughed out loud. 'So? Women wear better than men. Haven't you figured that out yet? We're stronger and we live longer. As toyboys go, Johnny Windham is already pushing his sell-by date.'

Daniel said nothing.

Brodie left him to ponder, followed her own train of thought. 'The problems with the horses may not have been confined to Barker & Walbrook but they certainly bore the brunt of them, to the point that they almost destroyed the business. Why? Not because Windham had a grudge against Stanley but because he had a friend in the yard who could collect the canisters and cover for any problems. Makes sense?'

She waited for a response but he wasn't ready to give one yet. That didn't stop her speculating. If Daniel was too reluctant to think the worst of people, perhaps Brodie was too ready. 'But Mary wasn't the senior partner. When Stanley realised what was going on he was going to put a stop to it. He didn't call the police precisely because it was Mary who was involved, and he couldn't shop Windham without shopping her too. So he threw Windham off the yard and then he had it out with her.'

Daniel had dragged himself back to the present and rejoined the conversation. 'And five days later he was dead and she was running the business. We know where Windham was, Kant says he was at home – but Mary was on the yard the night Stanley died. She was the one who found him.'

Brodie's cheeks were pale and hollow. 'Damn it, it does all hang together, doesn't it?' Then her eyes flared wide. 'So Mary not only killed Stanley, she tried to kill Ally!'

Daniel was nodding slowly. 'She had access to the house where Ally was staying. She brought her some clothes to the hospital, and later she left her a note on the kitchen table. She had a key. Ally hasn't many friends left: she left a spare key with one of the few she thought she could depend on.'

And then, almost before he'd finished the sentence, he slid away from it: tuned out, left the building and went to that place in his head where facts buzzed round like uranium atoms in a nuclear pile, banging off one another in their urgency to create a chain reaction.

Noticing, Brodie frowned. 'Daniel?'

He stopped her questions with a spread hand. 'Just a second. That's it – that's what was bothering me. She knew I'd talked to Kant. Rather, she knew he'd talked to me and wanted to know what he'd said. How did she know that?'

'I told her,' said Brodie.

He shook his yellow head – a little too emphatically: sparing him a sideways glance

Brodie saw his eyes flicker as the barbs of concussion twisted in his brain. He didn't let it distract him. 'No, you didn't. You were talking about what *we* knew, what *we'd* found out. But she looked straight at me and asked what he'd said. The only way she could have known I'd spent the evening with him was if he told her.'

'Kant?' Brodie's voice soared. 'You think he phoned her?'

'If they're partners, I think it's the first thing he'd do after he got away from Sparrow Hill. To tell her there'd been trouble, but he'd got the consignment and he'd deliver it as soon as he could make his way to Peyton Parvo. Brodie – that's where the factory is. A warren of outbuildings, power, running water, and now nobody around the place except herself. She didn't move into the flat there because she couldn't afford to live anywhere else: she did it because that's the centre of operations and she couldn't afford not to be there. And she couldn't have Alison move in there, even temporarily, for the same reason. Alison asked her after she lost the house and Mary said no.'

Brodie was struggling to take it all in. 'But tonight she didn't argue when Ally suggested staying over.'

'She wasn't really in a position to. We were bound to wonder why if she did. Also, this thing is moving towards the end-game.

351

Windham's under arrest – she can't count on him protecting her forever – and Kant's on the run. She needs to tie up the loose ends quickly – take what she can salvage and get out. And Kant's on his way there right now. I don't think Ally's life is worth tuppence to either of them.'

She couldn't in all conscience drive any faster – Ship Coomb dived away from the side of the road into a boulder-strewn chasm and if she killed them both Alison was as good as dead too. She glanced at her watch. They were still minutes from Barker & Walbrook's yard. Werner Kant might still be an hour away, or he might already be there.

'Call Jack,' she said, fumbling for her phone. 'He may be closer than we are.'

When she wasn't driving, Brodie could make a call on autopilot, her fingers going to the right buttons of their own accord. The last man in the civilised world not to own a mobile phone, Daniel always viewed the little thing with deep suspicion and looked to her for prompts, and seemed surprised when someone answered.

Expecting to hear Brodie's voice, Deacon was irritated to hear Daniel's. '*Now* what?'

Daniel didn't have the mental stamina left for an argument. If he told Deacon what to do, either he'd do it or he wouldn't; but Daniel knew Deacon pretty well by now and he thought he'd do it and ask questions, and probably do a lot of shouting, afterwards. 'We're heading back to Peyton Parvo and we need you to meet us there. ASAP. Mary Walbrook's involved in this. I think Kant's on his way there too, so you should probably bring some fire power.' Daniel had never used the term *fire power* before. It was oddly invigorating. 'And we left Alison there, and I think they'll want her dead.' Then he rang off and – first asking how – switched off the phone.

Then he cast Brodie a worried little glance. 'We'd better be right about this.'

She was past caring. 'If we're wrong and Jack turns up with the Seventh Cavalry, it'll be embarrassed smiles and apologies all round. If we're right and do nothing, Alison's going to die.'

Because that was the only likely outcome if she was there when someone who'd set fire to a horse-box with a man and a pony inside arrived with a consignment of illegal drugs. They couldn't hope to make her death look like another accident. But they had eight or nine hours before she'd be missed, which was time enough to dismantle the chemistry-set that was the Scram factory and pack it into Mary Walbrook's trailer hitched to her Land Rover. These were, Brodie had realised, immensely versatile little vehicles. A pony, a corpse or an illicit cottage-industry: if it needed moving and you didn't want it on show, a horse-box was your transport of choice.

'We're not wrong,' said Daniel in a low voice. 'It's the missing link, the bit that explains all the other bits that didn't quite fit.'

'Like what?'

'Like half an hour ago, when we drove into her yard with two strange cars and a trailer she wasn't expecting, and turned on all the lights, and even after that Ally had to get her out of bed. She lives alone there, quarter of a mile from the nearest neighbours, with a yard full of valuable animals. She should have been at the front door with a double-barrelled shotgun before we'd got out of the car.'

'She was asleep,' said Brodie reasonably.

'Like hell. If one of those horses coughs in the night she'll hear it. She was pretending not to have heard us because she didn't want it to look as if she knew we were on our way.'

He was right: it made sense. 'So the factory was in the yard all along?'

'I think so. She ran the yard, after all – Stanley lived in his big house miles away but Mary had a cottage just down the road. Like Windham, she probably had a local girl coming in to help with the horses, but nobody'd think to question her if there was a locked shed somewhere that only she had the key to. Certainly not after Stanley was dead and Alison was living in Dimmock.'

The scenario was evolving in his mind even as he described it. 'That's why it took months from the first supplies of the German tranquillizer being smuggled in – and we know when that was because it was the start of Stanley's problems with sick horses – to the first casualties of Scram overdose arriving at Dimmock General. Production had to be put on hold because the police were looking into Stanley's death. Even after they left, Alison was still insisting he'd been murdered. That's why they had to try and shut her up. If somebody listened to her, the police would come back and turn the yard upside down.'

'Mary was never going to persuade anyone that Alison fell into the water jump too,' said Brodie, picking up the thread. 'But people always assume a drug overdose is misadventure. If she was found dead in a house in Dimmock where she was living alone, depressed and irrational after her father's supposed suicide, and the autopsy found Scram in her system, the only reason the police would even talk to Mary would be to express their condolences. If she'd died when she was supposed to, the Scram operation would have run for year after profitable year.'

'But she didn't,' said Daniel, 'and now

they're going to lose everything they can't actually carry away with them. Except that the idea is still good. Give them time and they'll reappear in another part of the country under other names, and instead of dealing they'll be keeping show-jumpers or eventers or brood mares: anything that might go abroad on a regular basis. They'll find someone else on the continent who has access to the catalyst – after all, it won't be on trial forever, pretty soon it'll be widely available – and six months from now they'll be back in business. And the first anyone will know is when the clubs are suddenly flooded with tabs of Scram.'

By now they had crossed the coomb onto Menner Down and Peyton Parvo, not a light lit, lay in the blackness below. 'How are we going to handle this?' asked Daniel. 'If we get there before Jack?'

Brodie considered. 'I suppose that depends on whether we get there before Kant. If we do, I suggest we bluff it out. Say Jack sent us back for Alison because he needs our statements down at Battle Alley tonight. If Mary's on her own she won't challenge that. It could be true.'

'And if she isn't alone?'

'That could be harder,' admitted Brodie.

'Maybe you should stay in the car,' suggested Daniel in a low voice. 'Then if it all goes pear-shaped you can call for help.'

'Help's already on its way,' she retorted brusquely. 'And what the hell makes you think I'll hide in the car while you and Ally are in danger?'

He tried what had served before. 'You have Paddy to think of.'

She curled her lip at him. 'That only worked because it was an animal. This time it's my friends in danger. You don't really think I'll stand back and watch?'

'No,' Daniel said honestly.

'I should bloody well think not,' sniffed Brodie.

Her first instinct was to leave the car out of earshot of the yard. But subterfuge would immediately cast doubt on their cover-story. Whereas if they seemed casual and tired and a little irritated, if Alison herself had not been having parallel thoughts and jumped too eagerly through the escape hatch, above all if Mary Walbrook was alone, they would get away with it.

But there was no way to be sure what they would find. If they could talk Ally out of the house they would. If they couldn't, it was impossible to know how this would end. At least Deacon knew where they were, and why, and was – she was sure of this – on his way. And anyway they had to try. With the girl in imminent peril and no sign of the relief column, they had to try.

Brodie cast Daniel a last sidelong glance before they got out of the car. 'What do you think? Can we do this?'

'If we have to.'

She had just one last snippet of advice. 'Remember, it isn't lying if it means getting her out of there without a fight.'

'Yes it is,' he retorted sharply. Then, relenting: 'It's in a good cause. I can lie in a good cause.'

'Can you?'

'Yes,' he said firmly. 'Probably. At least... Oh what the hell,' he snorted, 'let's find out.'

Chapter Twenty-Eight

Talking loudly, grumbling about the inconvenience, they presented themselves at Mary Walbrook's front door and knocked. There were still lights on in the flat: they were unsure if that was a good sign. Brodie raised her voice and called up, 'It's only us. I'm sorry to disturb you again but Jack's sent us back for Ally. He wants statements from the three of us tonight.'

She wondered if that would serve. Would Mary Walbrook know that by *Jack* she meant the head of Dimmock CID? But if she made it clearer and less casual, wouldn't it be obvious that she was using his name as a weapon? She decided, on balance, this was one of those occasions when less is more.

Anyway, they were about to find out. They heard steps on the wooden stairs inside, then the door opened. It wasn't Alison, as Brodie had hoped, but at least it wasn't Kant. Mary Walbrook was wearing a disapproving frown. 'The police want to talk to Alison again? Tonight? She's exhausted, she's on her way to bed.'

'I know,' said Brodie apologetically, 'I was heading for mine as well. But they're adamant. They need the statements as the basis for a warrant.' She had no idea if there was any truth in this but the words had the ring of authenticity.

The woman gave an irritable sigh and stepped back from the door. 'I suppose you'd better come in. Alison,' she called over her shoulder, 'you have to get dressed again. You're needed in town.' She turned and led the way back upstairs.

For a second Brodie hesitated to follow. But success was within reach, she wasn't going to jeopardise it now. She set her jaw and went on up, Daniel at her heels.

Right up to the moment that Walbrook opened the living-room door and Alison was inside pulling on her sweater, Brodie half expected to be jumped from behind with a guttural yell of *'Achtung!'* They hadn't

359

wasted much time, either getting here in the first place or getting back, and the vet was on foot when he left Sparrow Hill. But he could have hijacked a car within minutes, in which case it was conceivable that he'd got here first.

But Ally was climbing into her clothes, not gagged with parcel-tape and roped to a dining chair, so it seemed he was still on his way. With luck, there'd be a reception committee waiting when he got here, but the main thing was to get Ally away. 'Step on it,' growled Brodie, 'the night's not getting any younger.'

Ally looked up in surprise at her manner. 'I don't understand. Why didn't Mr Deacon say he wanted statements before we left Sparrow Hill?'

'Because he had other things on his mind. Because he doesn't see why anyone should get some sleep when he's not going to. I don't know: ask him yourself. But get a move on, because I really, really want to go home.'

'OK – I'm coming.' Ten minutes after they trooped up the narrow stairs they were trooping down them again, and then they were outside and still no one had raised an objection. 'Mary,' the girl said over her shoulder, 'I'm sorry about all this. Thanks for your help. I'll call you in the morning.'

'Sure,' yawned Mary Walbrook. 'I'll be here.'

And then they were in the car, with the lights of the yard swinging round behind them and the darkness of the Downs sweeping in.

Daniel let out a breath he'd been holding, or thought he had, for ten minutes. 'Well, that was easier than I was expecting.'

'It didn't feel *that* easy,' muttered Brodie, wiping a dew of sweat from her lip.

Framed in the mirror, Alison's face was a study in puzzlement. 'What are you talking about?'

There was no reason not to tell her now – or only one, and Brodie was too tired and enervated to be kind. 'She's part of it. With Windham and the vet. We think it was Mary who killed your father.'

The silence grew like a balloon, stretching and growing thin until an explosion was only a breath away. Daniel twisted in his seat, reaching for the girl as if his gaze had been a steadying hand. 'I'm sorry, Ally. We could be wrong about it but I really don't think so. That's why we had to get you out of there. It was nothing to do with Detective Superintendent Deacon. We think Kant's on his way there now. We didn't want you to be there when he arrives.'

Her thin young face was a battleground for all the different kinds of information she was processing. Anger and a sense of vindication over her father; disbelief, shock and grief over her friend, because betrayal on that scale is a kind of bereavement; and a tremulous relief at how closely she had shaved disaster again. The poor girl couldn't decide if her guardian angel was working overtime to keep her safe or should be sacked without a reference for letting her get into these situations in the first place.

Daniel said gently, 'It's over now. You're safe, and the people who hurt you are going to pay. It won't bring your father back, but at least his murder won't be swept under the carpet.'

She began to cry. Soft as snowfall, desolate as a lost child. After a moment Daniel touched Brodie's arm, and she stopped the car and he climbed into the back with the sobbing girl and put his arm around her. Brodie drove on.

The road crossed the black maw of Ship Coomb and turned along its flank, heading for Dimmock and the sea. Brodie felt her eyes closing, had to shake herself awake. 'Fifteen minutes,' she said aloud, 'and we'll be home.' But no one answered. On the back seat Alison had stopped crying and was resting on Daniel's shoulder. Daniel too was drowsing, his yellow head parked protectively over her dark one.

A fog was coming up from the Channel, smearing the bright steel of the moon-shot water and turning the pinprick lights of the distant ships to shades of pink. The outlines of the hills were growing fuzzy. The road ahead had a strange amorphous quality in the rosy headlights so that she couldn't see for sure which way it turned. She was driving slower and slower, trying to puzzle it out. The steep-sided little gorge was too close to the offside wheels to risk guessing. Her chin bounced off her chest again.

Something was wrong.

She steered Deacon's big car to the side of the road and put on the handbrake. Even to herself her voice sounded odd, thin and breathy. 'Daniel, you're going to have to drive. I'm not feeling very well.'

When there was no reply she tried again. 'Daniel, wake up!' But he didn't, and neither did Alison. With considerable effort she turned in her seat and prodded his knee. But he was miles away, with no prospect – perhaps with no means – of returning. It took almost more strength than Brodie had left to get back in her seat.

Her mind wasn't working well but it was working better than her body. When she had the answer she let out a hollow little moan. 'Oh, you bastard!'

So Kant had reached Peyton Parvo ahead of them. Alison hadn't seen him because Mary had packed her off to bed while the man worked at dismantling the secret factory. When he was finished they'd have

363

dealt with her together before vanishing into the night.

But he'd heard their car return, seen them go to the door and heard what they said to Walbrook, and he'd guessed what it meant: that the time he'd thought they had to get out of the area was in the process of shrinking. Possibly to just a few minutes.

What he couldn't know was whether Daniel and his tall friend had already alerted the police to their suspicions or were waiting to see what they found at the yard. So much had gone wrong already today that they might have been reluctant to cry 'Wolf!' again, were simply acting on their own initiative. Which raised the attractive possibility that he could, by silencing them, regain his lead, those eight hours before any of them would be missed that was his buffer against disaster.

He'd had to think quickly, but he'd already proved adept at that. When they went up to the flat he'd slipped a Trojan Horse into their car. Something simple, unsophisticated but effective. Something he'd have with him: ether or chloroform would do, but probably the tranquillizer that all this was about would too. Somewhere under the seats was a rag soaked in the stuff. He'd thought she'd crash the car and solve all his problems at a stroke.

Well, she hadn't. She'd brought it to a controlled halt, and if she could open the window or door she could probably get enough fresh air in here to revive herself. If she couldn't, there was possibly enough vapour to kill them all. On these roads at this time of night, the chances of being rescued by a passing Samaritan were vanishingly small.

Deacon's car had electric windows. She couldn't remember where the switch was. She'd used it a dozen times, but now that it mattered she couldn't find it. She dipped the headlights and washed the windscreen, but the windows remained resolutely shut. She tried to open the door instead.

It was ridiculous. The handle was right there at her elbow. Brodie couldn't lift her arm enough to reach it. She watched her hand twitch laxly in the hazy moonlight and knew they were all going to die here if she couldn't make it do what she wanted.

She concentrated as she'd never concentrated before. Each muscle in turn she identified in her mind and issued with its instructions. Her upper arm to pull her elbow back. Her lower arm to drop her hand down beside her thigh. Her wrist to rotate and put her fingers where they could snare the handle, and the fingers themselves to lock onto it and pull. And pull. And when nothing happened, to pull harder. She felt a wetness on her face that was the tears of frustration. Salvation was inches away – but death was right here, in the car with them, and she was the only one left awake and she hadn't the strength to save them.

And then she felt the dull click through her fingers that was the lock turning, and the door edged away from her. Just a centimetre or so – but a centimetre all the way up, and it let the night air in. She inhaled. It tasted of champagne.

Then there were lights behind her, the deep throaty rumble of an engine, footsteps and someone standing beside the door. She tried to turn her head, to explain. No words came. Never mind, she thought, how much explanation does it need? You find three people unconscious in a car, you don't start a discussion, you call an ambulance.

As long as he doesn't shut the door again while he's waiting for it.

He didn't. He opened it a little further. He said, in a soft guttural accent, 'You must be Mrs Farrell. And' – looking in the back – 'Miss Barker and my friend Mr Hood. All my favourite people in one car.'

Brodie had been in desperate situations before, but never so desperate or so helpless. She couldn't have got out and run if he'd held the door for her. She couldn't have fought him off if he'd tied one hand behind his back. And she was in the best shape of the three of them. All their lives depended on her.

We are so dead, she thought.

And she *was* afraid – God knows she was afraid – but the fear was not the enormous, smothering, crippling burden she might have expected. Almost as if, finding it too big to deal with, her mind put it on one side with a note attached suggesting she try again later. A sort of promise to herself to be really, really frightened if she was spared to be. In the meantime she was preternaturally calm, analytical even, finding refuge from a terrifying, and brief, future in a last attempt to manipulate the present.

She said – whispered, rather, even the power of speech was failing her – 'You don't have to do this. Keep moving. They don't know where to find you.'

'Well, that may be true,' Werner Kant replied amiably. 'Or it may not. You may have informed the police of your suspicions before attempting to rescue Miss Barker. In any event, clearly they were not close enough to help. So perhaps you are right. For myself I do not need to do this.

'But Mrs Farrell, a man has obligations to his friends. You recognise this: you would not be here otherwise. I have obligations to my friends also. This regrettable incident, which cannot be laid at either of their doors – Miss Walbrook is even now speaking to Dimmock Police Station, notifying them that you are on your way, while Mr Windham has the even better alibi of being in a police cell – will seriously damage the case against them. Detective Superintendent Deacon may find himself in that most trying situation for any policeman, of knowing much more than he can prove.'

He failed to hide the satisfaction in his voice. But then, he wasn't trying very hard.

'Also, of course, his superiors will remove him from the case. It would be improper to allow him to continue with an investigation which has cost the lives of his mistress and her friends. A man, even a policeman, must be allowed to grieve.'

Brodie was no longer thinking straight enough to judge if his optimism was well-founded. What she knew absolutely was that it made sense to him, that he wouldn't be dissuaded by appeals to his conscience, his better nature, even his sense of self-preserv-ation. He'd thought the ramifications through quickly, because there hadn't been much time available, but thoroughly enough to satisfy himself as to his best course of action. He wasn't going to reconsider now.

Which at least spared her from spending her last dregs of energy arguing with a man who wouldn't be moved. She wrinkled her lip at him. 'Bastard.'

He had a rag ready. He wafted it close to Brodie's face – not close enough to leave its mark on her skin – and she felt her consciousness slipping once again.

Kant reached past her to make some adjustments in the car – turning the wheel to the right, taking off the handbrake. Then he opened the boot and removed something from behind the back seat. Then Brodie heard the vehicle behind her rev up and felt the jolt of a soft collision. Mary Walbrook's Land Rover, she supposed, the bumper padded to avoid damage to Deacon's rear-end. Deacon didn't go in for runabouts, his car was big and it was solid – but nothing short of a bin-lorry would be big and solid enough to resist a Land Rover.

Kant was right, Deacon would know this wasn't an accident. Losing three witnesses in one car crash was the sort of bad luck that would make even a very bad policeman ask questions. It had been a long day, and anyone could fall asleep at the wheel or misjudge a turn in someone else's car, but the circumstances were such that murder was a much more likely cause. But what could he prove? Only that, if they were run off the road, it wasn't by either Johnny Windham or Mary Walbrook.

Her mind slowing, Brodie had just enough awareness left to realise she had under-estimated these people. She'd thought they wouldn't risk faking another accident and so would run rather than fight. Now it was too late she knew that Mary Walbrook had no intentions of fleeing. She was talking to Battle Alley in the full knowledge that the time, duration and place of origin of her phone call would be recorded and refute absolutely any attempt to blame her for the crash. By the time the remains of Deacon's car and its passengers were found and squad-cars were squealing to a halt in the yard at Peyton Parvo, there would be nothing left to find there. Kant would have finished removing the evidence and moved on. By the time of Alison's funeral, at which Mary Walbrook would be the prime mourner in a smart new hat, he would have re-established the factory in some anonymous lock-up somewhere, with enough catalyst in the three plastic canisters recovered from Gretl to pay the rent for about a thousand years.

Brodie fought the creeping paralysis, struggled to use her last moments of will in defiance. If she could steer ... if she could pull on the hand-brake... But her hands stayed limp by her sides, deaf to the urgings of her brain.

Now the car was moving. As luck would have it – and it was purely luck, she'd stopped where the car came to a halt – it was on level ground where the road took a breather between two sharp descents. Not that it mattered. The Land Rover was well capable of pushing until either it picked up speed or ran over the edge of Ship Coomb, whichever came first.

Something else came first. At first she thought it was another effect of the knock-out drops: that after the rosy fog came the dazzling light. It was a couple of moments before she realised it was real, that it was headlamps. The vehicle was coming up the shoulder of the Downs from Dimmock, illuminating the drama like a stage-set.

God alone knows what the driver'll make of it, thought Brodie desperately. But if he only stops, or gets in the way, or takes a damn good look as he drives past, maybe it'll be enough. One fresh witness to replace three past their sell-by dates.

Or maybe all he would achieve, this inno-cent passer-by wanting to know why one car was pushing another towards a gorge, would be his own death. Half of Brodie was silently begging him to stop and help, the other half thought it would be the same for her and better for him if he drove on.

He didn't drive on. He didn't pull over and watch either, nor did he get out and remonstrate with the man in the Land Rover. Unhesitatingly he drove straight at the front of Deacon's car.

It was a big strong car, but with one vehicle pushing from behind and another impacting in front it jerked and shuddered, and the bodywork twisted and groaned, and some of the walnut trim popped off the dashboard and landed in Brodie's lap. And then it stopped, with the offside front wheel already over the hazard markings on the side of the road, just metres from the drop into Ship Coomb.

Kant might have gone on trying. But a moment comes when an intelligent man admits that luck is against him, and for the vet that moment came now. The Land Rover crashed into reverse and shot back up Menner Down as fast as the gearbox would take it. At an open gateway its lights slewed as it threw a three-point turn, then it was gone.

At that point Brodie had no idea who her saviour was, and whether he'd give chase or stay with her. If he left now she knew she'd be unconscious in just a few more seconds, with no idea whether any of them would ever wake up.

Doors opened and slammed and someone was hurrying to her side. 'Brodie?' His voice soared with disbelief like a rocket.

'Charlie Voss,' she sighed brokenly. 'Get me out of here. Get us all out of here.'

In the wash of headlights his freckled face was anxious. 'I shouldn't move you. You could be hurt.'

'We're *gonna* be dead,' she slurred emphatically.

It was enough. He threw open the door, unfastened her seat belt and towed her out

372

unceremoniously with his hands under her armpits. He laid her on the verge beside the road. 'Try not to roll.'

In a few moments she was joined first by Ally, then Daniel. Both of them were deeply unconscious and Daniel was snoring. But the fresh air was replacing, one cc at a time, the chemical miasma in their lungs and in their blood. Brodie felt the life seeping back into her, and knew it was seeping back into them too.

'Charlie,' she whispered. He bent down to listen. 'You want to be Chief Constable? I can fix it...'

Chapter Twenty-Nine

Dimmock General insisted on keeping them until the last of the drug had left their systems. By the judicious juggling of beds – old ladies going for ECGs finding themselves wheeled back to other wards – they managed to put Brodie and Alison in adjacent cubicles, but except that the thought was appreciated they needn't have bothered. Both women slept through what was left of the night and half the next morning.

When Brodie finally surfaced it was to a face as familiar as her own mirror image, if less lovely. When scenes like this appear in romantic fiction it turns out the lover has been keeping vigil by the beloved's side for hours if not days. But Deacon was a busy man, so two minutes after he arrived he started humming tunelessly and drumming his fingers on the table to wake her.

He knew what her first words would be, tried not to be disappointed.

'Daniel?'

Deacon jerked his head towards the door. 'Across the corridor, snoring his head off. He's fine.'

'And Alison?'

'The same, only she's right here. And less snoring.'

Brodie propped herself up to see but there was no reason to doubt what he was saying. The girl had a good colour and no machines recording her vital signs. She was just asleep. 'Good.'

Deacon was watching her soberly. 'That was a close one.'

'Too damned close,' she agreed. 'We were so lucky...'

'Luck didn't come into it,' he demurred. 'After Charlie took Windham into Battle Alley he was on his way to join me at Sparrow Hill. When the switchboard took Mary Walbrook's call Sergeant McKinney smelled a rat and diverted the nearest car to investigate, which happened to be Charlie.

He didn't know what he was going to find – possibly nothing – but when he saw a Land Rover trying to shove my car off a cliff he guessed the rest.'

'He saved our lives,' Brodie said simply.

Deacon shrugged. 'It's what he's paid for.'

She didn't want to argue with him. 'What about Kant? Did he slip the net again?'

'He did. But his time's coming. The police in four countries are watching for him. We'll get him. It may take a little time but it'll happen.'

'And Mary Walbrook?'

'At Battle Alley, saying nothing without her solicitor's approval. But she's going down, and between them her and Windham will tell us everything. He'll tell us everything she did, and she'll tell us everything he did.'

'Daniel was right? She was the one who pushed Stanley Barker in the pond?'

Deacon nodded. 'That's what Windham says. Pushed him in and held him down. Of course, everything he doesn't want to do time for himself he has to lay off on her. But actually I believe him.'

Brodie did too. 'What a crew! Mary and Barker were partners for fifteen years. They were lovers at one time. And she killed him for money.'

'Not exactly. She killed him to keep herself safe. But it was the money – drug money –

that brought her to it.' He leaned back in his chair, stretching out his thick legs, crossing his strong arms on his chest. 'Brodie, we have to talk.'

'I suppose we do. Now?'

'If you're up to it.'

She wasn't looking forward to it but there was nothing to be gained by delay. 'What are we going to do? What do you *want* to do?'

'I'm not sure I can have what I want,' said Deacon, keeping his voice low although no one was paying them any attention. 'I want all of you. I don't think half of you is enough any more.'

'That isn't fair,' she said softly.

'Maybe not. But that's how it feels. Every time there's a conflict of interests it's Daniel's needs that concern you. Not occasionally, not sometimes – every single time.'

'You were gambling with his life, Jack!' she cried. 'You put a price on it and decided it was worth paying!'

'I was following procedure,' he said stiffly. 'A procedure that evolved because it gives everyone involved the best chance of walking away. It was a good call. It was the *right* call. But you thought my decision was influenced by my feelings for you and yours for Daniel. I don't think that's a situation we can allow to continue.'

Brodie caught her breath. 'You want to call it a day?'

'You said that was what you wanted.'

'I was upset! I thought my best friend was dying!'

'That's kind of the point, Brodie,' said Deacon quietly. 'I should be your best friend. If I'm not, I'm not sure what it is we're doing here.'

It would have been easy to take the decision out of his hands. Both of them knew she'd find another partner before he would. She thought she owed him better. She thought she owed it to him – to both of them, to what they'd meant to each other – to fight for it.

'Jack, we've had this out before. Daniel is no threat to us. No more than if he was my brother. I care for him deeply: you know that. You knew it when you and I first got together. You knew I had other commitments. One was to Paddy, and one was to Daniel. And I didn't, and I still don't, feel anything for either of them that should spoil my relationship with you. It's absurd! You might as well ask me to stop caring about my daughter!'

'Daniel isn't your child,' he retorted forcefully. 'And he's not your brother. And the reason this has become an issue now is that things change. People's feelings change. That may still be the way you feel about him, but it isn't the way he feels about you. Not any more.'

She stared at him in amazement. 'Jack – I've no idea what you're talking about!'

He studied the depths of her eyes. 'No, you haven't, have you?' He sounded tired, defeated. 'Brodie, I don't know what to tell you. I know you think I'm being unreasonable. But that's because I know things you don't know, or don't want to know. Maybe before we finish this conversation you ought to talk to Daniel.'

'Daniel?' she exclaimed in exasperation. 'What's *Daniel* got to do with it?'

'Everything,' said Deacon. 'Trust me.'

He left then. Brodie sat alone for a while, just thinking. Then she got up and pottered along the corridor looking for Daniel.

He was still asleep. She didn't rattle around making enough noise to wake him. She pulled up the chair and sat quietly at his side for an hour until he moaned and mumbled and turned over and, already fumbling on the bedside table for his glasses, woke up.

'Hi,' she said softly.

'Hello.' A slow smile spread across his face.

'We made it.'

'Alison too?'

'Alison too.'

'What happened?'

'Kant happened. He was at the yard when we arrived. He put something in the car that put us all to sleep. He was about to push us into Ship Coomb when Charlie Voss turned up and stopped him.'

Daniel was nodding, but Brodie had the feeling she'd have to tell him all over again when he was more fully awake. And possibly this too. 'That's not what I wanted to tell you.'

He pushed himself up in the bed that was scaled to a much bigger man. The hospital gown made him look like a hand-puppet. 'What did you want to tell me?'

She picked her words carefully. 'That I heard what you were saying the other day. I'm sorry it took me till now to take it in.'

Groggy or not, he knew immediately what she meant. He wasn't sure what she expected him to say. 'It's been a busy week,' he tried lamely.

'Not that busy.'

'OK,' he said. 'So – what?'

'You mean, so what do we do about it?'

He shrugged awkwardly. 'I suppose.'

Brodie bit her lip. 'Daniel, I don't want to – mislead you. You know – you must know – that I think the world of you too. But not that way. I'm sorry, I wish I could, but I don't think I'll ever feel that way. So I guess the answer is, there's nothing we can do about it. But I wanted you to know that – well, that I wasn't pretending not to understand. At first I didn't. Now I do.'

When Daniel smiled it lit up half the ward.

'It's all right, Brodie. I'm not expecting a fairy-tale ending. It was just, it had been nagging at me and I was acting like an idiot round you and I thought it was time you knew why. That's all.'

'That's *not* all,' she said firmly. 'Somebody says he loves you, that's a huge big *not-all*. But to tell the truth it's not something I was expecting and I don't know quite what to do with it, where to put it. Can you be patient while I figure it out?'

Patience was his middle name – except on all those occasions when it wasn't. But what he'd given her was a declaration, not a proposal – he wasn't waiting for her response. 'I'm not sure there's anything to figure. I haven't *forgotten* about Jack, you know. I never expected you to take him aside and tell him you'd got a better offer. I was just trying to be honest.'

'I've told you about that, haven't I?' she admonished him with a kind of sombre grin. 'And to be honest in return, I'm not sure where me and Jack are heading now. Possibly, straight up a cul-de-sac.'

Daniel frowned, instantly wary. 'Because of me?'

Her first instinct was to lie and say no. Her second was to say yes, and that would have been a lie in its way as well. 'Because of us. Him and me. Because I keep disappointing him. I don't want to hurt him, Daniel – but if I'm going to, I'd rather hurt him once than again and again. I think maybe it's time to draw a line under it and part while we're still on speaking terms.'

For once he had nothing to say to help her. With a sad little smile and a shrug, Brodie headed back to her ward.

The doctor who'd run her tests was waiting, marking up her chart. 'Ah, there you are. I wanted a word with you.'

'Oh?' She climbed onto the high bed. 'You're not going to keep me in, are you? I'm feeling pretty well back to normal. A touch of nausea, maybe, but that's only to be expected, isn't it?'

'Oh yes,' he agreed. 'No, I see no need to keep you in after tonight. We'll get you in for a few more tests as time goes on, but it's important to be positive. What happened to you may very well have no effect whatever on the baby.'

Brodie went on looking at him way, way too long, nothing in her expression altering, waiting for him to slap his thigh and chuckle, 'Just kidding!' or notice that he was working with someone else's notes. He did neither. He was waiting for some kind of a reaction – relief, perhaps, or gratitude.

Finally she crashed her brain into gear and wrestled with the controls for speech mode. '*Baby?*' she echoed.

The publishers hope that this book has given you enjoyable reading. Large Print Books are especially designed to be as easy to see and hold as possible. If you wish a complete list of our books please ask at your local library or write directly to:

Magna Large Print Books
Magna House, Long Preston,
Skipton, North Yorkshire.
BD23 4ND

This Large Print Book, for people
who cannot read normal print,
is published under the auspices of

THE ULVERSCROFT FOUNDATION